LEGACY

Genesis of the Popular Nigerian 419 Scam

ERNEST BHABOR

LEGACY

First Edition

Copyright @ Ernest Bhabor 2018

Printed in the United States of America.

ISBN: **978-1986100731**

DEDICATION

This book is dedicated to my dad Isaac, for making sure I could read and write from a very young age.

CONTENTS

ACKNOWLEDGEMENTS

I thank all those who have believed in my ideas, and supported my dreams, even the crazy ones, all through the years.

According to Forrest Gump, from the movie *Forrest Gump*: "Life is like a box of chocolates, you never know what you are going to get".

PROLOGUE

"Every crisis presents both danger and opportunity" - Chinese Proverb

A young man in his early twenties, holding a paper file, dressed in a shirt and tie, is pursuing a large bus painted in peeling yellow and black.

As he grabs hold of the half open rickety door, running side by side with the dangerous looking vehicle, he lifts a foot onto the doorway.

He tries to climb in but loses his grip as the door comes off its hinge. He falls down hard on the tarred road bum first, peeling his butt. And as he struggles to get up a car coming from behind slams into him. He falls to the side of the road.

The bus continues down the road, as if nothing happened, with smoke billowing from its exhaust pipe towards the sky. The conductor, laughing, struggles to hook up the door on its hinge.

The young man, back on his feet, checking for injuries, dusts his clothes with a sigh. The car that slammed into him is well out of sight.

Another bus, identical to the last one, drives down. The young man performs exactly the same act. Other passengers join him in the encore, wildly. This time he makes it inside the bus in one piece, a weak smile on his young harassed face.

This is a typical bright June day in the most populous black nation in the world, Nigeria. The Niger-area, surrounded by the Atlantic Ocean in the south.

Nigeria shares land borders with the Republic of Benin in the west, Chad and Cameroon in the east, and the Republic of Niger in the north.

The extremely hot tropical sun hangs loosely overhead, looking wicked and fierce, ready to burn up everything in sight.

The people trod the streets with massive loads of sweat pouring off their bodies. Their foreheads glisten with a mixture of sweat, pain, and suffering.

A normal day in the life of the average Nigerian, the average Nigerian pulverized by lack, by deprivation, by squalor, by penury.

A suffering induced by selfish rulers, greedy rulers, thieving rulers; abject want in a land of plenty, a land of nothing, a land blessed, a land cursed, a rich land, a poor land, a golden land, a rusty land, a complex land, a simple land.

Nigeria is a nation of heroes, a nation of villains, a nation of ironies, a nation of indescribable-ness, a nation with abundant human and material resources, a nation where harsh lines of suffering—visible from many miles—powder the faces of the people.

But they trod on, unwavering. They pander on in pretense, belying the pangs of hunger gnawing at their insides; a proud people with forlorn browbeaten looks.

Heads of state and their sidekicks have been known to confiscate public property for their own personal use. Public buildings, farms, machinery and of course money have been stolen openly by these thieving monstrous sociopathic vermin that parade themselves as leaders.

These are no leaders but a gang of thieves from hell. What kind of man would steal a government project embarked on to feed a nation—to alleviate the suffering of the poor downtrodden masses? The very worst kind of the human race, that's who!

And there have been many of 'the very worst kind of the human race' at the helm of the affairs of this humongous nation of over 200 different ethnic groups, and well over 150 million citizens.

Some were from the armed forces, who supposedly swore to uphold the constitution and protect the nation from enemies both within and foreign. But turned out to be the country's very worst enemies. And the others?

The political class who were supposedly bastions of democracy? Well, lets just surmise that *Lucifer*, the devil himself, would be utterly embarrassed, and ashamed of the atrocities perpetrated on the nation by the aforementioned.

Yes, the devil himself is a saint compared to most of the so-called leaders of Nigeria, whether in uniform or in civilian clothes!

1 THE OLD MAN

"Perseverance is not a long race; it is many short races, one after another"
- Walter Elliot

A very old Volkswagen beetle with parts of different peeling colors is kaput in the middle of the road. The owner, a dirty, swarthy looking man in his early sixties — who is wearing old worn out clothes that have seen very many days — is tinkering with the engine in a futile attempt to get it rolling.

He glances up to see the traffic crawling to a stop behind his rickety jalopy; then skyward at the delicately fragile hands of a huge clock, etched on the frontal side of an imposing cathedral.

The hands of the clock are hovering around the five o'clock mark, a typical rush hour in the city of Lagos; Nigeria's former federal capital city and seat of government, but which still remains the nation's economic capital.

It is dry and scalding hot. The familiar breeze from the neighboring Atlantic Ocean seems to be on strike today, like everything else in this unpredictable country.

He takes off his prescription glasses and wipes his brow with his filthy shirtsleeve in frustration. He kicks the side of the vehicle in anger.

He mumbles incoherently to himself as he puts on the bifocals and goes under the hood again. He strikes viciously at the engine with a crowbar.

The drivers behind and around the beetle yell out obscenities to the man who seems oblivious of their tantrums. They struggle to maneuver their vehicles through the bulging traffic jam, cursing and swearing riotously.

Suddenly, very loud sirens pierce through the hot clammy day. A convoy of exquisite and exotic cars tears down the road. They screech to an abrupt halt behind the dilapidated Volkswagen beetle and the cars around it. The man, panicked, slams the hood over his head.

Armed policemen fly down from the vehicles before they stop completely, firing warning gunshots in the air. Several big brawny bodyguards, all dressed in black suits and dark glasses, jump out of the cars and rush at the man stuck under the hood of the beetle.

They yank him out violently and lift him off the ground with his feet dangling comically in the air. His glasses fall on the ground. One of them stamps on it with his big shiny black boots angrily. Crushing it brutally.

The man, frightened, pleads. Others grab hold of the dysfunctional bug and drag it to the side of the road roughly, parts of different colors are breaking off and falling on the ground.

The menacing looking policemen point their guns dangerously as they give cover to the bodyguards, daring any onlooker or passerby to attempt any heroic act.

At first glance, one would assume the convoy was that of a highly placed government official, because only distinguished people go around town with blaring sirens and a retinue.

But people are taken aback when a very wealthy looking young man, in his early thirties, steps out of the Mercedes Benz limousine in the middle of the convoy.

He walks daintily to the guards who are roughening up the old man.

"Stop!" he says.

They all freeze at once.

He commands them quietly,

"Let him go".

They put him down gently.

The old man, utterly afraid, looks down at his old dirty shoes. Too scared to look up.

He apologizes with a stutter,

"I'm very sorry sir. The car broke down sir. And I don't..."

The young man cuts in quietly,

"I understand"

He smiles warmly at the old man,

"Are you okay?"

The old man looks up at the young man for the first time, surprised at his age and humility despite his obvious affluence, and says meekly,

"I'm an old man, but yes I'm okay. Thank you"

The young man glances at one of his boys,

"John, give him something for his trouble"

John nods and walks briskly to the SUV in front of the convoy.

The old man protests,

"Sir, you don't have to do that"

The young man smiles and says with affection,

"I want to sir"

John returns with two bundles of *naira* notes, the Nigerian currency, totaling fifty thousand *naira*.

The young man gestures to the old man with his head.

John moves to hand him the bundles.

The old man's eyes almost pop out of their sockets with trepidation.

He says meekly,

"I... I can't accept this money"

"Why not?" asks the young man

The old man with a quivering voice says,

"I haven't done anything to deserve it"

The young man chuckles heartily,

"Just like my father would put it. Let's just say I want to apologize for this little misunderstanding"

He looks at the torn bug, then the broken pair of glasses on the ground, and says,

"I see my boys have damaged your car and your glasses, please fix the car and get another pair of glasses"

The old man glances around at the policemen, the guards and all the gathering onlookers — who are keeping a safe distance — and says quietly,

"You don't have to pay for anything, what happened is not your fault"

The young man still smiling says with finality,

"I insist sir"

He nods at John.

John takes the old man's hand and puts the money in it.

The young man nods at him, turns and starts to walk away, followed by his entourage.

The old man looks at the money in his hand, then at the young man walking away and calls out loudly,

"God bless you son!"

The young man stops in his track. His people freeze. He turns around and walks back to the old man slowly — like in a daze — a queer look on his face.

The old man, frightened, wondering what he said wrong, takes a step back.

The young man, no longer smiling, a strange glint in his eyes, stops in front of the old man and queries,

"What did you just say?"

The old man, confused and fearful, sweat breaking out across his brow, whispers almost inaudibly,

"I said God bless you, son"

The young man turns away thoughtfully. His followers, confused, hover around, exchanging perturbed glances.

He turns back to the old man who is ready to hand back the money if need be, even though in his swirling head he can just imagine the ton of things he can accomplish with this unexpected manna from this wonderful young man, who is at the moment acting rather strange.

He cannot remember the last time he had so much money in his hands. Life has not been fair to him he thought. His numerous creditors hound him, all the unpaid bills that have formed a permanent hunch on his back that weigh him down tremendously. Oh what a relief this money will be to his piteous self, he reckons.

And just then the young man turns back to him, staring at him intensely, that disturbing look still in his eyes asks,

"Are you...were you ever a teacher?"

The old man swallows hard, utterly confused. Wondering what is coming now. He nods slowly, and says with a quivering voice,

"I was a teacher"

The young man explodes expectantly,

"Mr. Jonah?"

The old man blinks wildly.

"Yes. That is my name. Do you know me?"

The young man grabs him in a bear hug, and exclaims,

"My goodness! I have looked everywhere for you. Where have you been!"

The old man does not remember him from anywhere. The young man looks at him all over and whimpers,

"Oh my God! Mr. Jonah, you don't remember me?"

The old man shakes his head sadly.

Tears well up in the young man's eyes as he says excitedly,

"You don't remember little Frank? Frank Audu, in your class in elementary school about thirty years ago, who you always told 'God bless you son'. You always protected me from the other kids when they beat and teased me about my uniform with holes. You bought me the first pair of shoes I ever had, a pair of brown sandals".

The old man, Mr. Jonah, is agape as he mutters in utter disbelief,

"No! Impossible. Frank? Frank Audu? Is this really you?"

Frank nods as tears roll down the corners of his eyes.

Mr. Jonah touches his face with his scraggy fingers and then hugs him tightly, in complete shock. He wonders when he would wake up from this beautiful dream about his former student.

He reckons his life has been too horrible for this one good thing to be really happening. He expects the rude awakening from this once in a lifetime dream of complete beatitude any second now.

But he remembers the bright little boy, Frank. The little kid who always sat near his desk to avoid the taunting from the rich kids — who were not so bright — in his class thirty years ago.

The kid who could answer any question he was asked, the kid who finished all the exams before everyone else, the kid who never played, the kid who never brought lunch to school, the only kid who scored a hundred percent in all his exams.

Is this fate? Is this destiny? Or is this a bad dream from the prince of darkness? Or perhaps a cruel joke from hell! Is this just a taunting dream about a messiah in the person of his beloved little Frank — the brilliant little malnourished kid back in the day of the chalk and the blackboard?

He had always wondered how God had packed that poor kid full with so much intelligence. Frank pulls away from him tenderly.

He looks at him all over again and asks,

"What happened to you Mr. Jonah? You were big and strong the last time I saw you"

Mr. Jonah smiles at him sadly, and mutters,

"My dear Frank that was thirty years ago. Life has been tough. I'm old now".

"Do you still teach?"

"No. I retired a few years ago. I'm waiting to die to go to heaven for my reward. They say a teacher's reward is in heaven"

Frank looks at him, glances at the badly beaten up Volkswagen beetle on the side of the road and asks,

"Is this the same car from thirty years ago?"

Mr. Jonah nods.

Frank gasps,

"My God! What happened?"

Painful memories flash across Mr. Jonah's face as he mutters,

"Long story son"

Frank takes his hand tenderly and pulls him gently towards his car.

"I have the time for a long story sir"

Jonah smiles, pointing,

"I see you've made good my boy"

Frank grins sheepishly,

"Long story sir"

Jonah sighs,

"I can imagine. I can just imagine son"

Frank opens the door for him to enter, and turns to John who is only a step behind,

"Cancel everything. Take us home"

John nods and closes the door. He rushes to his SUV in front of the convoy as he gives orders over a radio.

The policemen halt traffic. The convoy turns and head the other way — sirens blaring — tearing through traffic like an ambulance with a dying accident victim.

2 FLOOD OF MEMORIES

"Success comes from within, not from without" - *Ralph Waldo Emerson*

Driving through the streets of Lagos, with Mr. Jonah sitting beside him, Frank remembers how he was constantly bullied and terrorized by his classmates as a scrawny five year old.

He was intimidated for trying to help the other kids, he was persecuted for scoring the highest grades in class, he was tormented for knowing the answers to the questions the teachers asked, he was ridiculed for wearing torn clothes to school, he was browbeaten for not wearing shoes to school, he was oppressed for been the smallest kid in class, he was derided for being poor, he was scorned for being hungry, he was scoffed at for being Frank, he was harassed for every possible reason; and sometimes, rather incredibly, for no reason at all.

His little mind could not quite understand why he was disparaged so much, and with so much glee. But no matter how much they had disdained him, he had never told his parents at home for two reasons.

Firstly, he was afraid his parents might ask him to stay home if they knew how much grief he suffered. And secondly, he would rather have killed himself than to trouble his parents any more than life was troubling them at the time.

They were sacrificing so much for him that he had secretly vowed — to himself — to stay strong no matter what.

The only friend he had in school, back in the day, was Mr. Jonah. A man who was not related to him at all, but who had just believed he would be somebody someday if he were to harness his talent and gift for comprehending the lessons taught in class.

He remembers very vividly, everything this good kindhearted man — sitting beside him just now — ever said to him. He remembers every word this angel ever spoke to him.

He glances at him, but Mr. Jonah is lost in his own thoughts. He turns away to look out through the window and pictures — in his mind's eye — the other kids picking on him, and Mr. Jonah rushing to his rescue.

A little smile breaks across his lips as he remembers been called 'Jonah's son' by the other kids. He did not mind been called that at all. In fact he felt elated to know that the other kids thought of him so highly to call him Mr. Jonah Jr. To him, that was a privilege.

Then Mr. Jonah bought him those really beautiful pair of brown sandals when he scored one hundred percent in the English language exam. Something Mr. Jonah said nobody had done in his five years of teaching.

He was overwhelmed with joy the first time he wore those shoes — they were the only shoes he had ever owned. And he thought to himself, 'thank God, some of the kids will quit bullying me. I finally got some school shoes'. But alas, he was harassed a whole lot more for getting a new pair of shoes the very next morning.

His parents had been so proud of him for his brilliance and were willing to go the extra mile to educate him that he had made another private vow to himself.

He had vowed never to disappoint them, and to do whatever it takes to make his family comfortable someday, anything at all, as long as he is alive, he would do.

Nothing and no one was going to stop him. And with that vow, and that personal commitment he had struggled through life; working harder than the average kid on the block, ready to do whatever it takes to make good.

He had slept many nights on an empty stomach and woken up the following morning to go to school — a five year old — running wildly, clutching his books in one hand and his school shorts in the other; close on his heels are five burly looking kids — about his age — holding sticks and stones.

They pursue him, he runs frantically into a classroom — panting. The five rowdy kids stop at the entrance laughing. This happened every morning.

Most times they chased him inside the classroom, and Mr. Jonah threw them out. A few times they had actually hit him with the sticks and thrown the stones at him, hurting him in the process. He — Frank the poor kid — was their source of amusement.

Today, he is Frank Audu the multimillionaire in *naira*, in dollars and in pounds. The owner of over fifty businesses, magnificent real estate spread all over the world, and a countless number of exotic cars.

He is a renowned philanthropist, and a certified lawyer. Obviously, he was not always rich. He was not born with a silver spoon or any spoon at all for that matter. In fact, he was born poor. Not just poor, but wantonly poor.

He was raised in abject poverty like many other children of his generation. He is not a stranger to hunger, starvation and deprivation — these are very familiar relatives of his. He grew up without needs or wants.

All his childhood years were lived on an empty stomach not because he suffered from anorexia, but because his family just could not afford their basic needs. They worked hard no doubt.

They did menial, backbreaking jobs that could not take care of even fundamental elements like food and adequate shelter.

The youngest child of a family of five; his father, mother and two older sisters, he became grounded in the art of surviving at a tender age.

He had nothing but the strong desire to survive, the undying craving to endure the rough and tough endless days of lack, pain and suffering.

His two older sisters were married off at ages thirteen and twelve. Not for love or because of culture or tradition, but because it was a means to raise money for food and for his school fees.

He remembers those painful days with tears even though now he can afford anything at all he craves.

A moment later the convoy arrives in a secluded neighborhood. The cars cut speed but with sirens still blaring. On both sides of the streets are opulent castles and mansions as in a painting, or

9

storybook. All built with exotic marble and brick imported from distant lands.

The convoy makes a turn onto a side road. At the beginning of the road, is a large nameplate on top of a medium sized pole that reads: FRANK AUDU CLOSE.

Mr. Jonah looks at the plate and glances at Frank with sincere admiration. Frank nods at him with a smile.

The cars drive down the close towards the largest mansion in the neighborhood. As the cars approach the massive gates, they swing open as if of their own accord.

Frank grins at Mr. Jonah and says,

"Welcome to my humble home Mr. Jonah"

Mr. Jonah looks at him as if to say,

'Humble home? Are you crazy?'

The cars cruise through the gates and drive down the beautifully paved driveway with properly manicured flowers.

They stop, and in a second, John opens the door for Frank.

He steps out.

Mr. Jonah following behind, asks incredulously,

"This is your home? This is where you live?"

Frank nods, tears welling up at the corners of his eyes. He wipes them quietly, clears his throat and motions for Mr. Jonah to follow him.

He says with difficulty,

"I will show you around sir"

Mr. Jonah follows him, utterly dazed and speechless. Everything, and nothing, all fly crisply through his head in a tumble, at the same time, as he takes in the picturesque scenery.

An Olympic sized swimming pool, luxuriant flowers and the carpet grass that goes all the way out to form a miniature golf course.

A tennis court is just beside a basketball court. A large and wide garage with every kind of luxurious car imaginable, takes up a massive space near the imposing wall.

And the mansion itself — in the middle of this expanse of land — is mind blowing, exactly like something straight out of a fairy tale painting, no doubt.

Not even in his wildest imagination could he have ever dreamt of a place like this. His mind is completely blown to bits by what he is looking at.

He says to himself,

"Wait a minute. Is this heaven? Am I dead and in heaven?"

This does not seem like earth to him at all. This must be heaven, he reckons. He died and is perhaps in heaven.

Okay, if that is the case — glancing around — where should he go to get his reward for been a teacher for thirty-five years? After all they said 'a teacher's reward was in heaven'.

The last thing he remembers is being under his broken down bug somewhere in the city. After that, everything else is woozy.

He reckons,

"Maybe I got run over by some senseless and despicable driver on the street when I went under that dead beetle!"

He glances around furtively,

"Ha! That must be it. I am dead! But what is Frank doing here? He is only a young…"

He hears his name being called, he wonders if that is an angel calling his name to come receive his reward. He walks towards the perceived sound, but it is Frank.

Having walked down some distance and noticing Mr. Jonah standing way behind, he had stopped and called his name a few times.

Mr. Jonah walks and stops in front of him, startled — almost bumping into him — as if in the threshold of a trance.

Frank holds him gently, steadying him,

"Are you alright Mr. Jonah?"

Mumbling,

"What... what did you say son?"

"I asked if you are okay sir"

"Yes... yes... yes... I'm fine... yes"

Frank looks at him with concern,

"Perhaps you need some rest sir?"

"No... no... no. Pay me no mind. I'm fine!"

Frank smiles at him and continues to walk.

Mr. Jonah walks with him side by side, glancing around furtively,

"Son... can I ask you a question?"

Frank stops,

"You can ask me anything sir, anything at all"

Mr. Jonah looks over his shoulder discreetly, and though there is no one any where near them, he still whispers cautiously,

11

"Where are we son?"

Frank smiles warmly,

"My place sir. My home".

"Are you sure?"

"This is my home sir. I bought the place, and did some remodeling".

Mr. Jonah glances around one more time.

Frank looks at him with concern.

"Is something wrong sir?"

"No nothing is wrong. But where is this home of yours?"

"This is Victoria Garden City sir"

"So you mean we are still in Lagos, Nigeria?"

"Yes sir"

Mr. Jonah exclaims,

"That means I'm alive?"

Frank frowns slightly, confused,

"I don't understand sir"

Mr. Jonah quips,

"I'm not dead and we are not in heaven, right?"

"That is correct sir"

He grunts thoughtfully,

"Mmm".

He looks away for a second, then turns to Frank,

"That means I might be dreaming then"

"Mr. Jonah you're not dreaming sir"

He looks at him wide eyed,

"I'm not?"

"You're not sir"

"You mean this is real?"

"Very real Mr. Jonah"

Just then John walks up to them.

"Frank, food is ready"

"Good. Mr. Jonah, we will take a shower, eat and then play catch up".

"Okay son", whimpers Mr. Jonah, forcing a smile.

They walk towards the house.

Frank puts an arm around his shoulder affectionately as he says,

"Mr. Jonah, this is my friend John", turning to John,

"This is Mr. Jonah my..."

John interrupts him, grinning,

"I know. You must have told me about him at least a million times already".

Frank chuckles heartily.

John takes Mr. Jonah's right hand with both his hands respectfully, in a hand shake.

He says very warmly as he bows slightly,

"I'm very pleased to finally meet you sir"

Mr. Jonah shakes his hand and says,

"The pleasure is all mine son"

Mr. Jonah smiles at them both as tears trickle down his eyes.

Frank looks at him,

"You're crying".

Mr. Jonah smiles amidst his tears,

"Tears of joy my boy. Tears of joy".

Frank holds him close and leads him towards the mansion.

John looks at them walking together in front of him, like father and son although unrelated by blood.

He sheds a few tear drops himself as he looks on. He wipes his eyes, overcome by the obvious unspoken love between the father and the son.

3 IN THE BEGINNING

"I try not to live a lie" - Elizabeth Taylor

After a nice warm bath and a very sumptuous meal, the father and the son sit down to drink champagne from tall crystals under the star spangled night sky.

Mr. Jonah, now dressed in fresh warm clothes, and still unable to believe, or comprehend, his present situation, looks at Frank quietly — tongue-tied.

They are outside on the patio that is as beautiful, and as worthy, as any patio anywhere in the world can possibly be. They are ensconced in very fluffy and comfortable leather seats.

Mr. Jonah's feet are on a footstool like any other aristocrat of the time. He sips from his glass quietly as he glances up at the moon that seems to be smiling down at him.

He seems to hear angels singing 'hosanna' somewhere near the moon, perhaps on the right side. He glances at Frank quickly, wondering if he can hear the angels singing 'hosanna'.

No, they changed the song, he can hear the words from the hymn: 'Rock of Ages'.

'Rock of ages cleft for me; let me hide myself in thee...'

The words are indeed very clear to him. Perhaps he should ask Frank if he can hear the song, he reckons.

But just then, John walks out to them silently — breaking his train of thought.

He nods at Mr. Jonah with a smile and turns to Frank,

"I want to turn in now. Do you need me to take care of anything?"

Frank smiles,

"No thanks. I will see you in the morning"

Turning to Mr. Jonah, he says,

"Goodnight sir"

"Goodnight to you son", says Mr. Jonah.

John leaves as quietly as he had come.

There must be a host of angels singing in the sky, Mr. Jonah reckons.

"Or maybe I'm just drunk and confused", he figures.

He glances at the large empty bottle of champagne in the corner and then peers hard at the sky, hoping to catch a glimpse of the singing winged heavenly beings.

Squinting his eyes intently; he feels a slight touch on his arm, he startles — spills some champagne — and almost jumps out of his old taut skin.

"Are you alright?", Frank asks with concern.

"I'm sorry... I'm fine".

He forces a smile,

"My mind was doing a somersault".

Frank grins heartily,

"So do you want to talk, or do you want to go to sleep now?"

"Yes I want to talk. I can't sleep tonight. I don't see that happening by any chance".

"Alright then. Tell me everything that has happened to you in the last thirty years"

"No... no... no son. You tell me your story first. What miracle happened?"

Frank grins childishly; and then frowns slightly as pictures, very crisp clear pictures, form in his head.

Pictures he has fought hard to discard from his memory, but that have proven immutable or 'in-erasable'.

He looks at Mr. Jonah, almost tearful.

Mr. Jonah, feeling his pain, quips,

"Son if you don't want to talk about it, I'll understand".

Frank smiles wanly and says meekly,

"It's okay. I don't mind, though it hurts".

They sip from their crystals quietly.

Frank gazes at no where in particular and says almost inaudibly,

"You know how it was in elementary school..."

He almost loses his voice completely.

He sips from the sparkling liquid again. Hot sweat breaks across his brow, although a cool refreshing breeze hovers around.

"It did not get better".

He looks at Mr. Jonah and whispers,

"Things got worse Mr. Jonah".

Mr. Jonah bites his lip without a sound.

*

After six horrible years of elementary school, Frank, aged eleven, gained admission into high school.

On the morning of the entrance examination, after being awake all night, he had taken a bath and gotten ready even before his folks were up.

It was a Saturday morning, and the exam had been scheduled for nine o'clock. But he arrived at the venue, as the very first person, at exactly seven-thirty.

He did not have any breakfast, not because he had no appetite — or that he was anorexic — but because there was none to have.

He sat down in the hall even before the officials showed up. He remembers dozing a bit before the other kids started trickling in, followed by two officials — two complete opposites; one large and ugly, the other small and handsome, almost pretty.

As always some of the boys from his elementary school had teased him, wanting to know if he had passed the night in the hall.

That elicited some laughter no doubt. He too had found that reckoning amusing — and he probably would have actually slept in the hall if permitted.

The officials started handing out the exam papers at eight-thirty. And at exactly nine o'clock, they commenced the exam.

He did not forget to pray for success — maybe the third time that morning.

He had stuck to his prayer point that morning: 'Oh God; please help me succeed, so I can help my family and everyone else, amen'. He always prayed that very short but explicit prayer even to this day.

When he read through the questions — with a smile on his face as usual — he closed his eyes briefly to say the words: 'Thank you God for answering my prayer'.

He looked up, and around, to see many of the kids in a seemly confounded state.

He had smiled at them nicely, but they had glared at him in anger, perhaps wondering what the hell he was smiling about. Exams were not a smiling matter they must have thought.

But he always smiled, no matter what situation he was in. Good situations, bad situations, there was always a smile. He learnt that, or perhaps read that somewhere, though he could not readily remember from where at the moment.

As he thought of these things, he answered the questions and within an hour he had written all the answers. He looked at the question sheets and wondered if he had been given all the questions.

The kids around him were stretching their necks desperately — like ostriches trying to catch fish — in a frantic bid to steal answers from his paper.

He stood up and called out to the officials,

"Excuse me sir".

Walking towards him, the large, ugly and stern looking, middle aged official answers gruffly,

"Yes? What do you want?"

"Sir, I was wondering how many questions we are meant to answer"

The official, stopping beside him, glares at him angrily,

"What do you mean little boy? You don't know you should answer everything?"

The other kids burst into laughter.

"I know sir. But how many questions in all?"

Looking down at him threateningly and wagging a finger,

"Little boy, are you playing games with me?"

Frank shocked, pleads,

"No sir"

"Then shut up and sit down!"

"But sir..."

The official cuts him off rudely,

"I said shut up and sit down! One more word from you and I will throw you out of this exam hall this minute! Do you understand that?"

Frank says meekly,

"Yes sir", and sits down.

The brute walks away from him.

The other official, the small, handsome — almost pretty — effeminate looking man, approaches his desk and says nicely,

"What is the problem, my dear?"

Frank whispers,

"I just wanted to know how many questions we should answer sir".

Smiling warmly, he says,

"Everything, my dear".

"Yes. But how many questions, sir?"

Picking up his sheets,

"Why? You don't have all the questions?"

He flips through the sheets, wide eyed,

"My God! You have finished! Are you sure you..."

The first official turns to them, almost running, and exclaims,

"What?"

The effeminate man whispers,

"The young man has answered all the questions".

Glaring at Frank, the brute retorts,

"That is impossible! Hey! Stand up. What have you done?"

"Nothing sir. I just answered the questions", Frank says meekly.

Still glaring at him, the brute explodes,

"You have been cheating, right? Stand up! Stand up right now!"

The brute proceeds to search through Frank's papers, through his pockets and even through his socks.

Hot fumes spew from his large nostrils like a violent volcanic eruption in anger.

Finding nothing, he turns to the effeminate man, and bellows,

"What do we do?"

He chuckles, and says matter of fact,

"Nothing! If he has finished, he has finished. There is nothing wrong with finishing first".

He turns to Frank,

"Maybe you should go through your work again my dear. You still have..." glances at his wristwatch, "... approximately one hour left".

Frank whispers,

"Thank you sir, but I have to go do some work".

"Okay young man. I wish you good luck!"

"Thank you sir".

He picks up his writing materials and starts to leave the hall quietly.

The rude official glares at him as he walks away. He turns to the effeminate man and grunts, with Frank still within earshot,

"That is how they fail. How could he have finished in under an hour?"

The effeminate man smiles,

"You never know".

From the exam hall he had hurried to a building site — his writing materials still in his pockets. He was lucky to get hired for the day's work.

He carried bricks, and buckets of wet sand and cement — a harsh smelling mixture — from the mixing point to the bricklayers.

When this strong smelling concoction touches your skin, it burns it instantly and peels off the top layer after a while. But he did not mind doing this work at all. The meager wage at the end of the day goes a long way for him and his family.

The following day, which is Sunday, after church, he was going to work on a farm in the outskirt of the city. That should fetch some stipend too.

Not a lot, but something. Having nothing at all is worse than getting very little, he tells himself with a smile. As they say in Nigeria, 'at all at all na im be winch', which roughly translates to 'half a loaf is better than nothing'.

Although his parents objected to this kind of hard work for him, he still did it anyway. After all he is their only son. Most times they didn't know where he was, he couldn't tell them about any work until he had completed it.

From the corner of his eye, he watched his brown pair of sandals from dear Mr. Jonah; he cannot afford to lose sight of his only pair of shoes.

The thought of Mr. Jonah always brought him joy, and he tells himself, 'one day I will help him too. God will give me the strength to take care of my family, and all my friends'.

As he does the backbreaking work, he thinks of his father, Philip.

*

His father, Philip Audu, a God fearing man, has done about everything. He worked in a government establishment for many years until it was shut down when the chief executives embezzled the public fund under their care.

They were arrested and prosecuted, but since they could bribe the unreliable police and corrupt judges with their ill gotten wealth; charges against them were dropped.

They went ahead to start their own businesses and the likes of Philip Audu were left in the cold to starve to death. They were used, bled and abandoned with their families ignominiously.

Philip has been a driver for the government for many years, a security guard, a fisherman, a farmer, a construction worker, a bricklayer, a carpenter, a painter. You name it. He has done them all — at different times — to fend for his small family.

The government forgets about people like him after they put in many years of selfless meritorious service. In most regular societies they would be entitled to some form of settlement or pension but not in Nigeria.

You are *OYO* - 'On Your Own' - when your work place is duped and closed down due to no fault of yours; a very sad reality that occurs quite frequently.

Philip, a once very handsome man, frustrated from being kicked around willy-nilly by man-made forces and factors of annihilation; has become a shadow of his old self.

He is lean, scraggy and completely ravaged by penury. He constantly battles his ubiquitous high blood pressure; one of the very many vagaries of life he has to contend with.

Only God knows how many nights he has cried himself to sleep. Overwhelmed by seemly insurmountable upheavals, he has had to make several regrettable decisions for his family. Decisions that leave a horribly bitter taste in your mouth. Decisions that depreciate your manhood, unmanly decisions. Like when he reluctantly agreed to marry off his daughters.

Two young innocent children sold into marriage for money. Money for food, money for school fees, nothing luxurious. Under dire, uncanny pressure from friends and extended family members he had to concede.

But he has not had a moment's peace ever since. He hurts inside terribly, unable to reverse his loathsome situation.

He had to do something when Frank; his beacon of hope, was sent home from school the umpteenth time for unpaid fees. His heart broke to see his only son away from school when his mates were in class.

He believed, and still believes, that education is the key to success. He, a high school graduate, could not achieve enough. With a college degree, Frank would stand a better chance to fight. A college degree though not an end in itself, is definitely a means to an end, a favorable end, he reckons.

From the day the boy was born he had told himself, and God, that the boy must acquire a college degree by whatever means, even if it would kill him.

And in spite of all the odds, he had kept him in school, even when they could not eat. Thank God the little boy understands the situation at his tender age.

He thanks God for the child's uncanny gift to comprehend things, even their poverty, having to go to school in torn clothes, with bare feet, an empty stomach, et al. The boy understands it all, he never complains about anything, a true blessing from God to have such a wonderful undemanding son.

But at times their bleak condition casts doubts on his dream of sending this smart son to college.

At times he wonders if the college dream is not too tall to achieve. Perhaps it isn't an achievable goal he has set for himself. But every time he looks into his son's handsome eyes he sees a better tomorrow.

Something unfathomable and inexplicable tells him this boy is no ordinary child. He certainly isn't ordinary he reckons.

How many boys his age would want to do menial labor to supplement their family's income? How many kids score the highest grades even on empty stomachs?

Frank is certainly not an ordinary child. But does he have a better future? That remains to be seen. God knows he would do anything to make life more bearable for his family.

But what is there to be done? He has tried everything, or perhaps almost everything.

He has never stolen and never will. Everything he owns, his scarce and meager possessions, were all acquired from hard work or through some benevolent friend or neighbor.

He cannot depend on these folks though. They all have their own individual mountains and hills to climb over.

He cannot steal either. His conscience will plague him to death. He does not covet anybody, or anyone's property. He just wants a better life for his family.

He is a God fearing man who believes in God whole-heartedly in spite of all his woes. He knows God is not responsible for his predicament, but a bunch of extremely wicked humans here on earth. A group of demonic humans not concerned about the hues and cries of the poor downtrodden masses.

But in spite of all his sadness, and pain of death, he still derives some joy from knowing that Stella Audu, the pride of his manhood, wife of his youth and mother of his children; has and always will be there for him, through thick and thin.

Their marriage has no doubt epitomized the Christian union between a man and a woman. They have stuck together throughout their arduous trek in life.

The bible says 'a man and a woman shall leave their families and be cleaved together to become one flesh', that is exactly what Stella and Philip have done, he thought to himself with a quick smile.

Frank remembers everything his father told him. Even how his mother's family had tried, to no avail, to prevent their marriage, when they failed to change her mind, they had disowned her completely.

His maternal grandfather, Chief Timothy Okoro, a timber magnate, could not understand what his darling daughter was doing with a pauper like Philip Audu, an indigent man with no background of note.

But one day, one day in the near future, there shall be a reckoning. Even in his young mind, he could understand that there would be a day of reckoning for good, for bad, for all and sundry.

*

He had passed the secondary school entrance examination at the very top of the list. That morning, he had dressed up real fast and rushed out in tow of his father. They had walked into the ministry of education compound, hand in hand.

Many other parents and their wards were all over the place, with everyone straining to see the list of the successful candidates. Most of the kids looked as scared as rabbits on a street with a million cars running through, but Frank — as always — had his smile.

One of the troublesome kids from his elementary school spots him and shouts,

"Hey Frank!"

Frank and his father both turn around to see the rowdy kid, Andrew, running towards them.

He blurts out teasingly,

"What're you doing here?"

Philip looks at the kid queerly and retorts,

"What kind of question is that young man?"

Frank smiling, says,

"Papa it's okay. We were in the same class"

"Is that why he should ask you such a question?"

Andrew mumbles,

"I'm just teasing him, sir".

"Why do you have to tease him?"

"Papa, he is my friend", still smiling, "He's only joking".

He turns to Andrew,

"Did you see the results yet?"

"Yes"

"And?"

"Your name is on top of the list", he says, glancing at Philip.

Philip beams at him,

"Are you sure about that?"

"Yes sir".

He picks up Frank happily and attempts to throw him up. They almost collapse on the ground together.

He shrieks, tears forming at the sides of his eyes,

"My son! You make me very proud!"

He turns to Andrew,

"Thank you young man. You're a good friend".

He turns to Frank,

"Wait right here. I want to see it with my own eyes"

"Yes papa".

He hurries towards the crowd in front of the notice board.

Frank turns to Andrew,

"What about you?"

"My name is not on the list"

"What does that mean?" asks Frank, confused.

"It means I failed, dummy!"

"Sorry about that".

Andrew chuckles,

"There is nothing to be sorry about. My dad will take care of it".

Three other boys join them, accompanied by their parents. One of them points at Frank,

"Mummy, this is the Frank that scored the highest".

The lady, the boy's mother, a beautiful good natured woman beams at Frank,

"Oh my dear. Congratulations! Your parents must be really proud of you"

"Thank you ma", answers Frank, demurely.

The parents shake hands with him effusively.

Philip reappears, grinning widely, and the parents congratulate him as they all start to leave the premises.

The beautiful woman is overheard telling her son,

"Frank is the type of boy I want you to be friends with. Not some dull, no good, charlatan".

After the euphoria of Frank's success in the entrance examination had abated, his family is once again faced with the stark reality of their situation. They had to go borrowing to prepare him for high school.

There were specific requirements to meet if Frank was to attend high school. For one, there was the non-negotiable matter of the school fees, then uniforms, books and other numerous school supplies. Education was not free at any level.

Frank started taking up a lot more hard work to save up something towards his school. And although boarding was almost mandatory, his father had been able to negotiate for a day-student status.

Boarding — although a far better way to learn — was far too unaffordable for the Audus. Africans say: *'some people have heads, but do not have caps; whereas others have caps but no heads'*. Frank was an unusually bright lad with a head but no cap.

He got up as early as five o'clock in the morning, before daylight — with deep shadows still lurking menacingly — to hurry off to work at the same construction site. At times he got hired, other times he did not.

When he got hired, he worked as hard as any man three, four times his age. He carried — and lifted — building materials that weighed about five times his weight, over some considerable distance.

When he did not get hired, he went from site to site until someone gave him work to do. Then at night he would read books, books borrowed from neighbors, books that should be beyond his comprehension, high school books.

At age eleven, he went to sleep at twelve midnight and got up at five o'clock everyday, except Sunday. Sunday was sacred to him, a day to worship God, a day to glorify God, a day to thank God for all his mercies to him and to his family.

His mates were spending their vacation — before high school began — doing kids stuff, but he was too busy doing adult things to have any time for play.

When his parents got up late at night and saw him studying, they would force him to go to sleep. He would pretend to sleep, and when they went back to sleep, he would sneak back to his books with a smile.

*

By the time high school started, Frank was already two grades ahead of his peers. He had studied and understood every subject taught in the first and second grades of high school. He had even examined himself and passed. Some of his neighbors thought he was crazy.

His classmates — awed by him — concluded he was weird. As always, he scored the highest grades and answered every question asked in class, and tests.

And even when he pretended not to know the answers to the questions some of the teachers asked — to avoid making enemies — they would coerce him to speak for the class or be punished.

He did not have any close friend; his best friend was his book, any kind of book.

One time he stumbled across a book on philosophy, in the teachers' library. 'The Voice of Reason' written by the sage, Chief Obafemi Awolowo, a book many scholars find complex and complicated, but Frank describes as interesting.

Even one of the most confusing books of all time; 'The Man Died' by Wole Soyinka, was another one of his favorite books.

He read these really deep books with understanding, even as a child. His favorite quote, from 'The Man Died' was; *"The man dies in him who keeps silent in the face of tyranny"*.

Inside his young mind, he knew that their situation was oppressive, tyrannical, and caused by greedy evil people.

He also read and kept as his own, Chief Obafemi Awolowo's saying; *"Most young people today, waste their time and energy on fruitless ventures, the few who direct their energies towards purposeful employ, end up successful"*.

Frank read that and concluded that the sage was speaking to him. He took extra care to direct all his time and energy to good use.

His classmates, therefore, could not be close friends with him because they had divergent interests. While they preferred to play, he liked to read and work.

Many of them did try to be friendly to him because he was smart and always helped with their homework, and their tests.

By the third year, Frank was known by everyone in school as the guy with the big books. Anyone with any academic or scholarly concern sought him out for consultation.

He taught his mates; he taught his seniors, he wrote love letters and poems for them. His interests were only academic.

As the boys chased the girls, Frank picked the prizes for best student. He was the kind of student teachers loved to have in their class.

He metamorphosed into a very strong handsome looking teenager. The constant hard work, the carrying, the lifting, the building, the breaking — of heavy stuff — had built his muscles into a well-formed mass of strength.

He was no longer the little helpless kid bullies liked to pick on. He had a very firm six pack abdomen. His arms were strong and powerful like a boxer's.

4 GAME ON AND OFF

"Family life is full of major and minor crisis" – *Thomas Moore*

By his fourth year in high school he got involved in a money making scheme. The final exam for every high school student in West Africa, the West African School Certificate (*WASC*) Examination, was — and still is — a dreaded final test for graduating high school students.

It is usually taken in the fifth and final year. Many people write this examination for many years without passing a single subject. The ones who work hard enough — and with some luck — write this exam and pass the minimum number of subjects.

Five credits including Mathematics and English language make up the minimum passing level. With five credits, a high school graduate is qualified to take the almighty *JAMB* examination, the college entrance exam.

If *WASC* is dreaded, then *JAMB* — the Joint Admissions and Matriculation Board — is super dreaded. This is the exam that prevents poor people from going to colleges and universities. This is because, although many rich kids always fail this very difficult exam, they still go to college, or university.

They still get admitted because their rich parents are usually donors to the higher institutions; friends with the vice-chancellors, deans, and heads of departments. So even when they fail, they still find their way to a college.

But the have-nots, with no family connections, must pass this very tough exam with flying colors to secure a place in any higher institution. Although a few reputable colleges do not care about family name, or wealth. Once you fail, you do not get in, no matter who you are, or who you know.

These dull children, with more cash than intelligence, who must attend these prestigious and strict colleges, to pretend to the world that they are after all not dunderheads, usually seek out brilliant and smart people to write these exams for them. And for the service, a tidy sum of money is exchanged.

Therefore, Frank being a well-known terror to tough exams was a well sought after commodity by all the rich dullards in, and out of, town.

There are two methods to this very fraudulent scheme. Firstly; the mercenary exam candidate is stationed in a safe room not too far from the exam hall, where a prearranged runner brings the questions to him.

The mercenary answers all the questions before the end of the exam, and the runner takes it back to the hall for submission.

Secondly; the mercenary sits in the exam hall where he fills in the rich dullard's name and number, answers the questions, submits the answers like everyone else, and everybody is happy.

The smart one makes some money; the dull one gets the desired grades. The goal is achieved.

Some mercenaries liked to work with their own runners. This scheme, although it sounds simple, is actually one of the fastest ways to go to prison for young people in search of the proverbial short cut.

This is because it takes a lot of courage to do this deal, and in the exam halls there are usually security guards and police officers who might either be in on the deal, or be out to make the empty barrels fail.

When in, they facilitate the operation by protecting the runner, or mercenary inside the hall and there are cases where the invigilators and security personnel actually act as couriers between the mercenaries and the dullards in the hall.

When there is a lot of money involved, from the dunderheads, the officials orchestrate the operation. And it runs smoothly like clockwork.

They give out the questions to the mercenary or runner who leaves the hall and returns later to personally submit the answers to the official directly. Easy like 'Sunday morning'.

The more money involved the more high up — and more guaranteed — is the operation. But like every bad deal, many times the operation turns awry.

Some of the players become greedy, they do not grease enough palms, and the disgruntled parties blow the deal to hell. People are arrested and jailed. Some lose their jobs. They spend more money than they made, and are let off the hook in some cases.

Frank never went inside the halls. He always insisted on his own trusted runner. He waited in his secret, and safe, location for his runner.

At times the security in the hall is too tight and impenetrable that the runner is unable to get the questions on time, or at all. Fights ensued in such situations.

The dullard would want his money back for service not done, and for inadvertently failing the exam. Frank, in such situations, would want to return his part of the loot; but his burly and tough looking runner, John, would have none of that.

John's favorite line in such a situation is always the same,

"I'm not a bank. You don't give me money and expect to get it back. If you don't like my business, call the police".

And of course nobody would go to report their nefarious business association to the police.

Frank — at times — did the exam for them again the following year at a discounted price.

John, a tough kid in the hood with no interest whatever in education — but with the courage and tenacity of a raging mad bull — took a liking to Frank.

They met at an examination center; Frank was writing for some dunderhead, and John did the running.

They almost got arrested, but John saved the day. They became stuck together as partners. Their illicit business prospered, their association continued, and after a while, a friendship naturally sprouted and blossomed.

John, another deprived and homeless kid of the same generation, with no knowledge of his parents' whereabouts, and with no friends — like Frank — wanted more than anything else in the world, to succeed in life, no matter the cost, his greatest desire was to, one day, leave the African continent.

He breathed, ate, drank, smelt and dreamt of Germany every second of the day. He wanted to go to Europe so bad he would sell himself to any European that would buy him.

He liked Frank no doubt, except that they had different dreams. He wanted to migrate by all means; Frank wanted to go to college by all means.

Frank is a born leader, John is a born follower. They complement each other perfectly like 'yin' and 'yang' in Chinese philosophy.

John did not mind that he could not read or write very well. It did not bother him in the least.

Frank's brilliance was an asset to him. John got the exam deals, Frank did the exams, they both profited.

John saved towards his migration to Europe, Frank saved towards his college education.

John had a knack for sniffing up new ways of making money, more money. Life to him was all about making more money.

One evening, in a bus, on their way from an examination center in another town, John asks Frank,

"Can you write and pass *JAMB*?"

Frank glances at him from the book he is poring at with a tiny smile,

"Yeah. I think so. Why do you ask?"

"I know this family whose three kids are taking *JAMB*"

"And?"

Prods Frank.

John grinning, quips,

"I told them we can handle it".

Frank grins,

"We eh?" turning back to his book.

"Yes, partner", smiling.

"What're you reading?"

Frank shows him the book's cover page, and says with glee,

"Jurisprudence"

"Ju... what?" confused.

Frank grins,

"Jurisprudence".

John, wide eyed, exclaims,

"What language is that?"

Smiling, Frank responds,

"Latin origin. It is about the philosophy of law"

John, still wide eyed,

"Philosophy? Law? What business do you have with all that big stuff? You're still in high school!"

"Yes, but I will be a lawyer one day. I'm just trying to understand some subjects in law".

John and the other people in the bus look at him queerly, as if to say,

'Oh this handsome looking young man is losing his mind very fast. What a big loss to his mother!'

John glances around at the other passengers in the bus and whispers to him,

"I know I can't read or write too well, but do you really understand what you're reading?"

Frank nods at him with a smile.

John looks at him reading for a moment. He glances down at the words on the open page that seem like Greek letters to him.

He shakes his head as he turns to look through the open window. Germany and Germans automatically flood his mind.

By the time Frank was in the last grade of high school, he had written numerous *WASC* and *JAMB* exams for many dunderheads. And he had saved up quite a tidy sum of money towards acquiring his law degree.

His family did not have to worry about his first year in college, he reckons. And who knows, maybe in college he could find a runner who might be able to make things happen like John.

If only John would agree to go to college with him. They would have made a formidable pair, he reckons.

He had told John he would write every necessary exam — free of charge — for him to come to college with him, but John would have none of that. His unquenchable dream was to live in Europe, nothing else.

There was nothing in the world to change that dream for him. But he understands, after all nothing was going to change his own dream either.

A man's dream must live as long as he lives. As an everlasting burning light of hope that paves the way through even the darkest darkness for every mind with a purpose, a destination, and a goal.

A man with no dream is less than a man, not human and not fit to live, because a life without a dream is not worthy of living. That was his philosophy of life, and he respected everyone and their dream.

He loved John, his only friend, like a brother, the brother he does not have. Although five years older than him, John still respected him greatly.

It did not matter to him that Frank was his junior, an unusual thing in Africa where most people lived and acted out their lives with a heavy dependence on age and length of time on earth. This is the African age-grade syndrome.

*

Frank wrote and passed both the *WASC* and *JAMB* without hitch. The only incident was when Frank filled out the registration form for the WASC exam, and enrolled for eight subjects like everyone else, but rushed back the following morning to ask for his form back from the principal's office.

He was troubled the entire night that because he did not enroll for Christian Religious Knowledge — CRK — also known as Bible Knowledge, he would fail every other subject. He added CRK and was the only one enrolled for nine subjects.

The other students would have gladly enrolled for only five or six subjects if permitted, and could not, therefore, understand the strain of madness that had possessed Frank.

Some people actually told him, to his face, he would fail for enrolling that many subjects. Even Philip, his father, was concerned. He asked him if nine subjects were not too much to handle in one exam, Frank politely told him — like he told everyone else — that he would fail if he did not register for CRK. They left him alone.

And for the first time in the history of his high school, Frank passed all nine papers with distinction. And JAMB came, Frank jabbed *JAMB*.

He scored way above the cut-off mark for admission to the law department of the *University of Ibadan, Ibadan, Nigeria*; Nigeria's first and best institution of higher learning.

One of Africa's first colleges of repute, a former college, and affiliate, of *London University*, a well known institution reputable for producing students of 'great learning and sound character'. An excellent citadel of learning simply referred to as *UI*.

Being in UI back in the day was like being in *Oxford*, or *Harvard*. Some of Africa's finest intellects passed through UI. You can, therefore, imagine Frank and his family's elation at his success, at obtaining admission to study law at the '*greatest of the greatests*' UI!

Frank became an instant 'hit movie' in his small town in the Niger-delta region of Nigeria.

Everyone wanted to see him for two reasons. Firstly, because only very few people from the Niger-delta region ever made it across the country to UI.

And secondly, because he was the youngest to achieve the feat, only sixteen going on seventeen. An incredible feat without doubt.

He was due to start in UI in a few months. He went about preparing for the all-important voyage.

His friend John had gone off to Lagos, the commercial capital of Nigeria, a city just like New York City in many ways.

Overcrowded, the yellow cabs, the very expensive standard of living, the fast pace of things, the tall sky scrappers, and the sleeplessness.

A 24 hour round the clock bustling city! A city where everything is bought and sold, the good, and the bad.

And as New York City is to the Western World, so is Lagos to Africa. A real bustling modern city with thousands of visitors every year.

A city everyone loved to live in, or at least loved to visit. John had gone off in pursuit of his dream. And it is only in Lagos you can get traveling papers, at this time, genuine or fake.

If the embassy would not give you a visa, you could go to *Oluwole*, a tough hood in Lagos, to get any kind of document made, as long as you have the money.

You pay, you get the 'right' papers, you board the plane, you arrive at your destination, with, or without stress.

Many young Nigerians do this and succeed. They spend the rest of their lives in these foreign lands, because they might never be able to return home for a lack of real travel papers.

The not so lucky ones get to their destination and are sent back home, deported, only to start all over again.

Nothing stops a desperately determined man. No right thinking young man wants to live in 'hellish Nigeria', they say.

John moved to Lagos with his unquenchable desire to actualize his burning dream. Nothing was going to stop him as long as he could still breath, he says.

Before he left for Lagos, he had made a vow to always be there for Frank. He told him he would see him through college as soon as he got to Germany and started making some money.

Considering Frank's sterling performance in both *WASC* and *JAMB*, one would have expected, or at the least thought, that the quasi-government would consider him for some type of scholarship, a complete or at least partial scholarship. But this was not to be.

The wealthy folks, who can afford the massive college costs on their own, without a pinch, still get the scholarships for their dull wards, and dunces.

This is like a man with no head having two caps, and a man with two heads having no cap at all. A total travesty!

Of course Frank had applied for a scholarship, and true to type, the scholarship administrators had told him very candidly that he could not get any.

The list was completely full they said. The administrators received gifts in cash, and in kind, from the rich parents and put all the dullards on the list.

But that did not deter Frank, for he believed God would see him through, no matter what. He had saved up a tidy sum from his examination scheme; a handsome amount that could see him through, at least, the first year, if managed prudently.

He was a frugal teenager, no doubt. He did not have any luxurious cravings like many people his age; he did not have a girlfriend either, and was still a virgin.

He never tried to impress anyone, he could wear the same clothes everyday the entire year, and it would not matter to him. He just wanted to study, that is what mattered to him.

He wanted knowledge, for knowledge is power, and knowledge is strength; he wanted the power, and the strength, to free his family from the stranglehold of penury.

He knew the journey he was embarking on was a long arduous one, but that did not faze him in anyway. He believed God would make a way where there seems no way.

He was prepared to work very hard. He was prepared to do whatever it takes to get the degree in law.

He always wondered what he would be as an adult. He read every material he could find on choosing a career:. He considered medicine, he considered engineering, he considered banking, and he even considered teaching — in memory of the great Mr. Jonah.

He would have gladly become a teacher just like Mr. Jonah, except that teaching did not seem very lucrative. His family's needs were way beyond what a teacher's salary can handle.

He needed much more than a teacher's salary to triumph over their endless woes.

But he finally decided on law after reading a book. Not a book on career choice, but the all time classic bestseller: 'The Godfather', by Mario Puzo.

After reading that book, he knew for a fact that he only wanted to be one thing; a lawyer. Yes, he made his unequivocal choice from reading that book.

There was no going back after reading 'The Godfather'. He chose his path, his course, and his way of life, without any doubt in his mind.

*

One month to leave for UI, seventeen years old; bag packed, school fees and books ready, disaster strikes.

Philip Audu, a man with a broken spirit, collapses in the bathroom, struck by a massive heart attack.

He is rushed to the hospital; family and neighbors run around helter-skelter. It is pandemonium.

They fetch Frank from a job site.

A choice must be made, and must be made very fast too. Leave Philip in a government hospital, he dies, unambiguously.

Take him to a very expensive private hospital, he might live, he might die, but there must be enough money to make a non-refundable deposit, whether he lives, or dies.

Now this is a community of indigent people, a people who can barely survive, a people who must scrounge for what to eat, a people with no money or resource to their name or to their existence here on earth.

This is a community with no access to readily available medical care, or any sort of health insurance whatsoever. This is a cash only, 'PAYGO' - Pay As You Go - society in its purest form.

And in the bare and despicable government hospital, Philip is laid down on a stretcher on the floor, dying slowly with every passing second, unattended.

Frank, Philip's only son, has to make a decision for the family.

He glances at his mother, Stella; a woman overwhelmed with anguish, a woman inundated with pain, a woman crying helplessly, a woman pulverized by her inability to bring back her heartthrob — of many years — from the threshold of death.

He goes to her, lifts her from the floor and says meekly,

"Mama don't cry. Papa will be fine"

"My son, how? How will he be fine? We can't even eat?"

She holds him tight, and wails helplessly.

Frank forces a smile,

"Mama he will be fine, believe me".

He turns to their neighbors who are hovering around like hapless frightened dogs with their tails in-between their thighs, and pleads,

"Please help me take him to Holy Cross. I'll meet you all there in a few minutes".

They look at him as if he is out of his mind.

His mother pauses from crying, turns to him, and queries gently,

"Holy Cross? Are you sure?"

He smiles at her,

"Yes mama. I'll meet you there. I need to get something from the house".

He turns and runs out of the hospital before another word can be uttered.

She turns to the men,

"You heard him, let's go to Holy Cross!"

The hapless men pick up the stretcher from the floor and move to leave the building. They hurry into Holy Cross Hospital, just around the corner, privately owned, no doubt the best and definitely the most expensive healthcare facility in the community.

They put down the stretcher in a corner.

A robust female medical assistant walks up to them, and asks without sympathy,

"Can I help you?"

Stella answers, holding Philip's dying hand,

"My husband needs urgent help....it is a heart attack"

The medical assistant queries without empathy,

"Is he a patient here?"

"He is now", retorts Stella.

She glares at her like a robot,

"Does he have a card here?"

Stella whispers tearfully,

"No"

"Do you want to make a deposit and get the card so we...?"

One of the neighbors, Robert, cuts in angrily, out of frustration,

"Why don't you help the dying man first before you talk about cards and deposits?"

The robotic medical assistant retorts,

"I'm sorry I can't help you. Hospital policy requires a deposit before treatment is commenced. You either make a deposit to start treatment, or leave".

She turns and walks away from them angrily.

Philip grunts, dying even faster.

Just then Frank runs in and dashes to his father on the stretcher, he holds his hand, smiles at him, tears in his eyes,

"Papa you must stay alive! It isn't your time yet. Remember our dream?"

Philip tries to speak,

"My son..."

Frank puts a finger to his lips, and says lovingly,

"No papa, don't speak yet. We will talk later", wiping away his tears.

The neighbors wipe their teary eyes too.

Stella looks at her little boy with the eyes of a very proud mother. She watches him take charge like the truly strong African male child he is, a soaring eagle, a truly indestructible warrior.

Frank goes over to the counter and pulls out a wad of money. He hands over the deposit and fills out the admission form.

Then, and only then, almost two hours after, did the heart attack victim, Philip Audu, get any help.

Holy Cross Hospital crew went to work on Philip, the ravaged man; with no guarantee of the outcome whatsoever.

Frank, the selfless young man, had to dig very deep into his college fund to save his dying father, even when there was no certainty of his surviving the heart attack.

Having been left unattended for that long, Philip was dangling precariously between this world and the next.

Although no amount of money could guarantee his survival at this point, Frank was willing, and actually did bring out everything he had to the last penny.

He had even brought out all his expensive law books for conversion to money. He did not, even for one second, pause to consider the end of his own personal dream.

His dream was running down hill, very fast, at an uncontrollable pace, beyond redemption, before his very eyes, and he still had a sincere smile.

His whole world was crashing around him, and he could still smile. He could still smile sincerely.

He gave up his dream, spent all his savings, sold all his books and took up an overload of work to pay for his father's life. Even when his mother reminded him of his dream, he had told her, with a pleasant smile,

"What is the joy of success if there is no father to share it with?".

The long time neighbor and family friend Robert, who had snapped at the robust robotic medical assistant when they arrived at Holy Cross two weeks before, cornered Frank one evening and whispered,

"Frank, I know you love your papa. We all do. But you see, you're a young man with a bright future...with a dream...you must not sacrifice your dream and your future for your old man. He is in coma now for two weeks, only God knows if he will survive or not.

But you must live your dream. If your father lives, thank God. But if he dies, he will be unhappy in his grave to know his illness thwarted your dream. Your admission to UI is a once in a lifetime opportunity. You must not give it up. Not for anything, not for anyone".

Frank looks at him quietly as he continues.

"I wish this did not happen. And I wish we could do something to help the situation. But we are old and poor, and helpless, your parents and I are old, but you're the next generation, our hope for tomorrow, and our hope for a better day.

If you give it up now, you will be falling into the same abyss of failure and lack that our generation lives in. You'll be mortgaging the lives of your own children, their happiness, their opportunity, because if you succeed tomorrow your own children will succeed the day after tomorrow".

Frank smiles at him wanly and says,

"Uncle Bob, I thank you very much. I really appreciate your concern, but you see I don't really mind forfeiting my dream to save my father. I will never be happy if I succeed and lose my father"

Uncle Bob urges him further,

"What if you miss this golden chance and your father still dies? God forbid"

Frank smiles,

"Well, I'll take it as the will of God"

"That is my point. We don't know what will happen, only God knows"

"Yes. I have prayed to God. And I'll do my best for papa".

Uncle Bob looks at him, tears forming in his old troubled eyes,

"I want you to think about it"

Frank smiles brightly,

"I have. And I have decided to stay here and take care of my family, no matter what"

"You're a good child. A real blessing. Every father's wish. But you see, our people say; 'it is a taboo for a father to bury his own child, a child buries his parents'. Think about everything I've told you. Good night child".

Frank mumbles,

"Good night Uncle Bob", and watch him walk away.

5 GAME ON AGAIN

"You cannot control success or failure, only how you react to it" – Chris Gore

Three weeks from the day Philip suffered a heart attack, one week to UI's freshman date of resumption, college fund spent, law books sold, being out of coma, they bring him home still weak, and halfway to recovery, not by choice, but because it is less expensive than having him stay at the hospital.

Stella, Frank, extended family and friends can not thank God enough for sparing their husband, father, relative and friend.

Tears of joy flow freely, unhindered, and uninterrupted, from old eyes, and from young eyes, half blinded by a mixture of pain, of loss, of sadness, of happiness, of anger, of excitement.

These unleashed tears of a mixed variety were being released for two reasons. Firstly, for Philip's happy and successful return from the threshold of death.

And secondly, for Frank's sad loss, and absence from the line-up at *Trenchard Hall* — the main auditorium — in UI.

In two weeks, gaily dressed young men and women in free flowing blue academic gowns, and square shaped hats with flat tops, will be signing the matriculation register in front of the Vice-Chancellor of the University of Ibadan, with their families and friends acting as witnesses, at a matriculation ceremony.

These ceremonies, usually preceded by some ritual performed by the *'stalites'* — old students, on the *'jambites'* — new students, were

41

always something to look forward to, according to legend, and eyewitness accounts.

The term *'jambite'*, a connotation from JAMB, which means a new student who recently jabbed, or passed JAMB, is derogatory, and is used to refer to a new student who is presumably a *JJC* — a 'Johnny Just Come'.

A *JJC* is supposedly a stupid person with no sense of direction around campus. A person who is always asking for direction even to a place right in his face.

Also, *'Jambites'* are rumored to have very bushy tails that are cut off on the morning of matriculation.

'Jambites' are pretty easy to spot around campus, *'Jambitos'* for females. They usually walk together in clusters holding very neat and straight paper files that contain their registration forms and receipts.

Their frightened tails are tucked in between their thighs, and they are ready to fly out of their skin any second.

'Stalites' walked by themselves, or with a partner — a boyfriend, or a girlfriend, and you could never see their registration forms in their hands, they folded them into their back pockets, or pocket books. They did not care if the forms were crumpled up or not.

Jambites will not dare crumple their forms and receipts.

The *stalites* went around campus in search of the folks with clean brand new paper files, bushy frightened tails, and harassed them playfully in good humor.

Very early on the morning of matriculation, the *'stalites,'* dressed in their worst pairs of jeans, dirty and torn in most cases; would fill buckets and pails with water.

Some with dirty water, some with wet cereal, and they would form a barricade at the entrance and exit points of the hostels.

They stay there all morning, with their drinks, usually beer, or liquor, in wait for the *'jambites'*. And they terrorize the new students playfully.

The *'jambites'*, all well dressed in suits, ties, dresses, and academic gowns are barred from leaving the hostel for Trenchard Hall, venue of the academic ceremony, where the Chancellor, Pro-chancellor, Vice-chancellor, deans, heads-of-departments, Professors and distinguished guests are all waiting.

The only way out for the *'jambites'* is to participate in the initiation, or induction ritual, which includes a macabre dance, and a cutting of their tails.

The *'stalites'* make them do a gross dance in front of their visiting friends and family members, their tails are cut, they are baptized — a sprinkling of water, which may be dirty or with cereal, some are given a drink, and they are let out to go attend their ceremony; a ritual performed by a chanting of the word *'jambite'*, or *'jambito'*, repeatedly by the *'stalites'*.

Although a rather grotesque ritual, many people actually enjoyed it, and looked forward to it every session, either as a *'jambite'*, or as a *'stalite'*, it was, and still is, one of the very many rituals and traditions that make UI great, unique and different.

Frank knew about all this, and a lot more. He had read everything he could find about UI, written by 'non-*uites*','*uites*', and 'ex-*uites*'.

'Uites' were current students, and 'ex-*uites*' were old or former students. He had read numerous articles, essays and books about everything UI.

Students of UI, past and present, referred to each other as 'greatest *uite*'. He even bought a book called, *'Our UI'*, written by an 'ex-*uite*'. He knew all the great, all the weak, all the good, and all the bad stories about UI. He even had a map of UI, a beautiful city within a city.

He knew he would miss being a student of that great citadel of learning, no doubt; but he accepted the derailment and did not let it bother him.

He pushed that very painful thought to a remote corner of his mind, maintained his good nature, and with his forever present smile, he pandered on, unwavering.

He continued to work hard; he continued to care for his family, as much as he could, without any grudge. He put law, and UI, behind him.

Thank God, his father's spirit was restored, his flesh was responding to all the treatment, and to all the care, and to all the attention; but his soul was still greatly troubled on account of Frank's loss.

Philip felt personally responsible, naturally. He tried to talk about it with his dear son, but he would have none of it, all he had said was,

"Papa, I don't want us to talk about anything. Nothing else matters to me as long as I have you and mama here with me".

Philip could not argue with him because he had been grinning, and seemed very sincere, when he said that.

Even Stella had mentioned to him that Frank was very happy as it were, and that losing his admission was the farthest thing on his mind.

He just wanted his parents to live long, he did not care about anything else. In his reckoning; what will be, will be.

But the Friday, before the Monday *'jambites'* reported to the student affairs department in UI, something very strange and comically bizarre happened.

John who had been in Lagos in search of the *proverbial golden fleece,* in pursuit of his dream, suddenly returned home, after five months.

Frank had concluded in his heart, that his dear friend and brother, John, had succeeded and made it to Frankfurt, Germany. He was expecting a post card from Europe, in the mail, any day soon.

He was so taken aback when John appeared at his job site that he broke down and cried even before John could say anything.

He cried not for himself, but for his dear friend, because he thought John had been deported from Germany after the immense struggle, after all the risks, yet another failed dream, he thought.

John holds him lovingly,

"Don't cry Frank. What's wrong? Why're you crying?"

They hug themselves very closely, very warmly, very dearly, two long lost brothers, two suffering brothers, two hopeless youths, two helpless Nigerians.

It was very unusual, and normally unheard of for men to cry in Africa, especially in front of other people. It was taboo and an indication or a premonition of something bad, or evil, about to happen.

Among certain tribes of Africa it was considered a sign of weakness for a man to cry openly in front of a woman. A woman can not, and must not behold a man cry openly, even at the death of someone close.

It was, therefore, very precarious to see Frank bawl helplessly in front of John, who himself, confounded by this open display of weakness, is mortified gravely, and is moved to shed hot tears.

His own hot tears that stream down his cheeks freely and unencumbered, a taboo, a weakness, a failing by African warrior standards.

After they both take a moment to bawl quietly in a silent corner of the construction site, they wipe their eyes and look at each other quietly; embarrassed and strengthened at the same time by the strange but shared experience.

They had never cried before, at least not out loud, and not openly, and not in front of someone else shamelessly. It is one thing to shed tears without a sound, but another thing to bawl like a baby deprived of milk by the mother.

The sharing of this shameful act gives them a renewed affection, a renewed strength, a renewed vigor, a renewed discovery of a deep kind of oneness, and sameness.

These are two very identical young men thrown together by fate, and by destiny, a cruel, or a friendly, supernatural force, a crossing of paths has merged these two worlds into one inseparable unit.

One indivisible part, one unified tower under construction, an undetermined construction. A building without a plan.

A clueless journey through life by two identical men of like minds, who having identified the ills militating against the attainment of a just society, silently, and unwittingly, join hands together to build something out of nothing, even without a building plan.

Moment taken, eyes wiped, they look at each other quietly.

John clears his throat and asks,

"Are you alright?"

Frank smiles,

"Yes I'm fine. You?"

John laughs throatily,

"Never felt better. Maybe we should cry more often".

Frank laughs too, then looks at him with sad eyes,

"What happened? I believed you were in Frankfurt already"

"I know. Things didn't work out as planned"

"How?"

"They tried to dupe me".

"Dupe you?"

"Yes. You know, some of these guys say they will get you to Europe, they collect your money, give you very fake papers, put you on a plane, but as soon as you arrive there, they send you back right away, your money gone. Non-refundable!"

Frank says,

"So?"

"So I changed my mind. I will kill anyone that dupes me, and since I don't want to kill another human being, I came back home"

"Now what will you do?"

"I'm not sure yet. I'll probably wait until I find a reliable method. A fool proof method. But I'll work and save some more money. I met someone who knows someone at the embassy that can get me a real visa"

"A real visa?"

"Yes, but it is very expensive. When I've the money I'll go to the man"

"And you can trust this man?"

"I think so. He works at the embassy. But I'll make him understand that he dies if he dupes me. I don't care if I lose my life too, but he dies!"

Frank looks away for a moment and then turns back to him, smiling coldly,

"Is going to Germany worth dying, or killing someone for?"

"No. I'll kill him and then kill myself, not because of Germany, but because he would have killed my dream. If my dream dies, I'm dead, and the person responsible dies!"

Frank looks at him, and remembers Uncle Bob's words,

'... you must not sacrifice your dream, and your future... not for anything, not for anyone...'.

John looks at him and quips,

"Are you okay?"

Frank forces a smile,

"Yes, I'm fine, yes... yes very fine".

John grins widely,

"You must be ready for UI now. When're you leaving, Barrister Frank Audu?"

Frank laughs heartily.

John grins and says,

"You know, since I'm still around, I can come with you to Ibadan and stay until after your convocation"
"You mean matriculation?"
"Yes, sorry, matriculation. Convocation is graduation, right?"
"Yes", smiling.
"Okay, when do we leave?"
"We're not going"
"Why not, you don't want me to come with you? You think I'll embarrass you?"
"Not at all!"
"Then why don't you want me to come?" he asks, smiling
"Because I'm not going myself".
John grins,
"What're you talking about?"
"I can't make it".
John smiles as he says,
"Stop playing"
Frank grins,
"I'm serious. I'm not going anymore".
John frowns,
"What in the world are you talking about?"
Frank looks at him impassively,
"It's a long story my friend".
John looks at him quietly.
Frank clears his throat softly, and tells him Philip's heart tale.

*

The following day, Saturday, Frank went about his business. John too went about his business. They did not see each other.

Even Sunday came and went, they still did not see each other. John seemed to be avoiding Frank.

Frank went to church in the morning very upbeat. He is happy and smiling as always.

After church, he went to look for John, could not find him, went fishing, caught a big catch and prepared a nice decent meal for his family.

Philip — the miraculous victor of a heart attack, still sad, knowing the following day should have heralded his son's entry into UI, eats only a little bit.

Even when his dear son, and his loving wife, spare nothing in their attempt to comfort him, he still can not come out of his deep pit of sadness. He is depressed.

They talk for some time into the night until sleep overwhelms them. They bid each other good night.

Five o'clock Monday morning, Frank is still in bed, having privately made up his mind the night before, to stay home the entire day to mourn — once and for all, the death of his dream.

He had decided to take the day off any work, off any activity, and off reading anything, even newspapers — his passion.

He decides to only go to church in the evening to have a word with God, and His son Jesus Christ.

He would go to church, and then ask God and His son to sit down, and the three of them, with no one eavesdropping, would discuss his life.

About what to do; and to know if he should still dream, or to forget about dreaming altogether. They have to tell him what to do, since he no longer has any clue whatsoever.

He will not give up, no. He will hand it all to God and His son. He remembers his pastor saying sometime in the past that, 'when you have done all you can and failed, and you know you can not do anything anymore, you have a word with God and hand Him your life, and your life's situations'.

'You hand Him everything, then stand back and watch Him take control', yes, that is what the pastor said with zest the other day, he reckons.

Frank falls asleep with these thoughts flying crisply through his mind, back and forth.

That morning, around five o'clock, returning slowly from 'sleep-land', his mind stirring up gradually with the same thoughts from the previous night, he hears excited banging on their door, or perhaps he imagined he could hear something, or someone, banging, or knocking loudly, on their door.

He opens his eyes wide, and listens, trying to figure if the sound he heard is real or imagined. Not having to figure long, he hears the sound again, this time louder.

As he rises up from his sleeping position, his mother, herself a light sleeper, beats him to the door, she opens the door without even asking who it is.

Maybe an unusual thing in a country with above average crime rate. But when you know without a doubt that there is nothing of value in your possession, then you have no fear of losing anything.

She had opened the door for only one reason, the thought that a neighbor might be in urgent need, and if that be the case, it did not matter that it was only five o'clock in the morning.

Her house — although very meager and humble — is open to all her neighbors any time of the day. This is her character, a true Christian character, a giving and sharing character.

She will give everything she has to a neighbor in need without a second's contemplation, such is her spirit and her soul.

She opens the door, and standing there with a huge grin on his face, is not a neighbor, but John, who is carrying a traveling bag.

She is taken aback for a split second, but makes room for him to enter, as she asks,

"John? Is everything alright?"

John beams happily,

"Good morning mama!"

"Good morning dear. Are you traveling?"

Grinning,

"Yes. We're traveling!"

Stella, confused, queries,

"We? Who is we?"

John walks away from her, in search of Frank, Stella follows him from behind, curious.

He calls out loud,

"Frank!"

Frank appears from a doorway, very surprised to see him.

He asks,

"John? What is going on? What is the bag for? Are you traveling?"

Still grinning, John says,

"You're not ready yet? Hurry up boy! We have a bus to catch".

Frank exchanges perturbed glances with his mother.

John yells out happily, putting down his bag in a corner,

"What're you waiting for? Hurry up!"

"What're you talking about?" queries Frank, who is at a loss.

Philip woken up by all the noise, appears from another door and quips,

"What is..." he yawns, "... happening? John?"

"Good morning papa!"

"Morning. What's happening?"

"Nothing sir. Frank and I are traveling this morning"

Frank, Philip, and Stella, all chorus,

"Traveling?"

Frank, very confused, asks,

"Traveling to where?"

"We're going to Ibadan, to UI!"

Philip glares at him angrily,

"Boy, there are certain things people don't joke about, especially very early in the morning!"

John stops grinning,

"I'm not joking, sir"

"You're not joking?" pursues Philip

"No sir", John answers seriously.

Frank looks at him quietly, not smiling.

Philip looks at Frank, then at Stella.

She turns to John and asks quietly,

"What exactly are you saying my child?"

John glances at Frank, then at Stella, and says with passion,

"I want Frank to go to school. I can't watch his dream die while I'm alive, not in front of me, he is the only friend and brother I have. And because of him, I have a father and a mother that I did not have before", pointing at them.

Tears well up in Stella's eyes as she whispers,

"John, we love you as much as we love Frank, but I'm sure you know that we don't have the money to send him to school, and UI for that matter"

"I've some money", says John meekly, "once he registers and starts, it will be easy to continue, and by God's grace finish".

Philip clears his throat. Trying hard not to cry, he says,

"John, do you realize what you're saying?"

John retorts passionately,

"I know sir. I have thought hard about it for three days, and two nights".

Frank looks into John's eyes very intently, and asks,

"John, you're sure you want to do this?"

"Yes little brother, I want to do this", smiling.

"What about your own dream?", asks Frank.

"After you matriculate and become a lawyer, I'll travel to Europe"

"You mean *convocate*?"

"Yes, sorry, *convocate*, graduate. When you graduate, I'll go to Germany"

"In about five years, you know?"

John grins, "I don't care how long it takes little brother, as long as you graduate!"

Stella holds Philip's hands to stop them from shaking too badly as they watch these two uncommon friends.

John claps his hands urgently,

"C'mon boy, we don't have enough time for small talk now! Hurry up, pack your stuff!"

Frank flies into the adjoining room to get ready.

Philip, wiping silent tears from his eyes, holds John's hands and whispers,

"Why're you doing this?"

John looks at him. He looks at Stella, then at him again, and says quite frankly,

"If my little brother can give up his dream to save my father's life, I see no reason why I should not give up mine to rekindle his".

Overcome by emotion, Philip and Stella both grab him in a tight bear hug, and the three of them cry quietly as they wait for Frank to begin his journey — on a tears soaked road — to becoming one of Nigeria's most popular lawyers, and richest philanthropists.

6 PURSUIT OF THE GOLDEN FLEECE

"Eighty percent of success is showing up" - *Woody Allen*

Thus, Frank, accompanied by his only sincere friend and brother in the whole world, embarked on the pursuit of the proverbial Golden Fleece, a pursuit of his almost elusive dream.

After many gruesome hours in a bus, on the battered and abandoned roads connecting the Niger-delta region to the western region — and every other region — of Nigeria, they arrived, for the first time in their lives, in the golden and rustic ancient city of Ibadan, the very old but popular city that dates back to days of the old Oyo Empire.

A city on a hill that seems to have been hewed from a ragged mountain, a rugged but beautiful city with brown, rocky soil, and some roads as high as rooftops.

A city replete with fiery politicians, astute statesmen and very keen intellects. The largest city in West Africa.

A city of firsts. Home to the first radio station in West Africa, the first television station, and the first university in Nigeria. An unforgettable city without a doubt.

Their first contention is the issue of language. Ibadan is a city that prides herself very deeply on her cultures and traditions which includes an uncanny stubbornness and doggedness about communicating in their native '*Yoruba*' dialect.

Ibadan indigenes are by far among the most educated Nigerians, by and large, and that is not easy because Nigeria boasts a very large population of extremely educated people.

But their obstinate disregard for speaking the English language — Nigeria's official language and lingua franca — is inexplicable.

The first thing that grips you as you alight on Ibadan soil is a loud cacophonous rendition of the 'Yoruba' tongue all around.

It is spoken by the old, by the young, and by the un-weaned. As soon as they touch the soil, a massive sea of the strange sounding native 'Yoruba' tongue barrages their ears.

They look at each other, perplexed. They glance around — clutching their bags fiercely — at the huge number of people going about their business within *'Dugbe Market'* — the largest and most popular retail and wholesale market in West Africa, their drop off point. They feel very lost, unwelcome and nostalgic, all at once.

John takes Frank's hand and pulls him towards the brown, old and very dirty buses. The conductors are screaming at the top of their lungs, soliciting prospective customers.

They are yelling out strange words — strange to their ears — in a rhythmical singsong manner, pulling and dragging passengers, and even non-passengers, aggressively.

The 'warriors' from Niger-delta look about frantically, dazed by the language barrier. Although John had been to the overcrowded and fast paced Lagos, he still felt out of place in this sea of humans with a different tongue.

Communication in Lagos is predominantly in *'Pidgin English'* — an adulterated version of the English language. And Lagos also boasts a very mixed and diverse populace, unlike Ibadan.

They look at the conductor who grabs their bags, and starts to stir them towards a bus, suspiciously.

The conductor drags them towards a bus with the inscription, *'UP SHOOTING STARS!'*.

The 'Shooting Stars' is a soccer team whose home is Ibadan. You better support the team if you live in the city, or you would have yourself to blame.

They ask the conductor for direction to UI, he nods and runs off his mouth in a long flow of *'Yoruba'*. Confounding the duo further.

John, quick-tempered and irascible by virtue of the rather long uncomfortable journey, quips angrily,

"You don't speak any English?".

The conductor grins, and responds in another '*Yoruba*' narrative.

John glaring at him yells angrily,

"Doesn't anyone speak English in this town?"

The conductor turns to his colleagues and they all burst into laughter, pointing at the duo, and mumbling expletives in their native tongue, and comments like,

"*A won ebo re O!*" meaning, 'these are white men, or Englishmen'.

Exasperated, John pulls Frank away from the annoying conductors. They stumble through the crowd.

Frank glances at them from over his shoulder, smiling.

Just then, a very good-looking girl alights from one of the buses. She walks towards them.

The conductors whistle and yell obscenities in their direction,

"Excuse me, you seem lost. Do you need some help?" she says to the confused duo.

John turns to her and exclaims happily,

"Thank God, finally a Nigerian!".

She grins,

"Where're you heading?"

"We're trying to get to UI but don't know how," explains John.

She exclaims, "*Jambites*?"

John grins, "Not me, my little brother here", pointing at Frank.

She turns to Frank with a smile, "What department?"

"Law", says Frank

"Mmmm, '*efico*'! Welcome to Ibadan!"

Frank smiles at her, "Thank you"

"Come with me", walking away, they follow her,

"That's where I'm going myself"

John beams excitedly, "You're in UI?"

"Yes, two hundred level political science"

John frowns confused, "Two hundred level?"

Frank whispers to him, "Second year"

John grins foolishly, "I see".

They all enter the bus she just alighted from; she turns to Frank with a grin,

"You must be an '*efico*' to be admitted for law, you know?".

John whispers to Frank,

"What is *efico*?"

He whispers back,
"Someone who likes to read".
John exclaims,
"Oh yes! She is very correct, you're '*efico*'!"
They laugh, she asks Frank, looking at his young handsome face
with interest,
"What is your *JAMB* score?"
But John answers quickly,
"322!"
She exclaims,
"What? 322? Please be serious"
John continues with pride,
"I'm serious", he elbows Frank, "C'mon, tell her"
She looks into Frank's eyes,
"Is he serious?"
Frank nods shyly,
"My goodness! 322! You're definitely an '*efico*'! How many times
did you try?"
"Once", answered John.
"Once? You scored 322 on your first attempt? My God! How
did you do it? Did someone write it for you?"
John glares at her playfully, and quips,
"Never! Frank writes for..."
Frank elbows his side to shut him up.
She smiles at him,
"Frank? Your name is Frank?".
Frank nods, she smiles,
"I'm Nancy"
John cuts in, again, "I'm John".
She nods, still surprised, she mutters,
"322!".
She smiles at Frank sweetly, John elbows him lightly.
"And the cut-off mark for law this year is 275", she says out
loud, trying to put her voice on top of the rumbling sound from the
old engine in the rickety bus that has started crawling towards UI.
"275 and you scored 322! 47 marks above cut-off. Mmm '*efico*'!"
The old, brown, battered, Ibadan bus, finally stopped in front of
UI gate — after countless stops from Dugbe market.

The threesome — now a little more familiar, after Nancy's shock about Frank's JAMB score had subsided — get off the bus, and opposite them, across the street, on the Old Oyo Road, now UI Road, is the magnificent gate of the University of Ibadan, a truly beautiful gate that many stories have been written about.

And in the distance, within the campus, stands the famous towering Trenchard Hall, with its very tall tower almost touching the sky, keeping the time with its huge wall clocks that can be seen from almost everywhere within Ibadan metropolis.

Frank and John — both awestruck, cross the road, following Nancy closely, taken in by the splendor of the front of UI, and Nancy, grinning, says playfully,

"Welcome to UI!"

Frank's eyes glance all around the massive entrance, he tries to remember what is in his map, but looking at the campus in flesh seemed a lot more awesome, and just before he steps through the gate, he stops and whispers, almost silently, and unnoticed,

"Dear God, I have come here by your grace, even as an undeserving sinner, please Lord, guide my footsteps from this moment hence, make me useful to my family, to my friends, and to my community. Bless me Lord, so I can bless everyone else, in Jesus' name, amen".

He stops in front of the gate to say this prayer, unaware that both John and Nancy had walked ahead to a distance, from where they look at him, grinning, and calling him *jambite* repeatedly, not realizing that he is committing his stay in UI into God's able hands. They assume he is just overwhelmed by the grace and elegance of UI's architectural design.

He looks at them, smiling, and hurries to join them, a whole lot of other people walk around, back and forth, with massive loads, and bags of varying sizes.

Diverse people; all kinds of people, some beautiful, some not, some big, some small, all tribes, all nationalities, form the mixture of inhabitants of this intellectual community, this modern city within an ancient city.

Different cars, buses and motor bikes drive through the gates, some cruising with loud music blaring from gigantic speakers — speakers that are bigger and more expensive than some of the vehicles.

Nancy says to the duo,
"We've to get a cab. But I'll get off at Queens Hall..."
John wonders out loud, cutting her off,
"Queens Hall?".
Frank smiles, and says quietly,
"One of the girls' hostels"
Nancy grins,
"How do you know that?"
"I read it in a book, and I have a map of UI"
"Mmm! *Efico*! I see you've started your research, eh?"
Smiling, Frank replies,
"Well, I have been reading some stuff"
"Cool", she says, moving towards the line of clean campus cabs,
the duo following her trail,
"Do you know where you have to go?" she asks.
"I think we have to, em, go to the Students Affairs Office to see
what hall I have been assigned to"
"That's right!" exclaims Nancy.
Smiling, she says,
"You're a 'senior *jambite*' already!"
Frank grins,
"Like you, eh?"
Nancy giggles.
John queries,
"Which one is 'senior *jambite*' now?"
"Two hundred level students", answers Nancy.

John shakes his head in wonderment, trying to keep up with all
the new terms and phrases.

Their turn comes to board a cab, because although Nigeria is
widely unruly, it is still unheard of to jump the queue anywhere on
campus, not for any reason, especially not in UI.

They enter the clean, sweet smelling cab. Clean because
transportation is a thriving business within campus, and since no
commercial vehicles are allowed from outside, every cab has to meet
a particular standard, or else students, the very militant students of
UI, would protest and chase the cab, and its owner, away from their
soil in a heart beat.

And because of the huge returns the cabs made, many people
clamored for a piece of the cake; the university administrators, the

students union officials, members of staff, students, in short everyone of note, or with some clout, wants a piece of the racket.

As they drive down, Nancy, in the front seat, turns to them in the back, a piece of paper in her hand,

"This is my room number"

Frank reaches out to take the piece of paper from her hand.

She says sweetly,

"When you find your hall and move in, look me up. But you have to come in before 9pm though".

"I know", says Frank, smiling.

"Is there something you don't know?" quips Nancy.

"I wonder about that everyday", says John, grinning.

Frank chuckles.

Nancy turns to the driver,

"I'll get off at Queens. Please take them to Student Affairs", the driver nods.

She rummages through her pocketbook, looking for a bill to pay the driver.

John beats her to it as he stretches a *naira* bill over the driver's shoulder,

"I'll pay this time", says John, grinning.

She turns to him,

"You don't have to do that", smiling.

"Sorry, I already did", replies John, still grinning.

Nancy, Frank and the driver, all laugh.

The cab slows down to a stop in front of the beautiful Queen Elizabeth II Hall; an all female, undergraduate, hall of residence.

Nancy turns to them as she opens the door to alight,

"See you tonight?"

"Sure", answers John.

But she was asking Frank,

"Yes?" pursues Nancy, looking into Frank's eyes.

"Yes", says Frank, smiling.

She says, "Cool. Tonight then".

She alights, and shuts the door.

She waves at them as the cab drives off.

They wave back.

John turns to Frank and exclaims excitedly,

"That girl is hot for you little brother!"

Frank smiles, "No. She's just being nice, that's all"

The driver, peering at them through the rearview mirror, says chuckling,

"Ha young man, I don't think so O!"

"What?" they both chorus.

"Are you *jambites*?"

"Not me, him", answers John.

"Do you know the girl before?"

"No", answers John, the un-official mouthpiece.

"You just met her?"

"Yes".

"Well, congratulations! You just found yourself a girlfriend, my friend!"

"What?" exclaims Frank, not amused.

"That girl likes you my friend. It's in her eyes, and in her voice", says the driver.

John laughs heartily.

Frank, smiling, says quietly,

"How do you know that sir?"

"I've been driving a cab on this campus for five years now. I hear things, and I see things. I've seen many people come and go. I'm forty years old, and I've three children. My friend I've some experience, you see"

"Please tell him", teases John.

Frank, no more smiling says,

"I hope you're wrong, sir"

"Why?" asks the driver.

"I did not come here to find a girlfriend sir", says Frank quietly, "I came to study."

"That's what all of you say", chuckles the driver.

"Every *jambite* says that the first week. And by the second week you start the '*jambite* rush' with a wild fire burning in your groin like a dog in heat!" laughs the driver.

John laughs hysterically.

Frank looks out through the window with a straight face.

The driver continues,

"But the girl is not bad at all. She is very beautiful, and seems very decent"

"Not bad at all", agrees John.

"I'm sure you'll like her. And you should feel lucky to have a girlfriend, a *jambite* like you", teases the driver.

"Many boys stay here for four years with no girlfriend. Only 'bush meat'!" laughs the driver.

"Bush meat?" asks John, confused

"Non-students", says Frank quietly

John asks the driver, "What's *jambite* rush?"

"Ha, that is when all the male students try to catch a *jambito*, you know, a new female student. At the beginning of the session, all the boys try to find a new girlfriend. When they catch a new one, they abandon the old one", says the driver chuckling.

John laughs out loud.

Frank shakes his head, smiling, and says jokingly,

"Sir, please take us to student affairs, I'm tired of your stories".

"What's the matter?" says the driver, "You don't like girls? Or do you prefer boys? Are you homosexual?" laughs the driver.

John coughs as he tries to speak, from laughing too hard,

"He... he...", he coughs again.

Frank grins,

"You better stop laughing before you swallow your tongue".

John finally says,

"My brother... is... still a virgin", amidst laughter.

The driver exclaims,

"A virgin?", genuinely surprised.

Frank shakes his head, smiling wanly.

7 CAMPUS BLUES

"The world is advanced only by those who more than fill their present places"
- Wallace Wattles

They get off in front of the student affairs department, a not too impressive building, and join the long line of other '*jambites*' and '*jambitos*' with terrified looks.

They all have clean looking paper files in their hands, except for John and Frank. Frank who knows about the identifying traits of '*jambites*' is not prepared to be harassed by any '*stalites*'. He has formed a plan of action in his head.

Many '*stalites*' hover around the student affairs building. Some to fish for partners; others — who are in an undying kind of love with other kinds of 'creatures' like alcohol and drugs, and no interest whatsoever in the annual '*jambite rush*' — just hang around these places where '*jambites*' are many, to torment and harass the already terrified new entrants.

After waiting for a while, Frank walks inside the building. The officer in-charge hands him a form to fill out, and assigns him to Kuti Hall. A renowned hostel for gentlemen.

The cleanest hall in UI, named after the honorable Reverend Ransom Kuti, husband of the nonconformist freedom fighting first Nigerian woman to drive a car.

Reverend Ransom Kuti is the father of one of Nigeria's most popular indigenous musicians and social activists. The late Fela Anikulapo Kuti — you can say like mother, like son.

He thanks the man with a broad smile across his face. He walks outside. He pulls John from a corner of the building where he is chatting up a '*jambito*'.

They proceed to the admissions office to pick up his confirmation letter that contains his matriculation number — *matric* number for short, which is like a social security number.

In UI, to prevent tribalism and favoritism — which remains rampant anyway — students are only allowed to divulge their *matric* numbers at every point; for exams, for payment of fees, for allocation of any student privileges, etc.

Frank receives his *matric* number — which resembles a prison number — and proceeds to the bursary department for 'bleeding' — payment of fees.

Accompanied by his sponsor, John, they pay the first batch of fees; subsidized tuition, accommodation, students union dues, etc.

But paying for accommodation did not, and still does not, guarantee a room in the official halls of residence.

Many people pay and do not get accommodation, and they try fruitlessly to get the money back for four years — a scam obviously.

A few 'connected' or favored ones get a small room to share with as many that can fit in the tiny room.

Those who do not get an official space either become official or unofficial '*squatters*', or '*floaters*'; or end up paying a whole lot more for private rooming houses just outside and around campus. Or they pay the very expensive 'black market' rate for rooms on campus.

'*Squatters*' are those who live in a room where they are not officially assigned to. They may 'squat' in a room for three reasons, either because they have a tolerant friend in the room who does not mind being their 'landlord', or because they pay a 'landlord' — room owner — for 'squatting' rights.

Or, as a last resort, which is an extreme measure, by strong-arming the room owners into accommodating them. This last category is usually done by the seasoned un-accommodated '*stalites*'.

As a university policy, only first year and final year students are eligible to apply for accommodation.

The 'floaters' are a category of students who do not have their own space, or any squatting rights, but float from room to room. They have their belongings scattered around different rooms, or even different halls. They take their bath in one room, and dress up in a different room.

They also sleep anywhere they can find, usually in a room where a roommate is out of town for the weekend or for the night, and in situations where they can not find any spare bed, or floor space, they pass the night wherever they find; in the buttery, or common room, or in lecture theaters.

Accommodation in UI is a big deal and a very profitable enterprise for some people. In UI, there is always a cartel that deals in accommodation.

They somehow, through their connections to '*high places*', get as many rooms as possible, and in turn sell them 'black market' rate, which is often ten times the official rate.

The business is so big that everybody on campus with some power is involved in the illicit trade. From the vice-chancellor, to the registrar, to the bursar, to the dean of students, to the deans of faculties, heads of departments, hall masters, hall wardens, hall supervisors, and students. Practically everybody.

If you can swing it, you can sell it. The fact is, there are always more students admitted than the few halls can accommodate, a classic example of a very large demand for a rather scarce commodity. A commodity that is almost non-existent and seemly impossible to replenish.

The university administrators and power brokers all have a certain quota of rooms allocated to them at the beginning of every session, from the vice-chancellor down to the lowliest staff on campus, even hall porters and cleaners.

After they share a large portion of the space among themselves, the small part left is scrambled for by thousands of needy students.

The top guns of UI give out their rooms to the privileged children of their friends and relatives — who in turn sell them for very exorbitant amounts, and the under privileged wards from non-consequential families are left on their own.

This situation is synonymous to the scramble for, and partition of, Africa — back in the day — by the world powers.

Another source of accommodation in UI is the 'boys quarters' attached to homes of the university staff, and a low class suburb within campus.

An area that houses the non-academic staff, a place like the housing projects in Brooklyn, New York; a place called 'Abadina'.

'Abadina', by virtue of its category of inhabitants — the lowest earners in the academic community, was, and still is, nothing different from Bedford/Stuyvesant, or East New York in Brooklyn, New York.

The hood, dirty, ghetto and violent. A place economically and mentally repressed. Home to persons with a deep-seated inherent anger, and a high crime rate. You must be tough and rugged to survive in 'Abadina'.

Frank pays the first batch of fees. Armed with his receipts, his letter of confirmation and his *'matric'* number, all tucked in his back pocket, he proceeds to the very neat Kuti Hall. The abode of UI's gentlemen.

As he walks through the gate, John in tow, he is surprised to see the large number of 'paper file' holding *'jambites'* queuing up in front of the hall supervisor's office.

He glances at John, who asks,

"What in the world is going on here?"

Frank forces a smile,

"Waiting to get a room I guess"

"All these people? How many rooms are in this place?"

"I'm not sure. But not too many I think".

They join the line.

The sky is getting dark as dusk is setting in.

In UI, there are exactly ten halls of residence: *Queens* and *Idia* — females only; *Kuti, Tedder, Melanby, Bello, Zik,* and *Independence* — males only, *Awo* and *Tafawa Balewa* — male and female postgraduate students.

Some of these halls have wooden buildings that are old and dry, and in the threshold of crumbling down, or going up in flames, any second — a very real hazard.

The wooden buildings are solely reserved for the *'jambites'*, and some homeless *'stalites'*. Go figure!

Frank — standing in line — prays to God for a room; not getting a room would no doubt compound his already precarious situation. There is no way he can afford to buy a room 'black market' rate, or even contemplate renting a place off-campus.

After several hours in line, the moon just hovering somewhere in the sky, the hall supervisor — a very dark skinned, stern looking man, Mr. Mike — appears from his office to look at the sea of freshmen still waiting to be accommodated.

He clears his throat noisily and says matter of fact,

"Gentlemen, I'm afraid we have only ten spaces left. And considering the number of you still waiting, I have decided to have you ballot for the few spots left".

The *'jambites'* grumble and murmur in frustration as yet another mean looking man appears with a box that he puts down in front of the supervisor.

He looks at the people still in line — about five hundred admitted students, and says dryly,

"In this box are small pieces of paper. On each one is written either yes, or no. If you pick yes, you get a room, and if you pick no, I'm sorry you'll have to find an alternative"

John glances at Frank and queries angrily,

"What nonsense is this man saying?"

"We have to ballot for the remaining spaces"

"Ballot? Isn't that voting?"

"Yes, something like that. But we pick up the pieces of paper instead. And there are only ten 'yeses' and about five hundred 'noes' in that box"

"What kind of system is this? After passing jamb one cannot even get a bed space?"

Frank smiles at him.

He continues angrily,

"So who picks no will do what?"

"Look for an alternative"

"What?"

"Find a space somewhere else"

John glares at the supervisor angrily, ready to punch him to pulp any second even as the hapless *'jambites'* take turns to pick the pieces of paper from the box and hand them to the supervisor, who unfolds and reads the 'vote' out loud.

Frank picks his and hands it to him.

As the stern looking man unfolds the piece of paper, he glances at Frank's smiling face, and asks with a frown,

"What is funny?"

"Nothing sir"

"Then what're you smiling for?"

John cuts in angrily,

"Is it a crime to smile in this country now?"

The shocked supervisor glares at him,

"Who are you?"

Frank still smiling, says meekly,

"Sorry sir, this is my brother"

"Are you a student here?" he says to John angrily.

"I'm not"

"Are you a lawyer then?"

"Why're you questioning me? Just tell us what the paper says"

"And if I refuse?", quips the supervisor angrily.

"You can't do that!" retorts John stubbornly.

"Do you want to test my will?" asks the supervisor wickedly.

John whispers to Frank, "Can he do that?"

Some of the 'jambites' burst into laughter in spite of their tired and frustrated selves.

Frank clears his throat and says humbly,

"Well sir, that won't be fair"

"What do you know about fairness young man?"

John glares at him angrily.

Frank smiles at him.

The tired and frustrated 'jambites' in line grumble and murmur under their breath, through their teeth — too afraid to make any loud sound that might deprive them of the opportunity to ballot for 'ten spots' out of five hundred 'no-spots'.

The supervisor unfolds the piece of paper in his hand as he says,

"I didn't think you would know anything about fair…" his voice trails off as he looks at the piece of paper in his hand, then looks at Frank with sudden admiration.

He beams and says,

"You must have prayed young man. God just answered your prayer"

Frank grins widely,

"Yes I prayed sir"

"You're a Christian?"

"Yes sir".

He points to John and says sarcastically,

"You should take this one to church with you, he needs special prayers".

John moves to respond harshly, Frank elbows his side gently — to shut him up.

The supervisor grins at Frank,

"How old are you son?"

"Seventeen sir"

"You're very mature for your age. Congratulations and welcome to Kuti Hall. I hope you have a good time here. Go inside the office and my secretary will assign you to a room".

"Thank you sir", replies Frank with a grin as he pulls John to follow him.

The supervisor turns to the folks still in line and bellows,

"You all see the power of prayer? I hope you have all prayed too. If you've not, you better do so now. You should pray to God, or to Allah, or to whomever or whatever you pray to now before you pick".

Frank collects a form from the bleached-skin female secretary who smiles at him warmly. He fills it out, hands it over, and receives a key attached to a piece of cardboard with the number: E4 written on it.

He receives the key from her multi-colored fingers — bleached by toxic chemicals. A real eyesore.

He walks out to search for room E4, Kuti Hall, his new abode.

Walking down the corridors; John — who is by now very hungry and still seething with anger from the encounter with the hall supervisor — follows closely behind.

Their dusty bags dangle from the straps across their tired shoulders. Several tough looking 'stalites' watch them from their doorways and windows, some glaring at them for an unfathomable reason. Some are grinning at them cunningly.

They walk to E Block and stop in front of room number four.

Frank grins at John as he fumbles with the lock on the door with the key from the bleached-skin lady, but the key seems to be the wrong one.

He looks up at John smiling,

"I think she gave us the wrong key"

John snatches the key from him playfully,

"Move boy! You can't even open a door?"

Frank grins.

John fumbles with the key in the lock with no luck, and grunts,

"What in the world is..." his voice trails off.

They freeze as a huge scary shadow suddenly falls over them.

They turn around slowly. Standing behind them is a large guy hovering over them menacingly — no doubt a 'stalite' — with a deep frown set on his face like an ugly bronze carving made in anger.

He barks angrily,

"What do you think you're doing?"

"We're trying to get in, what do you think we're doing?" retorts John fearlessly.

The large guy frowns deeper and yells,

"You're what?"

"This is my room. I have just been assigned here" says Frank nicely with a smile.

The guy looks at them from head to toe and bursts into laughter.

John glares at him angrily and drops his bag on the floor,

"Is something funny?"

"You're a tough guy, eh?" retorts the menace.

Frank moves to stand in their middle smiling, and says,

"We're tired and would like to just go in to rest now, if you don't mind".

The guy snaps angrily,

"I mind 'jambite'! And if you don't scram from here this minute I'll kick your butt all over this corridor".

John really pissed now, lunges at him without hesitation. They grapple fiercely with John besting him.

Frank struggles to separate them. Other students rush out from different rooms to help tear them apart.

The commotion attracts many students. They fly down from every angle like starving eagles hunting for prey.

Fighting in Kuti Hall is unheard of — and in no time word gets to the hall supervisor.

He abandons the 'jambites' waiting in line and rushes towards room E4 with his potbelly bouncing up and down like a faulty pendulum.

The large guy shouts angrily, fighting to break loose from the strong arms pinning his hands to his side.

John stands in a corner behind Frank, panting and ready to pounce on his opponent again.

The supervisor appears, with a mean scowl on his face. He charges at John as he lashes out with his tongue,

"How dare you disrupt the peace and tranquility of this hall?"

Frank tries to explain,

"Sir…"

He cuts him off sharply,

"Shut up boy! I warned you about this tout, didn't I? I told you he needs special prayers. Nobody fights in this hall damn it! Tell me why I shouldn't throw you out of this hostel this minute!"

Frank says quietly,

"Sir if you will…"

He snaps at him again,

"Keep qui…"

Frank snaps back angrily,

"Let me finish! How can you pass judgment without listening to anyone?"

The shocked supervisor steps back — tongue tied with surprise.

The large guy shuts up too.

John looks at Frank with awe as he continues reasonably,

"This was only a misunderstanding and nothing to be so mad about".

The supervisor clears his throat and says quietly,

"What happened?".

John cuts in,

"That's what you should have…"

Frank snaps,

"Shut up John!".

John recoils, surprised by the new Frank.

He continues coolly,

"We were trying to open the door. This guy came here and started yelling. My brother yelled back and they grabbed each other".

The supervisor looks around and says, pointing,

"You were trying to open this door?"

"Yes. And the door won't open. I think your secretary gave me the wrong key".

The supervisor smiles and says,

"There is nothing wrong with the key. You're in the wrong block".

Frank looks at the key with a tag in his hand,

"Isn't this room E4?"

"Yes. But there is another E4 behind this building"

"What?" asks Frank, confused.

The other students yell out excitedly,

"Jambite! Jambite!! Jambite!!!".

Frank glares at them and snaps,

"Why don't you all shut up and go about your business!".

The supervisor continues gently,

"Your room is in the wooden block".

Frank snatches the bags that had fallen on the floor during the melee and walks away from the crowd.

John follows quietly.

They go towards the back of the hall, the *'jambites'* section.

They find room E4 and walk in through the unlocked door.

Inside the room are four official bed spaces and several *'squatometers'* — extra mattresses — lying on the floor.

The room that is originally built to accommodate two people officially accommodates four, and unofficially houses at least ten people every night.

Standing in the doorway, Frank looks at his residence for the session. He smiles at the folks already settled in.

He walks in, drops the bags and moves to introduce himself to his roommates,

"Hello. My name is…"

The six guys in the room all chorus,

"Frank Audu!"

Frank exchanges glances with the equally surprised John.

He turns to them, smiling,

"Have we met?"

One of the guys, Leopold, a lean looking guy with shifty eyes, grins mischievously,

"News travels fast in UI my friend".

Still grinning, he says playfully,

"You're the most popular *jambite* in Kuti Hall right now, maybe around the entire campus even!".

Frank shakes his head smiling.
The lean guy grins heartily,
"I'm Leopold Anamo your room mate".
They shake hands.
John shakes his hand too and says comically,
"I have only one question Leo".
Leo looks at him queerly,
"What's that?"
John yells playfully,
"Where in the world can I find something to eat here?"
Everyone in the room bursts into laughter.

8 HARD MEN RULE

"The best way of getting good at something is doing it" - Chuck Gloman

Frank becomes quite popular from his very first day in UI. Although he tries pretty hard to be humble, he most certainly isn't a weakling by any reckoning.

He is, in fact, an extremely fearless and uncommonly brave young man — a true warrior. He does have a frightful dark side.

He goes about the business of settling down quickly as classes were starting in a week. His roommate Leopold, Leo for short — born and raised in Abadina, UI — turns out to be a quick friend who puts his vast knowledge of UI at Frank's disposal.

They go around campus together with John, who, after the incident with the large guy, has become more subtle and reserved.

He looks at Frank differently — realizing his inherent fire and inner strength. This is the new and improved Frank, he reckons.

The first place Leo shows them is the famous 'black market' — a flea market — within the confines of UI. It is a place where the below average members of the academic community shop, or just hang out.

It has several eateries, bars and stores that all deliver at a good bargain even though some of their wares are really sub-standard.

Everyone in Frank's socio-economic class is welcome. And they are very comfortable within 'black market'. The business owners and their clientele are simple, down to earth people with no pretenses.

The wares and services here are reasonably priced and relatively affordable by the poor students as opposed to the other expensive shopping areas.

Those in the upper-class, 'the haves', do everything from eating, shopping and hanging out in another very famous UI landmark — the SUB, the Students Union Building.

The SUB is a place that houses the students council chamber and executive offices, a beautiful building that has everything from high class restaurants, to bars, to night clubs, to designer shops, to reading rooms, to game centers, and even an Olympic size swimming pool.

Many people go through UI for four or five years and never even set foot in this beautiful student complex for fear of being drawn in by this place fabled for fearsome stories.

The SUB is good, bad, wild, treacherous, and always awake. Some people drink away their future in this place. They sell, buy and use every kind of drug from marijuana to heroin — and every other kind of varying potency.

Just in front of the complex is a short flight of steps under an Indian almond tree where anything and everything happens. People have sex on these steps, they fight with guns and knives, they smoke weed — marijuana, they smoke heroin and they sniff cocaine.

The steps are so popular that they are called: '*Freedom Steps*' — because this is where people supposedly get high and '*free*'; which is ridiculous, because there is really no freedom without responsibility.

Only '*hard men*' and their cronies sit on these steps, you dare not go near '*freedom steps*' if you are not part of the elite class of '*hard men*' — an unusual assortment of daredevils synonymous with the '*made guys*' of the *Mafia*.

Most of the '*hard men*' are not from the bourgeoisie, or wealthy class themselves, but they get every privilege because they are dreaded and feared by all and sundry.

They date the finest girls on campus. They are invited to every party. They get the best rooms on campus. They always have money in their pockets, and they can make UI unbearable or uninhabitable for anyone who crosses their path.

These daredevils are members of some really tough, merciless and sometimes very violent fraternities — which are also erroneously referred to as 'secret cults'; because most of their activities are supposedly very secretive, and completely shrouded in mystery.

The fraternities in UI includes; *The Pyrates Confraternity*, *The Buccaneers Confraternity* — a break away from the *Pyrates*, *The Eiye Confraternity*, *The Neo Black Movement* — or *Black Axe Confraternity*, *The Mafia*, *The Vikings Confraternity*, the all female *Red Bras* and *The Amazons*, and several other smaller groups.

These groups can be very deadly because of their huge number and their possession of very sophisticated arms and ammunition that can be unleashed on any perceived enemies in a heartbeat.

Their reign of terror in Nigerian universities is frightfully renowned. If you mess with a member of any of these gangs, you will have to contend with all the other armed members.

Some of the members are children of top military officers and the stupidly rich that can afford guns and smart lawyers when they get in trouble.

Some of them are known to steal, kill and destroy anything or anyone in their way without remorse. Some of them are rumored to have participated in armed robberies, rapes and other heinous crimes.

Burning and looting is synonymous with some of these fraternities that started in good faith in the year nineteen hundred and fifty-two, (1952), by seven like minds hungry for equality.

That year, considering the spate of tribalism, nepotism, and socio-economic segregation — which unfortunately still remains unabated today — seven young men, all students of UI, known as the '*big seven*', sat down together in a bid to find a solution to the oppressive situation prevalent at the time, and they came up with the idea for the *Pyrates Confraternity*.

They formed an association of people with the desire to combat the ills militating against the attainment of a just society. And thus, the first confraternity in UI, and in Nigeria as a whole, was founded.

The members organized many peaceful demonstrations to challenge all the negative policies and activities of the criminally minded clowns in charge of government and the university administration.

The members then were all very eloquent, intelligent and selfless freedom fighters only concerned with the total emancipation of man from the pit of 'neo-slavery'.

They define a *Pyrate* as *'a liberated mind who having identified the ills militating against the attainment of a just society, shows a resolve to combat these ills, and is initiated into the Pyrates Confraternity to join others of like mind'.*

Although some other students at the time were a little concerned about their militant attitude, they could still identify with their goals and objectives that are summarized in a manual known as the *'4-7 Creed'* — *The Four Compass Points* and *The Seven Rudder Blades.*

The *4-7 Creed* is a piece of brilliant writing that can be compared to the Ten Commandments of the Bible. Apt and succinct.

The Four Compass Points are: against oppression, against tribalism, against moribund convention, for comradeship and chivalry.

And the Rudder Blades are: deck before ego, all before self, sense before slogan, truth before can't, learn before leap, change over stasis and act over yap.

This simple but altruistic concept is the founding principle of the *Pyrates Confraternity.* It is the guiding light and principle of their way of life. They were bold, brave and fearless back in the day.

They took up names without tribal tones or connotations. Fearful names like *Captain Blood, Long John Silver, Billy Bones,* etc. — names from the book: *Treasure Island,* a contributive background to the formation of the fraternity.

But as all human associations usually turn out eventually, about twenty years down the road, a major problem occurred. Five members were found wanting in relation to the *'4-7 Creed',* they were *'black spotted'* — expelled from the *Pyrates Confraternity.*

This did not go down well with them. They felt wronged. And because of their desire to continue to live as fraternity men, they formed their own — the *Buccaneers Confraternity.*

They formed this group with the objective to undermine the *Pyrates.* They wanted blood from their perceived enemies.

A few years later another group — the *Eiye Confraternity* — was born. Then another, and yet another, thus heralding the proliferation of too many confraternities. Some good with strong principles, others worse than gangs of unscrupulous thieves.

And with time some members of the fraternities deviated from their original calling and embraced a decadent way of life; they concocted different methods of exterminating their perceived enemies or rivals.

It was not a fight for the oppressed anymore, it was now a fight for superiority. They became an oppressive and malignant incubus, a bizarre metamorphosis no doubt — something like the *Mafia* in *Sicily*.

The founders — *the original seven* — have been widely accused of creating a reprehensible and indestructible monster, a cancerous nightmare that will not go away.

Parents worry about their children becoming members of these supposedly accursed gangs. University authorities are plagued by the increased crime rate in their institutions, and the government is afraid that the criminally minded members might someday overthrow them with the massive fire power in their arsenal.

*

Leo — an innate coward — explains to Frank why he must never go to the SUB. He, who is himself a 'UI born and raised', never goes there.

He is too afraid he might get jumped or mugged by the '*hard men*' — a very likely possibility no doubt, because he isn't one of them.

But Frank finds it amusing because he can not understand why he must not go to a certain part of campus out of fear. He is not completely fearless himself. He has his own personal fear, but it is not a fear of man.

His fear is a different but deeper kind. He has an encompassing fear of failure. There is not an iota of fear of any human alive in his heart, or body, or soul. His greatest fear is not achieving success in life. He is deeply afraid of failure.

Frank loves the SUB. He is attracted to the place the way moths are attracted to bright lights. He blends quite easily into the UI community in every way.

One evening he strolls into the SUB to have a drink, he orders a drink and sits down. Just then this very large fellow walks up to him and asks for his seat.

Frank smiles at him, thinking the fellow is joking. But apparently he is not.

"What are you smiling at, you bloody *jambite*?", he snaps.

Frank maintains his smile, ignoring him.

"I said get up. Are you deaf?"

Frank says softly,

"I'm really not in the mood for any '*stalite*', '*jambite*' imbroglio tonight"

The large fellow yells,

"You bloody *jambite*!" as he grabs Frank's shirt.

Frank strikes his throat with a deadly *aikido* strike, that he learnt from a book, with a growl.

"You miscreant! I said I'm not in the mood"

The large fellow holds his throat, coughing painfully,

"You hit my throat..."

Frank growls,

"And if you don't get away from me I'll bring out your heart and liver"

The large fellow backs away, shouting,

"You will pay for this... I will make you pay"

"Send the bill and I will pay, you punk", retorts Frank.

Several '*hard men*' in the area observe the scene quietly. Some whisper to each other, pointing and gesticulating towards Frank.

He ignores everyone, minding his business and thinking about his friend and brother John, who is turning into UI's number one pimp.

Two '*hard men*' walk up to him, one to his left, the other to his right; they smile at him, he nods at them.

The one on the left looks at him and says sarcastically,

"You're a *jambite*, right?".

Frank glares at him.

The one on the right smiles,

"He just wants to know if you're a new student."

Frank turns to look at him without a word.

He sips from his glass, unperturbed.

The one on the left continues arrogantly,

"You know that was a mistake, what you just did to that guy?".

The one on the right quips,

"You need friends in this campus to pull stunts like that".

"That's right. Real friends", says left.

"By the way, where did you learn that technique?" queries right.

"What is this? The good cop, bad cop routine?" asks Frank.

The '*hard men*' exchange glances and burst into laughter.

They shake hands with Frank, order drinks and chat with him like old friends would.

Since word travels fast in this world, especially in the underground part, he becomes very popular with the '*hard men*'.

They all want him to be a member of their fraternity. Some court him, others threaten him. Join or burn, '*partici-come*' or '*partici-go*' they tell him.

He thinks hard about becoming a frat man. He knows what it entails. He is aware of the consequences of joining or not joining. He weighs the pros and cons.

Academically, Frank quickly attains a respectable student status with his professors and colleagues. He attends all his classes on time, submits his assignments and does every test, acquiring all the available knowledge.

But John, his friend and brother, does not help the matter. He just wants a way to make money and date the hottest girls, perks of being '*hard*'.

John, although not an official student of UI, lives in the hostel with Frank like any other student. He attends classes with any girl he fancies. He dresses even better than some students and picks the habits of undergraduates pretty easily. It is not unusual actually.

Many young people in Nigeria's universities are not official students. They just live the life, act the part, but are not looking forward to acquiring any degree or diploma.

They just waste their time and energy pretending to be students. Some for many years, others for a few months until they can figure out what they really want to do.

Frank hangs out with '*hard men*' of different colors — this is dangerous because when there is a tussle for power he could be mistaken for any color and hit by anybody.

When the pressure from the fraternities gets too much, he decides to become a member. But he does not know which one would be of more advantage.

The frat men basically tell him every thing he would gain by becoming a member, but he can tell they are lying. It is all a sales pitch. They just want him because he is a brilliant student and perhaps a brave one too. He is viewed as an asset, a commodity.

On his way to an early lecture one morning, he sees something that will forever change his life.

Posted at a major street corner on campus is a billboard with a large painting of the popular skull and cross bones insignia of the *Pyrates Confraternity*.

His eyes are immediately drawn to the billboard. He walks and stops in front of the notice that reads something like,

Are you brave?
Are you bold?
Can you dance with the foregone terrors?
Then bring 20 toes and 50 fingers with an image to:
Kuti Hall D17.
I weep blood for you!

Frank is the only one brave enough to stand and read this scary notice that appear to be written in dripping blood.

Other students glance at it from the corner of their eyes and scurry off fearfully.

He reads it about three times, looks around with a smile and hurries off to his lecture.

In class, he barely listens to the lecturer for two reasons. First, he already knows the topic. Second, the *Pyrates Confraternity's* challenge and call to duty flashes through his mind constantly.

The very strict lecturer asks a question, expecting someone to answer. Nobody answers. He threatens to leave. He gathers his papers angrily and moves to walk out of the class.

Frank looks up to see every one staring at the lecturer leaving.

He asks the girl beside him. She tells him the question.

He calls out to the lecturer who is almost at the door.

"Sir!"

"What?" retorts the irritated lecturer.

"That is by Karl Max"

"Karl Max," says the lecturer, walking back into the class.

"What is your name son?"

"Frank"

"Frank who?"

The class laughs.

"Frank Audu sir"

The lecturer nods his head, turns to the class and bellows,

"Frank Audu here just saved your dull behinds. Be grateful fellas".

The students murmur under their breath. The lecturer puts back his papers on the table, picks up a chalk and writes on the board:

Religion is the opium of the people, the sigh of the oppressed...

Frank's mind wanders away again.

*

That evening, pretending he is going to the reading room, he finds his way to room D17 in Kuti Hall.

He knocks on the door, it opens, with thick darkness spilling out, a shadowy face appears in the door way and grunts at him,

"What?"

Smiling, he says,

"I saw a notice on..."

Before he can complete his sentence, semi-invincible hands pull him into the dark room violently.

They slam him on the floor, and unseen feet trample on him.

A voice growls in the dark,

"What have you got?"

"What?" replies Frank angrily.

"You said you saw the notice. What do you have for us?"

"I don't have any..."

"Nothing?"

They slap and kick him wickedly.

"You think this is a game?" growls another voice.

Frank snaps angrily,

"What is wrong with you guys? I just came to ask a few questions and you attack me? What kind of thing is..."

They cut him off,

"Shut up! You bloody lubber!".

Strong hands yank him off the floor and fling him towards the door.

Another voice grunts,

"Come back when you are ready".

They toss him out of the room. And slam the door shut behind him.

Frank looks around as he dusts his clothes. The unseen faces in the dark room smile to themselves.

Frank walks away thinking about the incident. Two things cross his mind. First, these *Pyrates* do not care if you join them or not. Second, people who have something to offer do not try to impress you. There and then he made up his mind to become a *Pyrate*.

After all, *Professor Wole Soyinka*, one of the founders of the confraternity is and has always been his role model.

He reads the professor's books all the time. He has followed the man's career like a stalker. He reckons that if the *Pyrates Confraternity* is good enough for a man like Soyinka, then he would be honored to be accepted in its fold.

Later that night he returns to room D17, Kuti Hall with the *20 toes, 50 fingers* and an *image*.

They let him in. They slap and kick him around. They threaten him, all in a bid to discourage him from applying to join the confraternity. But like the strong willed man he had become, he persisted.

*

Joining the *Pyrates Confraternity* can literarily be compared to a cow's attempt to pass through the eye of a needle. First, there is an extreme physical fitness requirement. You must be in an almost perfect physical condition to pass the hazardous physical test.

Second, academic and mental proficiency is held very highly. You cannot become a *Pyrate* if your grades and IQ were not above average.

There are a series of mental tests to rattle your composition. Many doctorate degree students have failed the tests countless times. And third, you must be above board morally.

Pyrates do not lie, steal, or cheat in any way, except in dire situations where it is in the best interest of mankind. It is truly difficult to become a *Pyrate*, especially for the affluent and egoistic person. Humility, self sacrifice and a sense of public service will take you a long way in this altruistic race.

Every night for about a month, Frank will run off to continue with the tests to becoming a *Pyrate*. About five hundred young able bodied students applied with Frank. But by the third day, there were three hundred.

One hundred and fifty by the first week; fifty by the second week, twenty the third week, and eighteen by the fourth week, '*many are called few are chosen*' they say.

The weak and cowardly who can not take the brutalization, disappear of their own volition. Only the strong and brave remain.

The applicants — now referred to as *rowers* — are beaten, threatened, frightened, and deliberately maltreated. They lay flat and roll in bushes and shrubs.

They jog; do push ups, sit ups and every conceivable exercise known to man inside deep, dark, and dangerous forests in the middle of the night, all the time getting flogged with horse whips.

They get punches and kicks from many faceless *Pyrates*. This is to show you what it feels like to be brutalized and oppressed. To be deprived of your rights and justice. To be victimized.

It is believed that when a person is subjected to all these despicable conditions that some people actually live in, he will be able and better equipped to defend the downtrodden. How can you right a wrong you don't know, or understand?

A *Pyrate* is supposed to be fearless. They sleep in graveyards. They sing and dance in dangerous forests without fear.

On the last day, before the initiation, they have a *curfew*, when they wear the bright red beret with the skull and cross bones insignia, black pants and white shirt, colors of the frat.

They dress up in this combination called the *half regalia* and go around campus without a word to *lubbers* — non-*Pyrates*. There is no exchange of word with any *lubber* — not even family members or close friends.

As Frank, in his *half regalia,* walks around campus in the bright sunlight, as ordered, he automatically and inadvertently makes many seen and unforeseen enemies.

Mr. Mike, his hall supervisor, who has developed a liking for him sees him walking out of the hall, says hello but gets no response. Frank regrets this, because he knows he will need this man very soon.

The essence of the curfew is to tell the world that you have become a *Pyrate*, to stay away from you, to put the fear of death in perceived enemies if you may.

And finally, the same night, the official initiation into the confraternity takes place in a deep dark forest by *zero hour*—

midnight. There is a big bonfire; there is oath taking, signing of the 'scroll', 'rumming' and 'sailing'.

A wild night no doubt, usually on a weekend, because of the aftermath of the strong brew referred to as *Bloody Mary*. You are only allowed to get drunk this one time in your entire life as a *Pyrate*.

You get drunk, go to sleep and wake up as a *deckhand*, the next step up from *rower*.

Frank officially becomes a '*hard man*'— a '*made guy*'. He cannot be messed with without serious reprisals from his brothers in the fraternity.

John only finds out about his frat allegiance on the day of *curfew*. He is too scared to even approach Frank in his scary looking *half regalia*.

Although now a frat man, Frank on his own personal recognition, is also a very '*hard man*'. Everyone who gets close to him feels exudes of his inner strength and his unusual courage.

He is fearless and bold, *Pyrates Confraternity* or not. In no time he becomes one of the most influential '*hard men*' on campus. Nothing happens on campus without his knowledge.

Frank gets the nickname '*Voltron the Defender*'. He stands up for the oppressed or harassed. Other frats that believe in stealing, and extortion, clash with him every now and then, because he prevents their members from extorting money or goods from poor students.

He tells them to take on the oppressive government, or the moneyed class that is responsible for their losses, but not fellow indigent students who scrounge to barely survive.

When students have problems, they look for Frank. A young student, the same age as Frank, a typical mommy's boy, Segun, comes to him one evening. Some '*hard man*' took his *Sony CD player* that mom gave him as a going away to college gift.

Frank looks at him as he tells his story.

"He took the player and requested money from me. He said I should go home if I don't have the money by tomorrow morning".

"Don't worry about it. You will have it back tonight," says Frank.

"You don't understand. He showed me a gun", whispers Segun.

"Don't worry. You will get it back", says Frank with a smile.

He turns to his friends, Gene and Paschal,

"Let's go to SUB."

These days when Frank walks into the SUB, people get up from their seats and leave. Some out of hatred since he became a *Pyrate*, others out of fear.

He walks in, followed by his cronies, Gene and Paschal.

At the far end of an open bar is the culprit who took Segun's CD player.

He nods at his friends. They walk towards the thieving '*hard man*'. A '*stalite*' who has been around campus for a while.

Frank pulls a stool and settles it beside the culprit. He climbs on it and whispers to the thief,

"You have my friend's CD player. He needs it back tonight"

"What do you mean?" the thief grunts angrily.

"I'm not in the mood for games. Just return the player and I'll forget this little misunderstanding".

The thief flares up angrily, standing up from his seat,

"Are you threatening me? What do you mean?"

"Why should I threaten you?"

The thief shows him a gun strapped to his waistband.

Frank looks at it and smiles,

"Like I said, why should I threaten you? You're too small to threaten".

The thief explodes angrily,

"Are you mad? Who do you think you are?".

Frank still smiling, and very calm, says quietly,

"Yes I'm very mad my friend. And I'll show you just how mad I am if my friend does not get the player back tonight".

He gets off the stool and starts to walk away, followed by his surprised cronies.

The thief calls out after him,

"You can't do anything. You met me in this school. You think I'm afraid of you?"

Frank turns and walks back to him,

"Listen, my friend. I don't care whether you've been too dull to graduate after eight years here. Or whether you're not afraid of anyone. That is neither here nor there, and I frankly don't care. Just return my friend's player by tonight or this campus won't contain both of us".

The thief pulls out the gun from his waistband, a .38 colt automatic pistol. People take off in different directions. He waves the gun in the air threateningly.

Frank smiles at him,

"You have pulled a gun. What is your next move?".

The thief grunts, unsure of himself,

"Don't mess with me man. Don't mess with me".

Frank retorts calmly,

"Take my advice, don't pull out weapons you can't use".

"You think I can't use it? You think so?"

"I don't think so. I know so. Tonight dude, not a minute later", and he walks away boldly without glancing back at all.

The thief puts back his gun and sits down angrily,

"Damn this crazy *Pyrate*. Who the heck does he think he is?"

Later that night, an 'anonymous person' drops off the CD player in Segun's room, unannounced.

Two weeks later, the same thief, Matt, sells another CD player to an unsuspecting *'jambite'*. As he walks to his hostel through a dark path not too far from where he had just paid for the player, a 'masked man' robs him at gunpoint.

The following morning Frank goes to the thief's room and knocks on the door.

A big black dude opens the door.

"Where is Matt?", asks Frank.

"Sleeping" replies the dude.

"Wake him up?"

"What?", surprised.

"Are you deaf? I said wake him up now".

Just then, Matt, the thief, appears in the doorway, rubbing his eyes.

He glares at Frank,

"What do you want now?".

"Last night? CD player? *'Buying and cramping'*?", retorts Frank.

"What?", asks the flustered Matt

"You know, you sell something hot. And you retrieve it yourself or through some one else. That is *'buying and cramping'*", explains Frank.

"What's wrong with you man? Why won't you leave me alone?" asks Matt angrily.

"My friend, you know how we do. Just return the money or the player and we are good", says Frank with a smile.

"Who are you to order me around?"

"I really don't care what you think dude. The player or the money not later than 12 noon today, dig?".

He glances at his wrist watch,

"It's about 8.30am, you've got exactly 3 and a half hours. Tick tock. Tick tock",

Frank winks and walks away.

Matt slams his door shut angrily.

9 WISE GUYS FEED TOO

"People are responsible for their own joy" - Lisa Nichols

John wakes up one Sunday morning and tells Frank he wants to go to church with him. He has never been to church any day of his life before.

Frank looks at him and wonders what is happening to him. They go to church. On their way back to the hostel John makes Frank sit on a bench in the park.

"Frank I have been thinking"

"Really?"

"Yes"

"About what?"

"Everything"

"Everything?"

"Yes"

"Is something wrong?"

"No. Nothing is wrong," he says, avoiding his eyes.

"Something is wrong. Right?" Frank says, looking at him quietly.

"Well em… I don't know how to tell you this"

"You don't know how to tell me what?"

"Okay. I em…"

He looks away uncomfortably as his voice trails off.

Frank holds his hand.

"John. We are brothers. What do mean you don't know how to tell me? What have you been thinking about?"

"I'm just confused that's all"

"Is it something bad?"

"I'm not sure Frank"

"Are you in trouble?"

"No I'm not in trouble"

He looks at Frank.

Frank smiles at him quietly.

"I em…" clears his throat "I want to go to school Frank".

Frank looks at him quietly.

"I want to study for *WASC* or *GCE*, you know, *JAMB* and do something with my life".

He glances at Frank's smiling face,

"I'm not sure if it is the right thing to do. But somehow, being on campus here seems to have changed me some what. I think I can learn something. It doesn't have to be a degree. I can enter for a diploma or certificate program".

"Do you believe you can do it?" asks Frank, matter of fact.

"Yes. I think I can. But I'm not sure if it is what I want to do"

"John I will tell you the truth as your brother. Education is the key to open doors. If you believe I should get education, why shouldn't you too?"

John hugs him and whispers, "Thank you little brother".

Frank grins widely, and says, "Thank you big brother".

*

It is Frank's second semester in UI. His results for the first semester just came out. He took seven exams and scored seven A's. To celebrate, he goes to the SUB with John, Gene and Paschal for a few drinks.

John wanders to a corner of the complex to gamble. For several weeks he has been earning very tidy sums of money from poker. Tonight is especially lucrative.

As soon as he sits down, his winning streak kicks in and within an hour he has well over ten thousand *naira* in his coffer. This is a very neat amount from one short game on campus.

The losers eye his bulging pockets angrily.

He stands up to leave, they will not let him.

One loser, a mean looking 'hard man', growls angrily,

"Where do you think you're going?"

"What?" asks John.

"Are you deaf? Boy sit down and play card"

"I really have to go. My brother is waiting for me"

"I don't care if your pop is standing behind you. Just play the damn card. You think I will let you leave here with my money?"

"I won. If I want to go, I will go" replies John.

Another loser quips, "I won't be so sure if I were you".

John sits down angrily, and says,

"You want to play cards? Let's play. How much do you have left?"

"Why?"

"Everything I have and everything you have" says John.

The three losers exchange glances.

"You're sure about that?" asks the hard man.

"Let's get this over with", quips John.

He whips out every naira bill from his bulging pockets and puts the bundle on the table.

The others rummage their pockets and put out everything they have left, a paltry sum.

"This is all you have?" asks John.

They nod.

"Okay. Deal the cards folks", says John.

The first hard man deals the cards, eyeing John intently as he gives out each card. The others adjust in their seats uncomfortably.

John picks up his share of three cards and looks at them impassively. The others play their hands nervously.

John puts his cards face down.

They look at him.

The first hard man grins widely, revealing dirty brown tobacco stained teeth, as he holds up his cards with his left hand. He stretches out his right hand to pull the heap of money towards himself.

He quips gleefully,

"21 palm".

"Not good enough" says John.

"What?" retorts the hard man angrily.

The others shake their heads sadly.

"See for yourself" says John as he grabs the money from the table.

The *hard man* throws down his cards, grabs John's cards from the table and turns them face up.

He exclaims angrily,

"Oh crap! Two keys"

"That's right," says John, stuffing all the money in his pockets.

He stands up, smiles at them and quips,

"Goodnight gentlemen. It was nice doing business with you".

He turns to leave.

The first *hard man* stands up and calls out,

"Hey. Hold up boy".

John stops and turns around to look at the *hard man* approaching him with a bottle of beer in his hand. He drinks from the bottle and stares at John menacingly as he stops in front of him,

"You really think I'll let you go with my money?"

"What?" asks John incredulously.

"Don't act stupid. Do you know who I am? You want to take my money? Do you have any idea what that means?".

He lights a cigarette with one hand, in slow motion, and blows smoke in John's face threateningly.

John coughs uncomfortably,

"I don't want any trouble. We played cards and I won", says John quietly.

The *hard man* laughs heartily, looking around at the other guys,

"Is this guy funny or what? He actually wants to take my money".

He glares at John,

"Do you know who I am?".

Frank struts in like a stallion and answers from behind John with a smile,

"Who are you?".

The *hard man* glares at him angrily,

"Mind your business dude. This doesn't concern you"

"Oh really?" says Frank stopping beside them.

"Give me back my money", says the *hard man* menacingly

"I can't do that. I won the game. And I'm not a bank", retorts John.

"Hear that? Well said I must say", says Frank.

He takes John's hand and pulls him away.

The *hard man* smashes his half empty bottle of beer on the side of the wall and yells angrily, one half with sharp edges in his hand,

"You think I'm joking? Give me my money!".

Frank stops in his track. He turns around and walks back towards the *hard man*,

"You've broken a bottle. Now what?"

"I want my money now!"

Frank looks at him quietly.

John hovers behind him.

"I'm not joking. Give me my money or blood will flow right now"

"Whose blood?", quips Frank.

"I don't care whose blood damn it. Just freaking give me my money".

Frank bends down to pick up a large piece of the broken bottle.

He looks into the *hard man's* eyes as he puts the piece of bottle in his mouth.

Smiling, he chews on it noisily.

The *hard man* looks at him wide eyed. He throws down the other half and runs away into the night, screaming,

"Crazy weirdo! Freaking psycho!"

*

A few days later, Leo, Frank's roommate, corners him as he returns to the hostel from his last lecture for the day,

"Franco man. I've looked everywhere for you"

"I had classes the whole day"

"Yeah?"

"Oh yeah. What's up?"

"I need your help man"

"What do you need?"

"It's Kemi. Remember Kemi?"

"Kemi?"

Leo nods.

"I should remember her?"

"You don't remember Kemi? The girl at that cafeteria inside 'black market'? The dark pretty girl?"

"Okay. Kemi. Cafeteria. Black market. What about her?"

"You have to help me man"

"Help you how?", getting exasperated.

"You remember? I told you how I eat there. You know, for free"

"Okay you eat there for free"

"Yes. Now she won't give me anymore free food. She says I have to pay"

"That's sad. But what can I do? I don't even know this person"

"That's the point"

"What's the point?"

"You"

"Me? Leo look I don't have time for this crap. I've got a lot of work to do. What're you talking about?"

"Please don't be mad at me"

"I'm not mad. Just say what you have to say or let me go take care of business. I'm not sure if you realize we're in school or not. I have to study my brother. I don't have time for too many games. Especially some crazy game like this one right here"

"The thing is Kemi likes you and…"

"Are you crazy? I don't even know this person"

"But she knows you…"

"Knows me from where? What's the matter with you? I don't have time for this crap…" he starts walking away angrily.

Leo follows him, explaining,

"Do you remember the night I took you there?"

"What night?"

"That first night…"

"What?" stopping.

"That first night you and John got here, and I was showing…"

"My first night in UI?" asks Frank incredulously

"Yes. And I took you to black market?"

"That was six months ago. You expect me to remember some cafeteria girl from six months ago?"

"But she remembers you. Every time I go there she asks about you. Then she told me she likes you very much. That she wants to meet you…".

He looks away.

Frank looks at him thoughtfully,

"What did you tell this girl?"

"Well... I told her I would hook you guys up"

"Hook us up?"

"Yes. Now she won't give me any more freebies without seeing you"

"Leo I'm not interested in her or any girl right now. I just want to study man. I don't have the time..."

"Please Frank. Just talk to her at least once..."

"Are you crazy? Tell her what?"

"You know, that you like her too. You'll be her boyfriend..."

"Sorry man. I can't lie to her. I can not deceive her or..."

"It's not deceit. Just do it for me, please"

"Sorry Leo I can't do it. Ask me something else, not this".

He walks away.

Leo calls out after him,

"Frank I will starve if she stops feeding me. You know my situation".

Frank stops. He turns and walks back to him.

Leo whispers painfully,

"I have not eaten since morning Frank".

Frank smiles, looks at his wristwatch,

"C'mon lets go. You have exactly thirty minutes".

"Thirty minutes? That is too...", they walk towards black market.

"Hey don't push your luck brother"

"But thirty minutes is too short"

"Okay one hour. No more"

"That's what I'm talking about", says Leo, laughing excitedly.

Frank shakes his head, smiling.

They arrive at Kemi's 'buka' — cafeteria, and take their seats. The overly excited Kemi stops everything she is doing and devotes all her attention to Frank.

Leo grins from ear to ear. She offers them the best meal they have, drinks, etc. And she blushes every time her eyes meet Frank's.

A moment later Frank and Kemi walk away into the night, talking. She tells him how much she looked forward to seeing him again, and again. She has fallen for him, she explains.

Frank, confused, wonders how she can fall for someone she barely knows. Matters like these are really not part of his interests, not his forte. But in order not to offend her, or spoil Leo's 'bailout program', he flows with the flow; although deep inside he hated himself for being used for this outrageously despicable scheme.

When the time for him to leave comes, she attempts to kiss him. He is shocked, but plays it cool. And from that night onwards Frank is welcome to eat at Kemi's '*buka*' anytime, for free. John and Leo too.

Frank eventually gets with the program. But although Kemi wanted more from Frank, he was not ready to get intimate with anyone at this time. Well, at least not until he met the girl who changed his life forever.

*

A few weeks later Frank runs into Nancy, his first female encounter at the University of Ibadan, around campus. He is glad to see her; but she is very upset.

She is upset because since their first brief encounter she had thought about him night and day; but never set eyes on him again until now.

Although upset, she still felt very strong feelings for him.

She glares at him playfully, he grins at her cheerily.

"Nancy. What a pleasant surprise?"

She frowns, "Oh really?"

"Yes. I'm glad to see you"

"Really?"

"Really. And you look great too".

She fights a smile playing around the corner of her mouth,

"Mmm. I'm surprised you even remember my name".

"Remember your name? Are you kidding me?"

She retorts almost angrily, fighting her feelings for him,

"You tell me."

He frowns slightly as he asks,

"Are you okay?"

"What?"

"Are you okay? You seem a little upset."

"A little upset? Why would I be a little upset? Because you stood me up? Or because the first and last time I saw you was over eight months ago? Why would I be upset Mr. Frank?".

He blinks uncomfortably,

"I apologize".

"You apologize. How sweet. I guess that makes it all great. Right?"

She starts to walk away from him.

He follows her,

"Nancy wait".

She stops, and says almost angrily,

"What do you want from me Frank?"

"Nancy…"

"What?"

"But…"

She starts to walk away again.

He steps forward, takes her arm, and turns her around gently.

He looks into her eyes and pleads,

"Please wait. Nancy I'm sorry".

She looks into his eyes and melts. Her legs weaken, her insides warm up, a sudden wetness starts to drip down her thighs, and her face glows with heat.

She almost reaches out to kiss him, to break off a piece of him, to eat him up. But she stops herself, with immense difficulty.

He implores her,

"Nancy I tried to see you a few times".

She frowns,

"Don't play with me Frank. You're not the hottest guy on campus. Don't play with me".

Frank grins,

"I'm serious. I tried to see you".

She retorts,

"What're you talking about?"

"I came to your room. Different times and…"

She snatches her arm from his hand and starts to walk away, upset that he would lie to her.

He calls out,

"I saw your room mates. I left messages…"

She stops and walks back to him,

"What?"

"I saw your room mates. Bimbo, Yetunde, and Aisha. I left messages. You didn't get any of my massages?"

"No. Those damn bitches. Nobody told me anything. I'm sorry. I thought you were messing with me".

She looks at him and suddenly kisses him.

He kisses her too.

He pulls back, and grins at her,

"What was that for?".

She chuckles,

"That is for thinking you were lying to me".

He takes her hand as they walk away together.

He quips,

"How've you been girl?"

She chuckles again,

"Excuse me? When did you start speaking like that?".

They laugh heartily.

Then he asks again,

"But really. How've you been?"

"Not good", she says.

He stops to look at her,

"Not good? What's wrong?"

She smiles at him,

"I've being thinking about you night and day. I've been to your department many times, hoping to catch a glimpse of you".

"Mmm. Stalking me, uhn?"

"Sort of"

She kisses him again, and whispers in his ear,

"My roommates are out of town. Do you want to come with me?".

He whispers in her ear too,

"You're sure about that?"

"Yes. I literally want you to come with me. Are you game?"

"Wow. Feisty. Feisty".

"Frank I've waited for this for a long time. Are you with me or not?"

"Nancy aren't we moving a little too fast?"

She retorts,

"I'm not asking you to marry me. You're too young for that anyway. I just want to spend some great time with you. Do you want to do that or not?"

Frank grins, takes her hand, and leads her towards her room in Queens Hall. As they walk through the door, even before locking it, Nancy *'jumps him'*.

She tears off her clothes and peels off his. And she breaks off a piece of him, as she unwittingly 'dis-virgins' Frank.

His first experience is no doubt the wildest thing he has ever experienced. Nancy knows exactly what she is doing and more.

It is an earth shattering experience for Frank. And this rendezvous continues for sometime. They are both apparently very compatible with each other; at least sexually.

10 LOVE AT FIRST SIGHT

"What love we've given, we'll have forever. What love we fail to give, will be lost for all eternity" - Leo Buscaglia

Frank becomes quite popular within a few months in Ibadan. All kinds of people come to him with all kinds of requests and for everything under the face of the earth, even for the weirdest reasons imaginable.

He is both feared and respected within the community. He is 'in the know' about happenings around campus. Matter of fact, he makes many things happen. And he stops many things from happening. He is indeed a *'made guy'* in every sense of the term.

But the most remarkable development is the metamorphosis of his relationship with Nancy. They have somehow become completely inseparable.

They are now like the proverbial *'5 and 6'*; always together, almost every time of the day. Every time you see one, the other is only a few feet away, or both together holding hands.

They have fallen in love and just can not do without each other. They are a formidable couple. Nancy is a very beautiful, almost six feet tall campus beauty queen from a very wealthy background.

And Frank is an handsome daredevil with very charming looks, but from the opposite end of the economic spectrum. An unusual thing in a society with a very strong socio-economic class dichotomy. But never the less, they are glued together by love.

Nancy fell in love with Frank from the very first time she set eyes on him.

Frank is a young ambitious precocious teenager in search of knowledge and a better tomorrow. He was not smitten by her right away, but has grown to love her deeply. Especially after she '*dis-virgined*' him.

She is the first woman he has ever been intimate with, and naturally developed very strong feelings for her.

Nancy's very forthright, guileless, outgoing, vocal and sincere nature made it very easy to fall for.

She is an unusual type. She is not shy by any means. She goes after want she wants. She is from a very affluent family, but extremely down to earth, unpretentious and caring.

She is an almost perfect human being with a great sense of humor. She is richly endowed with a sensuous voluptuous body and a deeply passionate persona. Every man's dream mate, no doubt.

Frank is, therefore, envied by many, and certainly despised or hated by a lot more for his relationship with Nancy.

Many would gladly fight Frank for Nancy's affection; if they dare. Even some females try all manner of tricks to get her to leave him.

They tell her lies and tall tales of how Frank is supposedly '*a secret cult leader*', a criminal, a no good, etc. But she laughs it all off. She is in love.

And ironically, she always tells him what anyone says to her about him. Even the dudes who have tried to 'hit' on her are 'ratted' out too. But only after making Frank promise he wouldn't say or do anything about it.

She only cares about him, and no one else. He can see that, and he believes her completely. He has never been loved this way before, ever. He knows that.

Nancy changes departments shortly afterwards. She leaves Political Science for Law, so she can see Frank every day.

Their relationship has gotten really serious. She invites him to her home in Lagos, to meet her mom.

People don't do stuff like that in college, well, unless they are not just fooling around.

Nobody takes their campus boyfriend or girlfriend home to meet their parents unless they are extremely serious. She does it, and that says a lot.

Her friends on campus go a step further. They start telling her family all kinds of damning stories about her supposed *'secret cult'* boyfriend, Frank.

Her family members are of course very concerned, as would be expected. Nobody wants their child, their only daughter, to be hobnobbing with a supposed criminal.

Her two older brothers are completely incensed and livid with rage. Word gets to their father, a traditional ruler and King of a certain Kingdom. A man who is also a former high court judge. Things are not pretty when he finds out.

But Nancy remains very committed, loyal and steadfast to her heartthrob. She isn't going to give up on him, or leave him because practically everyone says she should.

She is her own woman. She makes her own decisions, and can care less about all the ruckus. She is very happy with him. He has never maltreated her in any way. He never yells or curses at her like all her friends boyfriends do.

He doesn't cheat on her either like her friends boyfriends all do, she figures. Frank is practically always with her, holding hands, kissing, and almost 'eating each other up' any where and everywhere; to the chagrin of everyone around.

They have somehow become the yardstick for measuring 'campus love'. A feat not easy to accomplish in a huge campus like UI.

Ironically, all the so-called friends who always have something terrible to say about Frank are the same very ones who come crying to her to ask Frank to help them when they get into a jam with some other *'made guy'* around campus.

But as it turns out, some of her friends do not only want Frank secretly; they actually make passes at him behind her back. Why? Nobody can answer that.

But perhaps because they want a taste of the 'bad boy' Frank. Or maybe they have a need, or an unquenchable urge, to understand whatever the 'beauty queen' finds so irresistible about the supposed criminal. Curiosity they say sometimes kills the cat.

Some of them start to conjure up stories about her to him, and practically throw themselves at him brazenly, every time her back is turned, even when she is only a few feet away.

They make up stories about how she is cheating on him, and not really serious about him after all, etc.

Unfortunately, Frank falls for this treachery a couple of times. He sleeps with a couple of Nancy's friends behind her back.

And as far as he knows she is unaware of this betrayal. But does she know? Has he been 'ratted' out? Until this day he is still not sure.

She has never brought it up. She has never asked. And he has never confessed.

But he realizes too that Nancy, in spite of all her wonderful attributes, can be a devil if she wants to be. His favorite nickname for her, after all, is 'the wicked witch'. And that is for a reason. A really valid reason at that.

The very loving Nancy can be extremely vindictive if she chooses to be. She just might be waiting for the opportune moment to bring up that terrible indiscretion and despicable act of betrayal.

He still quivers every time the thought crosses his mind. But then, only time will tell.

*

The first time is when Nancy had gone to Lagos for a photo shoot as a model for a popular oil and gas company. Something she does quite frequently to make some extra bucks.

Something she is very proud of, making her own money that is. Even though she does not have to work for anyone, or anything for that matter, considering her background.

But she does it anyway, and she would usually give all the money to Frank to do whatever he pleases with it.

Frank is returning from the library on that cold rainy harmattan night when he comes across the voluptuous and stunning, very moneyed, pampered, and overly spoilt Halimat; Nancy's friend and roommate.

They exchange pleasantries and start to walk together. She says she is looking to get something to eat. He says he is on his way to his room after a long stint in the library studying.

The library is something he always makes time for in spite of his very torrid life in Ibadan. He never jokes with his primary purpose of being in Ibadan in the first place.

She invites him to dinner with her. He declines. But she insists, claiming it is a perfect opportunity for them to talk because she is having some difficulty with 'jurisprudence', since she is also a law student, although a year his senior.

And everyone in the department knows 'jurisprudence', amongst many other subjects, is like a piece of cake for him.

It just happens to be one of Frank's major strengths. Not wanting to refuse to help someone in need, he acquiesces. And that is the first mistake.

She takes him to an exclusive and top class eatery within the SUB; a place that ranks amongst the classiest and priciest on campus.

They take their seat in a private area of the spot. They place their order. And then she orders a bottle of Bordeaux red.

That is the second mistake, because nothing good can possibly come out of two young adults after a bottle of wine on a cold rainy night. Especially when one of them is a very gorgeous and elegantly flirtatious young woman, and the other is a naïve young man that just recently discovered the pleasures of sex. Absolutely not a good mix.

The waiter brings the bottle of wine, opens it, and pours it into their glasses. They clink glasses and sip from the delicious age old romantic elixir.

Her eyes are affixed on his face all the time.

Frank smiles, as he tries to avoid her very strong mesmeric gaze.

He manages to say unconvincingly,

"I'm really not sure if red wine goes well with jurisprudence"

She chuckles loudly, touching his hands and fingers.

He let her hold his hands, not sure what to do since he is not very experienced in these sort of matters. He is smart enough to admit when he doesn't have a clue about something. This is the third mistake.

He makes a mental note to do some research about this sort of thing later on. He realizes he is in a completely uncharted water. He has no idea how to react to what is happening to him.

He should speak to John, the unapologetic pimp, about this encounter, he reckons. John will have the answers he seeks.

Her hands linger on his as she stares into his eyes very intently; all the time massaging his fingers gently. He becomes really uncomfortable as something starts to stir in his pants, around the groin area.

He clears his throat and mumbles,

"So what problem are you having with jurisprudence?"

She giggles and quips,

"You sound just like the professor"

Frank grins sheepishly.

She squeezes his hands lovingly.

She whispers erotically,

"Why don't you tell me about you instead?"

Frank smiles, as always, but very confused now,

"Really?"

She nods, smiling lasciviously, her eyes not leaving his face.

He mumbles uncomfortably,

"There isn't really much to tell…"

She giggles,

"That's not what I've heard"

"What have you heard?", says Frank demurely.

"Well, I've heard stuff…"

"Like?"

She chuckles, and says,

"It's girls talk. Nothing to be concerned about"

Frank smiles, very confused,

"I see"

She giggles, winks at him, and sips from her glass.

Frank sips from his glass too as he makes a mental note of his questions for John. And just as he is thinking if perhaps he should leave, their food arrives.

He has somehow become quite famished all of a sudden, and he is not sure if it is because of the wine, or because of Halimat's intense gazing, or her massaging his fingers, or the activity currently going on in his pants; or a combination of all the aforementioned.

But be it as it may, he starts eating right away. Trying to cut off the massaging and intense gazing.

Halimat starts to spoon-feed him from her plate, and barely eating anything herself.

They continue to eat, drink, and talk about everything except jurisprudence. They finish the bottle of Bordeaux red. And she orders a bottle of champagne.

They are both really plastered by now. It is also very late.

Then they leave the restaurant.

As they walk down the street Halimat keeps bumping into him. He isn't quite sure if it is on purpose or not.

But a moment later she kisses him smack on the mouth. He is too shocked and too drunk to react.

He isn't sure if he should kiss her back or not. Another question for John pops in his head.

She takes his face in her hands, looks intently at his face and queries almost pleadingly,

"What's wrong? Don't you like me?"

He is tongue tied.

He mumbles,

"Em…"

She mutters seductively,

"I like you Frank. I really like you a lot"

And with that she kisses him again passionately.

The stirring around his groin area returns, and he can't help but kiss her back; even though at the back of his aroused and drunken mind something is wondering if this is right or wrong.

Another question for John he reckons.

Frank, still unsure of what is happening, continues to make out with her wildly on the street corner.

In between mouthfuls of Frank's face, she whispers something like,

"I'm alone this weekend. Lets go to my room…"

He wanted to say with all his might,

"No! Absolutely not. I can't do that. It is wrong"

But he hears himself say meekly,

"Ok".

And he is led like a sheep to the slaughter.

*

The second incident occurred shortly after the tryst with Halimat. But not before asking John all the questions he had.

A discussion which did very little to help his predicament, because John as it turns out was really a pimp daddy after all. Rather than tell him he was wrong, John had high-fived him over and over again; practically condoning and encouraging the indiscretion.

He was certainly not a healthy relationship counselor by any reckoning. He is, matter of fact, a very bad influence. His advice to Frank is that he keep his mouth shut and never to mention anything about the incident to Nancy. He is absolutely no help at all.

Then it happens again when Nancy is away visiting her mom in Lagos. Nkiru, Nky for short; Nancy's supposedly very good friend, shows up in front of Frank's room on Saturday morning.

She knocks on the door loudly and repeatedly.

Frank who is alone and trying to read a book, hurries to open the door thinking someone might be in trouble.

He is taken aback by the very seductive and very oiled ebony skinned Nky standing in the door way.

She is wearing a very flimsy top without a bra, with her very hard nipples and curvaceous bosom straining the very thing material of the top to breaking point.

The very skimpy top is over a pair of very short shorts; the kind Jamaicans call 'pumpum shorts'.

Without wasting any time for small talk, or niceties, or pleasantries, or finesse, none of that, she pushes Frank back inside the room.

She locks the door with the key in the lock.

Frank is mouth agape, totally astonished and blown away by the boldness.

She continues to push him towards a bed.

A waft of her very sensuous and erotic perfume envelops the entire room even as a full blast of hormones take over his senses.

A tornado starts to swell around his groin area. He is fully automated now, and perhaps not liable for his actions going forward.

He swallows hard and manages to blurt out implausibly,

"Nky what're you doing?"

She shuts him up with a finger to his lips, and a catlike whisper, "Shhh"

She pushes him all the away to the bed. And with one smooth motion she removes her almost nonexistent top, and then the shorts too. There is no underwear.

He glances up at her dark smooth oiled sweet smelling skin and he melts completely. She climbs on top of him and goes to work.

He closes his eyes as she gently ease him into paradise.

11 THE MAN

"Whatever the mind can conceive it can achieve" - *W. Clement Stone*

John, true to his word, has made a complete 180 degree turn. He registers for *GCE - General Certificate of Education - classes,* a *WASC* equivalent for adults. And is preparing to take the exam that would make him eligible for *JAMB*, and perhaps some sort of degree program. Frank is of course very elated by this development.

He has offered to write all the exams for John. But he is declined. John wants to test himself. He wants to see if he is in fact capable of acquiring any education all by himself.

But he accepts extra private tutoring from Frank. Something that makes a lot of difference really, and which Frank gladly provides.

John takes all the relevant exams all by himself, and he does rather well. He becomes eligible for JAMB. He passes that too, and is admitted to study computer science and economics, because; apparently, he has a natural knack for mathematics and computation.

Perhaps because he always knew how to 'compute and generate' money. John is a congenital economist imbued with entrepreneurism. He just has a gift for sniffing out business opportunities, albeit some with very questionable legitimacy.

His life however changes for ever when he meets another young man named Edward. A young man who is about his age and also an innate entrepreneur.

They meet in a JAMB preparatory class and a friendship quickly develops, especially because Frank has become rather scarce and rarely available, no thanks to Nancy.

Edward who, like John, wants to *'hammer by all means necessary'*, make money at all cost, introduces John to a new scheme. A rather straight forward scheme.

Laughable, idiotic even; but very criminal, yet extremely effective as it turns out. A rather simple scheme Edward calls: *letter writing*. Yes, letter writing.

Edward writes tons of letters everyday to unsuspecting victims nationwide. Letters making comical promises. A *'maddofesque'* type letter with promises of stupendous profits with only a nominal cash investment. This is a typical *'advance fee fraud'* scheme that preys on greedy folks who are induced by promised wealth.

The letters usually claim that if you invest a small amount of money, you would reap millions within a short period of time. But the reality is that there is no profit to be made, the fraudsters are only after your 'small investment' that you will never see again.

It sounds funny, but believe it or not there are actually some very many greedy and gullible people around. And it adds up.

Imagine collecting the equivalent of only a hundred dollars from about one thousand unsuspecting people. Or perhaps five hundred dollars from about ten thousand people. Do the math!

The foregoing is how the famous, or rather infamous *419* was born. Greedy people with an insatiable desire to profit where they have not labored usually fall victim to this scam.

Imagine receiving a letter from out of the blue with a promise of selling you shares in the *Nigerian National Petroleum Corporation (NNPC)* at a very reduced rate. Or shares at *Coca Cola* for instance. Or the *Nigerian Airways*.

The sensible thing to do in a case like this would be to either destroy the letter immediately, or at the very least make an attempt to verify the authenticity of the so-called offer with the appropriate authority.

The caveat is usually for the recipient of the letter to keep the letter and its content private and as a secret, because it is an 'under the table' deal for only a 'pre-selected group of people'. Go figure!.

Agreed, some folks would receive a letter like that and immediately shred it. Or perhaps make an effort to verify its efficacy.

But many receive this letter and are immediately blinded by the prospect of making huge returns on a seemingly fraudulent investment - by supposedly buying 'discounted shares' in either a federal government owned company, or a global entity like *Coca Cola* for example.

What about the even more brazen letter that claims to be from a bank soliciting for a willing partner who would front as the owner of a supposedly dormant account that contains millions of dollars?

You receive a letter claiming to be from a bank that is supposedly in possession of millions of dollars under a deceased's name; and that they want you to come forward to claim this supposed largess as the beneficiary.

Many people get this type of letter and the first thing that crosses their mind is what they can buy with all that money. They respond to the letter right away.

They go back and forth with the supposed bank via letters, then via phone, and then several fictitious and very fraudulent documents are faxed, all with promises of a big pay out. The prospective 'beneficiary' sends over all his personal information, etc.

The bait is thrown; the hook, line, and sinker is swallowed and it is time to reel in the catch, which is the *'maga'* or *'mugu'*, the fool. The 'bank', having sworn the *'maga'* to secrecy, proceeds to make demands of cash settlements paid up front to accelerate the process.

Little sums of money are demanded. A thousand dollars here, five thousand dollars there. Then ten, twenty, hundred thousand dollars are thrown away, gone.

Because all the time the *'maga'* is reminded of the millions of dollars that is coming to him or her. Blinded by greed, the *'maga'* with vivid pictures of all the millions coming to him in his mind, continues to pay out thousands of dollars. This is the classic *'Advance Fee Fraud'*, or the 'Nigerian *419'*.

And if for whatever reason the *'maga'* becomes suspicious, the 'bank' arranges a face to face meeting with the *'maga'* inside an actual bank building. Some 'palms' of the officials of a real bank are greased with a few hundred dollars, and they make a conference room available for a meeting between the *'maga'* and the 'bank'.

At the meeting the *'maga'* is convinced that the 'deal' is real, and is happening.

Happy and satisfied, the '*maga*' doles out even more money to complete the deal that will conclude any day now. He continues to pay out.

He even borrows money from his family and friends, without ever letting them know about his forthcoming 'big pay day'. And he waits.

Already broke now, after committing over a million dollars to this endeavor. Meanwhile, the 'bank' is living very large. Buying homes, exotic cars, and the finest clothes and jewelry. The 'bank' continues to milk this '*maga*' while they throw out other baits and hope for another '*maga*' to bite.

When reality starts to sink in, the '*maga*' who is unable to report the situation to the appropriate authorities or to anyone for that matter, broke, and indebted, starts to contemplate all manner of things, including suicide; especially when his letters and phone calls to the 'bank' are no longer answered, or returned unopened.

It finally dawns on him that he is a full blown '*maga*' when he goes to the bank building where he was in a meeting with the 'bank' only a few weeks before, and the security guards wouldn't even let him inside the building. He is told they don't know him, and never to return there.

All his money is gone. His business is dead. He is in debt. He is losing his mind. He has caught himself speaking loudly to no one. He is becoming unkempt. He is not eating, or sleeping. Now, what to do?

Having being completely schooled in the art of 'letter writing' by Edward, John completely falls in love with the scheme. This is what he has been looking for all his life.

He was born to do this, he reckons. And he naturally brings it to Frank's attention. Frank laughs it off initially, but on closer examination; and after considering the success rate of the scheme realizes that it wasn't a laughing matter at all. And he is hooked too.

John who is by now something of a computer genius, and a very practical entrepreneur, finds a way to make the 'letter writing' scheme more effective and cost efficient.

He comes up with the very first 'email letter'. He successfully reduce both the turn around time and cost of their 'letter writing' business. Emails are both faster and cheaper than snail mail. Emails have the potential of reaching a rather vast number of possible *'magas'* much faster than snail mail ever could. And at a much cheaper cost.

Frank, on the other hand, being the naturally brilliant and unusually intelligent one; comes up with much more inventive letters targeted at much bigger *'magas'*. He naturally becomes the *'chairman'* of their *'office'*, *'the big boss'* of their criminal enterprise. He successfully transforms the small business into a multinational industry. He brings in many others, and starts to create a financial empire.

Business is 'good'. Many more young brilliant undergraduates, and jobless graduates, are enlisted into this army. Several other 'offices' are established across the country. Every new office established has to pay a certain percentage of their income to Frank, the 'chairman'; so even when he doesn't have a paying *'maga'* of his own at any time, there is still some residual income coming in from one of his franchisees.

By the time he graduates from the University of Ibadan he is already a millionaire. And he naturally has several followers and dependents.

Within a few years he has become a household name. He is helping whoever needs his help. He makes contributions to poor communities.

He helps pay school fees for the indigent. He gives several scholarships. He builds hospitals, clinics, and medical centers for the poor. He provides them with clean water as needed. And naturally, the people are drawn to him like moths to flame. They bestow several chieftaincy titles on him from all across the nation.

But Frank's biggest achievement is successfully marrying his first love, Nancy, straight out of college; he reckons.

*

Mr. Jonah had listened to every word Frank had said for the last five plus hours uninterrupted; completely captivated and intrigued, with all his undivided attention, not moving, and not asking any questions.

Frank smiles as he exhales quietly.

The sun is rising, it is already morning.

Mr. Jonah looks at him with amazement and mutters almost to himself,

"That's one heck of a story"

Frank smiles at him.

Mr. Jonah continues,

"If I didn't hear it from you myself, I won't believe it"

Frank whispers,

"It's hard to believe"

Mr. Jonah retorts,

"You've come a very long way my boy. A very long way. Who can blame you for anything? Certainly not me son"

Frank looks at him quietly.

Mr. Jonah continues, he says matter of fact,

"You had to do what you had to do. Life happens my child. It is what it is"

Frank smiles.

Mr. Jonah reaches out and pats him gently on the shoulder, and mutters,

"It is what it is son"

Frank turns to him and asks,

"So what happened to you since the last time I saw you?"

Mr. Jonah frowns slightly.

He turns to Frank and says quietly,

"Son, lets leave that story for another day. Ok?"

Frank smiles,

"Ok sir. Another day"

Just then John walks out to join them on the patio.

He turns to Mr. Jonah,

"Good morning sir!"

Mr. Jonah gets up and walks over to John.

He grabs him in a tight bear hug with tears streaming down his eyes. He whispers in John's ear,

"Thank you John. Thank you for everything"

John smiles, as he mutters,

"Thank you too sir"

Frank stands up, smiling.

Mr. Jonah pulls him close.

The three musketeers hug with teary eyes for a long moment without a word.

And thus Mr. Jonah returns to Frank's life as a surrogate father, after a thirty year gap. A responsibility that Mr. Jonah embraces completely. And there couldn't possibly be a better son than Frank Audu anywhere. He starts to take care of Mr. Jonah just as he does his own biological father Philip.

Mr. Jonah lives in his household and lacks nothing. He doesn't have to worry about anything for the rest of his life, according to Frank. If he wants anything he just needs to say the word and it will be done.

Although Mr. Jonah has no biological children of his own, he understands that he couldn't have asked or wished for a better child than the one God Himself has blessed him with in Frank Audu, and now John Okhide as well. So he is now the very proud father of two great sons. And perhaps a daughter as well in Nancy, he reckons.

He was briefly married once. It didn't work out. His accursed wife from hell ran off with a politician who had more money than common sense. As he remembers those ugly days, he mutters to himself with a grin,

"Good riddance to bad rubbish!"

*

Life is 'good' for the next few years for Frank Audu and his empire. Business couldn't be better, with thousands of 'magas' and 'mugus' hooked and paying up from all across the world.

Everyone 'connected' to the empire is smiling to the bank. Even the wantonly corrupt politicians in power are all having a field day stealing the country blind, and wasting the nation's resources on the most idiotic policies and projects.

The poor downtrodden masses are getting poorer and hungrier; whereas the rich are all getting fatter and richer.

The extremely corrupt politicians and their cronies, including the police, the judiciary, etc., are all in cohorts with the likes of Frank Audu.

They turn a blind eye to the criminal enterprise called '419', ironically named after a Nigerian criminal law code for advanced fee fraud, and thereby making a mockery of the entire Nigerian judicial system.

Frank Audu and his ilk live like emperors and lords, even as kings. They have more money than some small nations around the world. They control many of the politicians, countless judges, and almost all the police force. They can get away with anything, including murder. They are law unto themselves. No one, and nothing, can stop them, they reckon.

Nigeria is in decay. The decadence is mind boggling!

*

Frank walks down a corridor — dressed in a very expensive suit and tie. John follows a step behind — also dressed in a suit and tie — holding a black leather briefcase with gold trimmings.

They stop in front of a door. John opens the door for him; he steps inside the opulent boardroom. Four men are already seated inside the massive room. Three Nigerians and a German national.

They stand up to shake hands with Frank as he walks around the large desk. He sits down at the head of the table; John puts the briefcase in front of him.

He clears his throat softly as he opens it.

John moves to sit in a corner quietly.

Frank glances around, and says,

"Gentlemen, welcome to Lagos. I would like an introduction before we proceed".

The first man to his left speaks,

"I am Engineer Tom Bagudu, representing the Minister of Petroleum".

Frank nods at the next man,

"My name is Alhaji Usman Yahaya, Governor of the Central Bank".

"I am Professor Bola Awofeso, Chairman of the Presidential Committee on Petroleum Resources".

The German smiles at them as he says,

"My name is Hans Ludwig, I'm a business man".

Frank looks around the desk from man to man,

"Gentlemen, if you would please open your folders, you will find every document that is relevant to this discussion".

They all open the file folders in front of them. They examine the papers diligently.

"I assume you're all familiar with this matter. My client here..."

Pointing to Hans Ludwig,

"...has shown interest in the shares offered for sale by the ministry of petroleum. I sent you copies of the proposal".

Engineer Tom Bagudu, a man in his forties, wearing a very thick pair of horn rimmed glasses squints at the papers in front of him studiously.

Professor Awofeso, a slightly balding man of letters, probably in his fifties, looks at the papers quietly. He taps his temple gently.

Alhaji Yahaya, a very dark and lanky man with a seemingly permanent frown — whose age is hard to tell because of his athletic figure — shakes his head from side to side.

Hans looks from one to the other and then at Frank, with sly eyes. Frank smiles at him slightly.

The Engineer clears his throat noisily, and says with finality,

"The papers seem to be in order to me".

The Professor smiles wanly,

"They are in order except that we may have to reword a few sentences".

Frank turns to the Governor,

"Alhaji?"

Alhaji bellows almost angrily,

"Walahi, I am not comfortable with the figures fa".

Hans glances at Alhaji uncomfortably,

"Is there a problem sir?"

Frank raises a hand to silence Hans.

Smiling, he asks,

"What do you disagree with dear Alhaji?"

"Frank, walahi, the figure proposed for the shares is too low. Our oil is one of the best in the world fa! We can get a better deal walahi".

The Professor chimes in,

"Alhaji I understand your concern, but Mr. Ludwig is the highest bidder we got".

Engineer Bagudu, adjusting his glasses, says,

"I will like to inform you, gentlemen, that our situation is precarious at the moment. We need a foreign partner urgently. The ministry of petroleum can not continue to operate the refinery in Warri without some assistance and..."

Alhaji cuts in,

"So we should throw away our oil ko?"

"Not throw away our oil Alhaji. I said a partnership sir."

Hans tries very hard to hide his satisfaction. A smile curl up at the side of his mouth.

Alhaji continues forcefully,

"Walahi, this partnership will be tantamount to throwing away our oil in the Atlantic Ocean fa!"

Frank, still smiling, says,

"Alhaji it is not that bad. My client is offering us..."

"Your client offers us nothing fa! He only wants to take our oil. He will make all the profit for nothing!"

The Professor smiles at Alhaji warmly,

"Alhaji, the presidency is in support of this partnership and..."

"You politicians come and go fa. When you go, the central bank will be blamed for every financial impropriety. The people will not understand. I'll be the man who destroyed the economy. Walahi, this is not fair fa".

Frank looks at Alhaji and asks with thinly veiled sarcasm,

"What do you want sir? Another fuel scarcity? Another crisis? Another string of nationwide riots? The petroleum corporation needs urgent help and my client is offering to turn around the situation".

Alhaji glares at Hans,

"Mr. Ludwig, do you have any prior experience in petroleum refining fa?"

Hans clears his throat,

"I have partners in Europe that have being refining crude oil for many years sir. And I listed all my partners in the initial proposal".

Alhaji shakes his head sadly.

Hans glances at Frank furtively, he smiles at him.

The Professor wipes off sweat from his balding head with a handkerchief—even though the air conditioner in the room is working perfectly.

The Engineer adjusts his glasses gingerly.

The scene above, which is like a bad script from a really terrible 'Nollywood movie', is indeed exactly that. A script. It is in fact a script written by Frank himself.

And all the participants, except for Mr. Hans Ludwig, the prospective '*maga*', are professional actors hired by Frank specifically for this meeting.

A meeting being held in a very cozy conference room inside the *Nigerian National Petroleum Corporation (NNPC)* headquarters, somewhere in Lagos, Nigeria.

*

Several weeks before the aforementioned meeting, Hans Ludwig is behind his desk in his simple but beautiful office somewhere in Frankfurt, Germany. The computer screen on his desk flashes the message: INCOMING MAIL. He glances at the computer screen for a moment and reluctantly opens the email. He is preoccupied with his personal thoughts.

At fifty-six he should be considering semi retirement from his business that he has done diligently for thirty years. His son, Himler—who is thirty now, should be getting ready to take over this business. He has not done too badly in business for thirty years, he reckons.

He started from nothing. With only a high school diploma, he had decided to take on the business world. He worked his way up the business ladder humbly. He cut lawns for a fee. He packed snow. Then he designed snow blowers and hired a few people. He had been fortunate that there had been a lot of heavy snow days in those early years.

As business bloomed, he had diversified into garbage collection. He acquired trucks and a disposal unit. With time he had branched into general construction and civil engineering. To his credit are countless buildings, roads and bridges all around the world—especially in the third world countries, and a very large bunch of fed families.

Families nourished from his purse, from wages to his countless employees. But he will not deceive himself that it was easy at all. It was not in any way easy.

There were times he was afraid he would fail. There were times he wanted to quit entirely. There were times his wife was the only one standing behind him with unalloyed encouragement and support.

She helped him persevere. She is like the proverbial rock, the silent pillar behind his success.

He metamorphosed into a successful businessman with a knack for sniffing up prospective ventures despite his very little formal education, but with loads of street smarts. He had succeeded where others had failed.

He had gotten married—at twenty-five—to his beautiful supportive wife, Helga. And together they produced a strong son. He hopes that someday, his son Himler will be able to run this conglomerate that he toiled to build. Himler should be prepared for the task no doubt. He had been properly educated with degrees in engineering and business.

In a nutshell, he is a happy man. A very content man without a doubt, he reckons.

He opens the email and is stunned by the content:

Att: Mr. Hans Ludwig

BUSINESS PROPOSITION

We wish to intimate you with a business proposal, as representatives of the Presidential Committee on Petroleum Resources.

The Federal Ministry of Petroleum of the Federal Republic of Nigeria, is putting up for sale a substantial amount of shares to the highest bidder.

We found your name listed in a reputable list of businessmen around the world compiled by the Nigerian Chamber of Commerce. If you are interested in this matter, please send a reply as soon as possible.

And be informed that our committee is going about this project very discreetly, for security reasons. We will appreciate it if you do not disclose this information to anyone else because we are contacting only very few people with this offer. If you do, you will be disqualified automatically.

If you are not interested, we will expect that you destroy this letter and forget about it. If you are interested; send us your fax and or telex numbers with your reply, to enable us send you the appropriate documents.

Sincerely yours,

Professor Bola Awofeso

Engineer Tom Bagudu

Co-Chairmen, Presidential Committee

For: The Minister of Petroleum.

Hans reads the email on the screen three times. He prints a copy. He stands up from behind his desk, with the email in his hand; he paces around the office, still reading the letter.

He moves to the desk, he picks up the phone. He dials a few numbers, stops midway. His eyes go back to the letter where it says, '...do not disclose this information to anyone...'

He drops the phone and moves to sit down again. He stands up and walks to the window. He peers through the window to the traffic beneath, deep in thought.

He smiles to himself as he starts to ponder what a fabulous retirement package this sudden 'largess' will be for him. He starts to pace the floor, hands folded behind his back.

Later that night, Hans is tossing and turning in his bed. Helga wakes up to see him sitting up. She moves close to him,

"Is something wrong?".

He turns to her,

"No...no... I'm fine. Go back to sleep".

She holds him tenderly,

"Are you alright?".

He forces a smile, "I'm fine".

"You were restless in your sleep"

"Really? I...I... was having a bad dream"

She looks at him, worried,

"Ha! You want to talk about it?".

He holds her gently,

"I don't remember what it was".

She looks at him quietly. He pulls her back on the bed slowly,

"Lets go back to sleep. Maybe I'll remember in the morning".

He kisses her goodnight, the second time that night. They cuddle. A little moment after, her chest heaving up and down, she starts to snore lightly. He glances at her, and then closes his eyes with some effort.

*

Hans is at his desk at the break of dawn. He types away at his computer—replying the email he received yesterday. As he sends it, he leans back on his huge leather seat. He stretches his left hand to open a box of cigars on the left side of the desk. He takes out a fresh thick *Cuban Havana*.

He sniffs it for a moment, his eyes closed, savoring the scent with relish—almost religiously. He opens his eyes slowly; they stray to the computer screen. He squints at the screen almost painfully—as if willing a message to appear on the blank screen. He turns to his right and picks up a cigar cutter. He nips a piece off the tip of the cigar, puts down the cutter and snatches up a lighter — with his right hand—as he gets up from the seat.

He walks towards the window, the cigar moving up to his mouth with fervent passion. As he stops at the window, he puts a short burst of flame to the cigar clamped between his teeth. He inhales deeply; holds a ton of smoke in his lungs for a brief moment, and then lets out a thick bluish cloud of smoke that swirls up to the ceiling like a rivulet — forming rings.

He looks up at the bluish carbon monoxide rings with peevish satisfaction — a fretful smile in the corner of his mouth. He glances down — through the glass in the window — at the people and cars on the street below, like some *demigod* seated atop some high throne looking down at his subjects.

He tucks his left hand in his pant pocket. The other hand clamps the huge cigar between two fingers — like a vice. Absentmindedly, he takes another long drag from the cigar.

He coughs violently, his body quivers like a small city struck by an earth tremor. His eyes water at the sides. Still holding the cigar, he moves to a corner of the office where different exotic bottles of liquor stand at rapt attention like infantrymen with valor and chivalry.

He picks up a glass and pours himself a large respectable manly portion. As the glass kisses his lips, the phone beeps loudly — startling him. He spills some of the liquor on his shirt. He walks towards the desk; the phone switches to fax mode, papers — facsimiles — spew out from the machine.

He peers at the first page and sees the words: *Federal Ministry of Petroleum, Federal Republic of Nigeria.* He smiles to himself, sips from the glass in his hand and pulls on the cigar again — this time subtly.

He goes round to sit behind the desk, putting down the glass and killing the cigar — in a tray — at the same time. He picks up the papers lovingly — with the tenderness of a newborn baby — a glint in his eyes.

And thus, Hans Ludwig unwittingly swallows the bait; hook, line, and sinker. He starts to remit thousands of dollars to the 'committee' who must bribe all the parties involved to make 'the deal' happen as soon as possible.

Shortly afterwards, the distinguished, very private and secretive 'committee' introduce Hans to a very reputable, respected, and very 'trusted attorney', a certain Frank Audu. The only person with the authority to negotiate any type of deal with the 'committee', on behalf of any interested party.

After paying several thousands of dollars as kick back to the 'committee', and having become restless and suspicious; Hans demands to meet with the 'committee', accompanied by his 'trusted attorney' and 'representative', Frank Audu - the *chairman* himself.

But then Frank 'advises' his client - Hans - that he would be better served to demand that the 'committee' grant him the right to take over the oil refinery in Warri, Delta State, Nigeria.

A multi million dollars government owned entity. Because, according to the 'trusted attorney' Frank, taking over the refinery would be a sure fire way to get back his investment made so far with huge returns within the shortest time frame.

Not wanting to lose what he has invested up to that point, Hans bites the second bait, hook, line, and sinker. He authorizes his 'trusted attorney' to prepare the proposal for the refinery takeover to the 'committee'. But of course, several palms must be greased as is always the case with doing business with the supposedly wantonly corrupt governments of the so-called third world countries.

Frank arranges for a guided tour of the Warri refinery, the whole package; which includes several helicopter rides over the entire facility. Meetings with supposed department heads, etc.

Hans, convinced that this deal was going to happen, starts to pay out huge sums of money, up to the tune of several million dollars. He couldn't eat or sleep anymore. He couldn't help himself. All he could think about was how he was going to become an oil magnate, just like the Saudi Arabian oil rich princes.

In his head, he has started devising methods of how he would short change the Nigerian people by diverting some of their crude oil vessels to be sold on the black market for more money.

But all the while, his once successful civil engineering and construction company is taking a big hit. He is destroying the business by taking out too much too quickly. The business is getting liquidated.

Even when his prior business partners speak to him about the dangers of his decisions, he is far too gone to heed their warnings.

Africans say '*a dog that will be lost does not hear his owner's whistle*'. Hans Ludwig has become blind and deaf to reason. He is lost.

He continues to make payments to Frank Audu and the 'committee', even as he is becoming broke and bankrupt. He believes too much in the oil dollars waiting to be made to back down. There is just too much oil money in the *Niger-Delta* region of Nigeria to ignore, he reckons.

Africans say '*those whom the gods want to kill are first made mad*'. Hans Ludwig has become seemingly irrevocably mad. Every one else could see it except for him. Even the love of his life from forever, Helga, after pleading with him endlessly had threatened to leave him if he won't quit the madness, and he still wouldn't bulge. All her pleas and threats had fallen on deaf ears. Himler, their son and only child, was completely in the dark about all this.

Not able to deal with any more of the madness, Helga leaves Hans. She moves in with her parents, hoping he would come to his senses and come for her. But he doesn't. He is really lost. He has unwittingly become the ultimate, and complete, '*maga*', supposedly.

12 SHOWDOWN

"Mistakes happen, but you move on" - Sara Caldwell

Hans, sitting at his desk, almost every day, calls the 'committee' several times without getting a response. Either the phone rings endlessly, or someone answers curtly,

"Please hold"

And then classical music comes on, which plays in his ear endlessly. Usually it is *Beethoven's Symphony No. 9,* and at other times it is *Mozart's Symphony No. 40 in G Minor.* The music just plays until he hangs up. When he calls back, the cycle repeats unabated.

And even his 'trusted attorney and advisor' Frank Audu is no different, he reckons. Every time he tries to call him, a very sweet female voice answers with a honey dripping tongue,

"Hello. You have reached the law office of Frank Audu and associates. How may I direct your call?"

He always wonders who that very soothing and enjoyable voice belongs to. He would really like to meet the owner of that blissful voice, he reckons. He wonders if the owner is as beautiful and perfect as the voice sounds.

His train of thought is cut off,

"Hello? Frank Audu and associates. How may I direct your call?"

He stutters,

"I'm sorry. Hi. May I please speak with Frank Audu?"

"Who is calling?"

"Hans Ludwig please"

"Please hold"

And *Christoph Eschenbach's Piano Concerto No. 1 in C Major* comes on, as he mutters,

"Oh no. Not you too…"

But the sweet sounding voice, still dripping organic honey, comes back right away and quips,

"Hello. Thanks for holding Mr. Ludwig. But I'm afraid Mr. Frank Audu is not available at this time. Would you like to leave a message sir?"

Hans, taken aback by her return to the phone. Not expecting her to come back, blurts out,

"Are you sure?"

The voice says,

"Excuse me sir?"

Hans retorts,

"I'm sorry. Please pardon me"

"Ok sir. Would you like to leave a message?"

"Em. Please tell him I called. And I've called many times already. Have him call me back".

"Ok. Mr. Hans Ludwig?"

"Em… yes. Hans Ludwig from Germany"

"Ok sir. I'll make sure he gets your message. You have a very splendid day sir. Bye".

And click, she hangs up.

He looks at the dead phone in his hand for a moment and smiles ruefully as he rests it on the cradle. He turns to the box of cigars on his desk. He begins the ritual of lighting up a large *Cuban Havana.*

A thick cloud of bluish smoke starts to envelop the room. He sips from a tall glass of whiskey sitting idly on the desk. He smacks his lips, and pulls on the cigar once more. He blows up the smoke towards the ceiling thoughtfully, and then rests the cigar in an ashtray gently.

He turns to the far corner of the large desk and picks up a medium sized black leather case. He opens it gingerly, and stares briefly at the .38 colt automatic pistol nestled inside it. He picks up the gun slowly and checks to see if it is loaded. It is fully loaded.

He cocks the mean looking gun and deliberately points the barrel to the side of his head, point blank range. Tears begin to well up on the sides of his eyes. With the gun still pointing directly at his temple, he starts to glance around the room very slowly, almost trancelike, making a visual sweep through of the office, as if for the very last time.

His roving eyes stop at a picture of his wife and son hanging up on the wall, close to the desk. And he starts to cry softly, tears stream down his face like a broken watershed, even as his finger begins to squeeze the trigger ever so slowly.

*

At the exact same time in the universe, somewhere in Lagos, Nigeria; John and a couple of his cohorts are in the middle of a '*wash wash*' operation.

John, flanked by two of his goons, is sitting across an opulent desk inside a rather flamboyant office, with the very important looking Chief Oturugbeke, a renowned businessman and political bigwig in these parts. The Chief is plopped in the massive leather chair behind the desk.

John had dangled '*the bait*' at Chief Oturugbeke several weeks before. His congenital and unscrupulous need to reap profit from where he has not sown has blinded him, and his greed has made it impossible for him to back away from this supposedly profitable business transaction in play.

The Chief has been convinced that a certain chemical element has the capability of converting paper cut in standard currency shape, and size, into US hundred dollar bills. The process is known as '*wash wash*' by the practitioners.

The truth is, dollar bills; real dollar bills, are covered in some type of harmless chemical that makes the bills look like ordinary paper, shrouding its original state. The bills are then dipped in a bowl of water mixed with some type of food coloring. The chemical is washed off, and voila, the real dollar bill is returned to its original state.

Greedy people fall for this trick every time. They are so blinded by the supposed profit they can make, as always, that they throw away every caution to the wind. Chief Oturugbeke is no exception.

John has shown the chief how 'ordinary paper' can be made into real dollar bills. He performed the 'experiment' right in front of him. The paper had turned to a real hundred dollar bill. He held it, looked at it carefully; and even kept it for a few days. He showed it to his friends in the banking sector, and even the ones who are in the business of money laundering. They have all confirmed that the hundred dollar bill is very real and legitimate.

Hooked, both line and sinker; Chief Oturugbeke decides to pursue the money making business with John, the supposed US trained engineer known to the Chief as Tim Anuku.

John, aka Tim Anuku, supposedly needs a business partner who can pay for the cost of the chemical needed to make the dollars. The chemical is so rare and expensive that it would cost *an arm and a leg*. Tim Anuku knows how to get the 'chemical' from Europe. He is willing to do the business with Chief Oturugbeke. They will import the chemical, and start to 'print' their own hundred dollar bills. Matter of fact, they would also try to print British pounds too; and even euros as well.

Tim Anuku offers Chief Oturugbeke fifty percent of the business; but the Chief wants more. They then settle for a 60-40 percentage share. Agreed, Chief starts to pay out. And he waits for the shipment to arrive.

Due to all the vagaries of the turbulent seas, compounded by all the unforeseen 'delays' of the shipment, e.g. problems at the laboratory that manufacturers the chemical, etc. the Chief winds up 'investing' about five million dollars. But of course, that is chicken feed compared to the 'humongous profit' they are looking forward to make, according to Tim Anuku.

Chief Oturugbeke awaits the arrival of the shipment expectantly. He waits and waits for days, weeks, then months. Having run out of patience, he starts to call Tim Anuku every day; but for some reason he seems unable to get a hold of him. His phone number seem to be disconnected, or out of service. Then a light bulb finally goes off in his head.

He realizes he has been *'419ed'*. He is a certified *'maga'*. But he is too embarrassed to admit it to anyone, not his friends or family members, and neither the police. But there are whispers amongst his people. They know something is amiss, but they just can't put a finger to what it is. They're all confused.

But he vows to take revenge. He would make it his mission to bring the criminal Tim Anuku to justice, one way or the other. But where would he find him, he wonders. All his sources are unable to find anyone named Tim Anuku. He either managed to disappear from the face of the earth, or he does not exist at all, he reckons. Go figure!

*

A couple of weeks later, Hans Ludwig, having been unable to completely pull the trigger of the .38 caliber colt automatic pistol jammed to his head at point blank range, returns to Lagos, Nigeria; in search of 'the committee'.

He takes a cab straight from the *Murtala Mohammed International Airport* in Ikeja to the *Nigerian National Petroleum Corporation (NNPC)* headquarters in Victory Island. He is immediately detained at the gate for trespassing. His claims of having been there for meetings in the past fall on deaf ears.

He is handcuffed and put behind bars at the security post. His request to meet with the so-called 'committee' is met with stone cold stares from the heavily armed Nigerian Army personnel on guard duty. Hans looks completely deflated as he holds his head in his handcuffed hands.

*

Frank is drinking champagne in his modest but very respectable looking office with an opulent looking young man. A man who is not much older than him, a political juggernaut, the one and only Chief Femi Badamasi; a real *'son of the soil'*, as they refer to the original natives of Lagos. An *'omo eko'*, in the local parlance.

Chief Badamasi, sitting with Frank on the couch, sips from his glass, smacks his lips and grins heartily,

"What do you say Frank? Can I count on you?"

Frank grins, then frowns,

"I'm not really sure Chief. You know me. I'm not the type. It's not my thing, and I don't have your courage…"

Chief cuts him off with a wave of his hand,

"C'mon Frank! You can do it. We believe in you. I believe in you".

Frank mutters,

"Mmmm. I don't know Chief"

Chief continues,

"I'll be with you every step of the way. You will not walk alone".

Frank smiles wryly, stands up and starts to pace the floor thoughtfully.

Chief Badamasi looks at him quietly. He sips from his glass of champagne, and looks up at the pacing Frank expectantly.

And just then the phone on the desk rings shrilly, piercing into the tension in the office like a very hot knife through butter.

Frank frowns at the phone, as he moves towards it. He glances at the Chief,

"Excuse me Chief"

Chief nods and waves his hand as he sips some more champagne.

Frank picks up the phone,

"I thought I said I was not to be disturbed?"

His voice trails off as he listens to the caller.

He frowns,

"Excuse me?"

He listens some more.

"Are you sure?"

Phone in hand, listening intently, he moves to sit in his chair behind the desk. He mutters almost under his breath,

"I'll be damned! Hans Ludwig?"

He glances over at Chief Badamasi on the couch, then at his wrist watch, and says quietly,

"Do nothing. I'll call you back shortly".

He hangs up the phone, stands up from behind his desk and walks towards Chief Badamasi. He smiles ruefully, and says matter of fact,

"I'm very sorry Chief, but we have to reschedule this meeting".

Chief Badamasi frowns,

"Why is that?"

Frank says, without mincing words,

"Something rather out of the blue has come up"

Chief grins,

"Something I can help you with?"

Frank grins,

"Thank you Chief. But it's nothing I can't handle"

"This is Lagos Frank. And as you know, I'm a son of the soil. Whatever you need. Just ask any time".

Frank smiling, bows his head respectfully,

"I know that Chief. And I appreciate it".

Chief Badamasi empties his glass of champagne down his throat, stands up and takes Frank's hand in a very firm handshake. He looks into his eyes and says seriously,

"Frank. Times are changing. We need every political power we can get"

Frank frowns slightly as he asks,

"Can you really trust these people?"

Chief answers without mincing words,

"Yes. Absolutely!"

Frank smiles,

"I'll think about it"

Chief grins,

"Fair enough"

They shake hands effusively, both grinning. They hug like really close friends.

And Chief says,

"Well, let me not hold you up. Call me"

Frank says,

"I will".

Chief Badamasi leaves.

Frank rushes over to his desk, and dials numbers on the phone furiously.

*

As it turns out, Hans Ludwig, having run out of options and being held in detention by fully armed Nigerian Army personnel at the NNPC Headquarters, decides to gamble by requesting a phone call to his attorney, a certain man named Frank Audu. And he also demands to speak with the highest ranking police officer in the state, and that happens to be the Lagos State Police Commissioner.

Usman Danladi, the Lagos State Police Commissioner is a no nonsense disciplinarian who is reputed to be very forthright in all his dealings. A man renown for his very hard stance against every form of corruption all around the country. He is a lone voice fighting against corruption within the police force.

The corrupt politicians in power, aided by some criminal elements in the police force, have tried several times without success to get rid of him.

They have tried to bribe him, tried to coerce him, tried to threaten him; but have all failed woefully. The man is simply incorruptible. He is a career police officer with an impeccable record. A man that cannot be moved or bought with money, only by the truth; and justice. He is God fearing, humble, and extremely honest; even to a fault.

Following protocol; but really because nearly every soldier in the country is disillusioned with the political class, and considering the Commissioner's reputation for being a straight shooter, one of the army officers on duty at the NNPC Headquarters gate had called to inform Usman Danladi, the Lagos State Police Commissioner, of a certain German national named Hans Ludwig who was demanding to speak with him. Bewildered and curious, the Commissioner agrees to speak with the man.

*

A high ranking official of the NNPC, who is on Frank's payroll, had placed a call to him as soon as Hans showed up at the NNPC Headquarters.

While Frank is scrambling and deciding what to do with Hans, the Police Commissioner had requested that Hans Ludwig be transported to his office immediately. So, by the time Frank decides to go to the NNPC Headquarters to meet with him, it is too late. Hans is already on his way to meet with the Police Commissioner.

Hans Ludwig, crying like a baby, tells Usman Danladi every detail of his business dealing with the 'committee' and his supposedly 'trusted attorney'. The Commissioner is livid with rage, and also very upset with Hans for his role in the deal.

The dreaded and highly esteemed Usman Danladi, the Lagos State Police Commissioner, immediately constitutes an investigation of the matter. An investigation he wants to personally oversee. He recruits a crack team of incorruptible officers that would report to him directly. Officers loyal to him, and that he knows very well. Officers that he trained personally. People that cannot be bought over, or easily influenced in any way. The proverbial die is cast.

When Frank hears this development, he knew right away that nothing good could possibly come of it especially because of who is in charge of the investigation. He immediately tries to find Hans Ludwig. But he seems to have disappeared. There is no trace of him, not even a sniff. All his people turn up empty, with no clue of his whereabouts. All his informants within the Police Force are just as hapless and useless.

This is most certainly a very serious situation, he reckons. He starts to make all the necessary calls. To the governor of Lagos State, to the Inspector General of Police, to some top guns of the government.

And then he waits for the inevitable, an invitation to meet with the Police Commissioner, something he would rather avoid by all means; but that he knows is coming very soon. What to do?

On the exterior Frank seems calm and at peace as always, but deep inside he knows the situation can balloon out of proportion real fast if not handled appropriately. He makes up his mind to make one final phone call, reluctantly. He calls '*the son of the soil*', the fixer, the political juggernaut, the one and only Chief Femi Badamasi, the original '*omo eko*'.

Now, Chief Badamasi has waited for this opportune moment for a long time. An opportunity to finally bring Frank Audu into his political caucus in readiness for his run for president soon. He wants Frank's immensely wealthy empire in his corner.

He has courted Frank variously, covertly and overtly, with no success. He desperately wants Frank to openly support his party, and his political aspirations; but that is something Frank would not do for his own personal reasons.

Frank is something of an apolitical pariah. Chief Badamasi is a renown political fixer who longs to have Frank in his debt. He knows exactly who and what Frank is; everything he does et al, and what he can bring to his party's inner caucus.

He hugely wants his support; along with the support of all his empire, and associates nationwide. Chief reckons doing this big favor for Frank would most certainly seal the deal once and for all. Frank would be in his debt, and in his pocket. So he goes to work.

*

Meanwhile in a matter of days the task force set up by the Lagos State Police Commissioner is within touching distance of making arrests in the Hans Ludwig case. And this is certainly nothing short of a miracle because the Nigerian Police Force is supposedly renown for being incompetent, and allegedly reputed to do everything at snail pace. So this lightning speed performance is most definitely unheard of, and a massive record.

All this time, the Police Commissioner is purportedly holding Hans Ludwig in a very secure undisclosed location as a material witness in the case he is building at the speed of light.

The Commissioner is seated behind his desk in a meeting with four of his handpicked taskforce officers. They are going over several papers and photographs when the telephone on his desk suddenly rings shrilly.

He frowns as he glares at the phone.

He ignores it briefly, then picks it up, and barks curtly,

"Hello?"

He listens and then frowns,

"Governor? How're you sir?"

He listens briefly, and says politely,

"Well, if it is not important I would rather not come"

He listens again, frowning deeply,

"Well in that case I will see you tonight"

He listens again,

"Yes. Ok. See you tonight"

He hangs up the phone as he curses in *Hausa*, under his breath,

"*Shege Danboroba!*", rough translation: 'Bastard'.

He turns to his officers who are all impassive, and blurts out angrily,

"The governor wants to see me tonight"

He glances from one to the other and says angrily,

"I can assure you he wants to talk about Mr. Hans Ludwig. These politicians are shameless bastards!"

He gets up from behind his desk and storms out of the office angrily.

13 YOUR EXCELLENCY

"If a child washed his hands he could eat with kings" - Chinua Achebe

The Governor's Mansion, the official residence of the sitting governor, located in the middle of a prime expanse of land somewhere in Lagos, is a no go area for just anyone without invitation; or if you do not belong in the governor's inner caucus.

The long tree lined road that leads to the mansion itself is always beleaguered with heavily armed 'mobile police' officers, 'mopol' for short. The 'mopol' are a special breed of police officers who are almost inhuman and very dreaded by all and sundry. They are reputed to be a very lethal force who are constantly mobile and always on the move, never in a location for long, hence their name.

They are supposed to be an elite force that is called upon in the face of a serious crisis; but that the corrupt politicians, and their wealthy cronies, have turned into their own personal guards.

To put it in proper perspective; the rank and file of the Nigerian Police Force dreads the elite 'mopol' unit. Even the entire nation's armed forces including the army, navy, and air force, all thread carefully around 'mopol' officers.

Mopol officers can be very unruly, unpredictable, and almost never held accountable for their actions because they are usually faceless and nonexistent, something akin to Adolf Hitler's Gestapo officers. Many of them have been to battle fields around West Africa and beyond. They have shed blood, they are not afraid to do it again, and they do not hesitate to do it with the littlest provocation. They are law, court, judge and jury all by themselves, literally. And they also can act as mercenaries for those who can afford their services.

Mopol officers can be relied on to carry out their assigned duties almost efficiently and effectively, except that they can be overzealous sometimes. They often get carried away, and perhaps overdo things sometimes. They are wont to do extra. But one thing is for certain though; every mopol officer is fiercely loyal to every other mopol officer. They will bleed and die for each other before they will lift a finger for anyone else. A mopol can only trust another mopol, end of story.

*

And inside the Governor's Mansion; the Governor of Lagos state, His Excellency Bode Adeferasi, walks inside his very opulent and flamboyantly furnished living room with several of his cronies spread around different corners of the massive room.

The Governor beckons on 'the fixer' Chief Badamasi who is sitting with Frank Audu in a corner. They both stand up and follow the Governor through a door into an adjoining office.

All three men walk inside, the Governor stops by the door and shuts it behind them.

He turns and grins at Chief Badamasi widely, as he says,

"Chief Badamasi. The son of the soil!"

Chief Badamasi grins, bowing slightly,

"Your excellency!"

They embrace very warmly like very old familiar friends do.

Frank, standing erect, looks on with a slight smile across his face.

Chief Badamasi turns towards Frank and says matter of fact,

"Your excellency, this is my friend, Frank…"

The Governor cuts him off, grinning, as he stretches a hand towards Frank for a warm handshake,

"…Frank Audu. I have heard plenty about you…"

Frank smiling, shakes his hand,

"It is an honor to meet you sir"

The Governor grins widely,

"Call me Bode. And the honor is mine"

He points them to seats in the rather spacious home office.

"Please have a seat"

He walks towards a bar by the wall. He picks up three tall glasses, turns to them and asks,

"Whiskey?"

Chief Badamasi beams widely,

"Certainly!"

Frank smiles,

"Yes, thank you"

The Governor pours generous portions into the three glasses. He picks two up and moves to hand them to the men. One to Frank, the other to Chief Badamasi. He walks back to the bar and picks up the third glass.

He moves to sit behind the huge mahogany desk. He lifts up his glass in the air, and toasts,

"Cheers"

Both Chief and Frank lift their glasses up and chorus,

"Cheers"

The three men sip from their glasses momentarily.

The Governor clears his throat and grins at Frank heartily, and without mincing words quips,

"I understand you are in a little pickle?"

Frank smiles,

"Yes your excellency"

The Governor, smiling, glances at Chief Badamasi,

"My friend here vouches for you".

Chief Badamasi chimes in effusively,

"All day, every day, your excellency!"

The Governor grins, and shrugs, as he says,

"That is good enough for me. It is nothing to worry about Frank. Consider it handled"

Frank mutters courteously,

"Thank you very much your excellency"

Frank glances at Chief Badamasi. He nods and winks at Frank.

He clinks his glass with Frank's, as he bellows,

"Cheers my friend"

Frank smiling, mutters,

"Cheers".

The Governor raises his glass and says emphatically,

"To democracy!"

Both Frank and Chief Badamasi raise their glasses and chorus,

"To democracy!"
They all sip from their glasses.
Chief Badamasi smacks his lips and blurts out loudly,
"This is Lagos!"
The Governor chuckles, and says,
"This is our Lagos…"
Frank shakes his head, grinning.

*

Meanwhile the Lagos State Police Commissioner, Usman Danladi, reluctantly on his way to the Governor's Mansion, is still seething with anger about his phone conversation with the governor earlier that day.

He detests being drawn into any type of contact with the governor or any other politician for that matter. As far as he is concerned, he would rather maintain the most minimal contact with politicians.

He is a professional police officer who is completely disinterested in politics or politicians at any level. His job is to maintain law and order; and by his reckoning, politicians are not very lawful people. Matter of fact, many of the very corrupt politicians always sought creative ingenious ways to circumvent and obstruct the rule of law, especially in Nigeria; in his opinion, and he abhors that greatly.

As his vehicle approaches the Governor's Mansion he becomes more and more irritated. He glances at his wristwatch, shakes his head, and mutters to his driver,

"Shehu slow down. I'm not in a hurry to meet with this man tonight"

The driver nods, stifling a smile, as he slows down the vehicle,

"Yes sir".

He picks up the newspaper on the seat beside him. He squints at the words on the front page, as he attempts to take his mind off the upcoming meeting with the Governor of Lagos State. But his mind wanders off to the Hans Ludwig case.

His investigation has uncovered a grand scheme to defraud the German national, Hans Ludwig; and certainly thousands more all across the world he reckons. Although, as far as he is concerned,

Hans Ludwig had in fact facilitated his own defrauding. He has not quite being able to understand why a full grown man could be that gullible, and be willing to part with so much money just by reading some frivolously engineered letters.

He suddenly blurts out loud,

"Greed! That's why. The man is greedy! He wanted to reap where he did not sow"

Shehu, the driver, glances at him through the rearview mirror as he asks carefully,

"Did you say something to me sir?"

"Sorry. Not to you. I was thinking out loud"

Shehu continues,

"Is everything alright sir"

The Commissioner grunts,

"Don't worry about it Shehu. It's ok"

Shehu looks away and continues to drive down the road.

The Commissioner continues to ruminate over the Hans Ludwig case. He frowns as he thinks to himself,

'The man was very foolish. But that gives no one the right to steal his money. It is still a crime. It is fraud'

His frown deepens as he says inside his head,

'But who are the culprits? I must speak with that lawyer. That Frank Audu. Is he an accomplice? Mm, I wonder'

And just then, Shehu looks at him through the rearview mirror and says,

"Sir we are here"

The Commissioner looks through the window as Shehu turns the car into the long tree lined road leading to the Governor's Mansion.

The Police Commissioner is a very simple man who likes to travel very simply without attracting undue attention. And this night is no different. He is in mufti, just as his driver Shehu, and in an unmarked car. Because according to the Governor, this is not an official visit. He is here as a guest, not as the Police Commissioner.

As the unmarked car drives down the road, armed mopol officers flag it down.

Shehu, grinning, stops the car.

Two mopol officers approach the car, one on either side. They bend slightly to look to see the occupants.

As they recognize the Police Commissioner in the back seat, one of them, a Sergeant, screams at the top of his lungs,

"Attention!"

All the other mopol officers in the vicinity automatically jump up and stand erect like 'iroko trees'.

The Police Commissioner opens his door and climbs out of the car. Shehu follows suit. The mopol officers form a guard of honor right away, standing very erect, and seemingly not breathing.

The Commissioner looks at the officers, smiles and says,

"At ease"

The mopol officers relax slightly, still completely shaken by the sudden unannounced appearance of the Lagos State Police Commissioner, Usman Danladi himself. A man who is himself a former mopol Captain of many years. Here is the feared and dreaded Police Commissioner Usman Danladi in flesh and blood.

Many of the officers here tonight have never met him in person before; but they have certainly heard of his exploits. He is not a man to be trifled with. He is mopol through and through. And he is a legend.

The Commissioner chitchats with the men briefly, they salute him effusively with utmost respect, and he enters the car again, and Shehu drives him to the Governor's Mansion.

*

Inside the mansion, it is almost the same scene like before. Several cronies and minions are spread around and hovering over every kind of assorted exotic wine, liquor and food of all variety.

They were partying stupendously, and making all kinds of underhanded deals, just like they do every other night; whereas the poor downtrodden masses continue to sleep on empty unfed stomachs.

The Commissioner walks inside the huge living room, closely followed by his driver and aide-de-camp, Shehu. He glances around the various people sprawled all around different corners of the room.

He mumbles under his breath, with stifled anger,

"Shege. Danboroba!"

Shehu looks around from corner to corner, impassively.

And just then the Governor, accompanied by both Chief

Badamasi and Frank, walk inside the living room.

The Governor calls out heartily,

"Police Commissioner Usman Danladi"

The Commissioner turns to him and forces a smile as he says,

"Your excellency"

They shake hands.

The Governor introduces the men with him,

"Commissioner meet my very dear friends. Chief Badamasi. And Barrister Frank Audu"

The Commissioner shakes hands with them, forcing a smile,

"How do you do? How do you do?"

The Governor bellows,

"Please come. This way please"

He leads the way towards a door, followed by the Commissioner, Chief Badamasi, Frank Audu and Shehu. He opens the door and they enter a smaller living room. He motions them to sit down.

"Please sit down"

He starts to walk towards a bar in the corner as he speaks,

"Whiskey for me. Whiskey for anyone else?"

The Commissioner, stifling a frown, says matter of fact,

"Nothing for me thank you"

The Governor turns to him,

"Are you sure?"

The Commissioner nods,

"Yes. Nothing for me. Thank you"

The Governor turns to Shehu,

"What about you? Em... I didn't get your name"

Shehu smiles,

"Shehu sir. Captain Shehu"

The Governor grins,

"Ok. Captain Shehu. Would you like some whiskey? Or perhaps something else to drink?"

Shehu smiles,

"No thank you sir. I'm fine"

The Governor shrugs. He makes three glasses and walks two of them over to Chief Badamasi and Frank Audu.

He clinks glasses with both of them, as he says,

"Cheers gentlemen"

Frank and Chief Badamasi both chorus,

"Cheers!"

The Governor walks over to the Commissioner and beckons with his head,

"Commissioner, please come with me"

The Commissioner stands up reluctantly and follows the Governor who is walking out of the room.

*

The Governor leads the Commissioner inside the empty home office. The one he just recently occupied with Frank Audu and Chief Badamasi.

He points to a seat across from the desk,

"Please have a seat Commissioner"

The Commissioner sits down on the edge of the seat, and looks up at the Governor impassively.

The Governor walks behind the desk, glass in hand. He sips from the glass of whiskey and smacks his lips with satisfaction. He looks at the Commissioner and quips,

"Are you sure you don't want something to drink?"

The Commissioner, trying hard to hide his impatience and infuriation, forces a smile as he says,

"No. Thank you"

The Governor stands up from his seat, glass in hand, and walks to the bar in the corner. The Commissioner glances at his watch with thinly veiled contempt and disdain.

The Governor pours more whiskey into his almost empty glass. He turns to the Commissioner grinning,

"This's some really good whiskey"

The Commissioner forces a smile as he says sarcastically,

"Is that so?"

"Oh yes. One of the best I have ever had!"

The Commissioner glances at his watch again as he mutters, almost under his breath,

"Interesting"

The Governor walks back to sit behind the desk. He puts down the glass on the desk and clasps his hands together. He looks squarely at the Commissioner and asks matter of fact,

"What can you tell me about Mr. Hans Ludwig?"

The Commissioner looks at him straight-faced, and quips,

"Mr. Hans Ludwig?"

The Governor retorts,

"Yes. The German national in your custody"

The Commissioner completely taken aback by the Governor's brashness, stutters,

"Your excellency, I'm really not sure what you're asking me"

The Governor, not smiling, not frowning either, says matter of fact,

"Let's cut the crap Commissioner. You've Mr. Hans Ludwig in custody of some sort, and I'm asking you what you can tell me about the circumstance surrounding his detention or whatever you call it"

The Commissioner restrains himself from blurting out loudly the phrase '*shege danboroba*', instead he says calmly,

"Your excellency..."

The Commissioner almost cringes at the term 'your excellency' as it rolls off his tongue, but he continues with difficulty,

"...there is nothing to tell you. It's an ongoing investigation"

The Governor frowns and sips from his glass, then asks,

"It's an ongoing investigation?"

"Yes", retorts the Commissioner.

"And what is the investigation about?", asks the Governor.

The Commissioner quips,

"I'm still trying to determine that"

The Governor looks at him quietly momentarily. He sips from his glass again. He puts down the glass and clasps his hands together. He looks intently at the Commissioner and asks heavily,

"Do you like being the Lagos State Police Commissioner?"

The Commissioner frowns slightly as he says,

"I really don't understand your question your excellency"

The Governor smiles,

"Why're you playing dumb with me Police Commissioner Usman Danladi?"

The Commissioner retorts with suppressed anger,

"Excuse me?"

The Governor prods,

"I ask you a simple question and you choose to play games with me instead? Really?"

The Commissioner says calmly,

"Your excellency, I've been a police officer for over twenty years. That's all I've been. Nothing else"

The Governor smiles impishly,

"That's not what I asked you"

The Commissioner is completely shaken by the Governor's very tasteless tactlessness. He just stares at him quietly, not sure how to react. And trying very hard not to explode, something he knows he is reputed for, he struggles to maintain his composure.

The Governor sips some more whiskey from his glass. He looks at the almost empty glass. He stands up and staggers slightly towards the bar in the corner. The Commissioner trails him with his rage-filled eyes, seething with suppressed anger.

The Governor fills up the glass almost to the brim. He turns and starts to walk back to his seat. He stops and turns back to the bar. He grabs the bottle of whiskey and walks back to the desk with the bottle and glass in his hands. He sits down behind the desk, grinning. The Commissioner just looks on quietly at the seemingly inebriated Governor of Lagos State.

The Governor drinks some more whiskey, clears his throat loudly, and bellows,

"Police Commissioner Usman Danladi. You'll personally report everything about Mr. Hans Ludwig to me directly…"

The Commissioner tries to interject,

"But…"

The Governor cuts him off rudely,

"I'm not finished!"

The Commissioner glares at him wide eyed.

The Governor continues arrogantly,

"I want to know everything about this Hans Ludwig and his allegations. Matter of fact, I think the man should be prosecuted for trying to buy government property illegally. I want a report on my desk immediately!"

The Commissioner shakes his head from side to side.

The Governor glares at him with drunken eyes as he asks,

"Do you understand me?"

The Commissioner nods and says quietly,

"I understand you sir"

The Governor snaps impudently,

"Good. Very good!"

The Commissioner quips,

"But I'm afraid I can't do that sir"

The stunned Governor, not believing he heard correctly, asks incredulously,

"Say what now?"

The Commissioner says very calmly,

"I cannot do that sir"

The Governor stands up abruptly, staggering slightly, and asks angrily in a drunken rage,

"Do you realize who you're talking to?"

The Commissioner, realizing the man is drunk, says reasonably,

"Your excellency, I do not report to you"

The Governor yells,

"I'm the chief executive officer of this state. You work for this state. And you'll report to me. You must obey my order!"

The Commissioner stands up and says matter of fact,

"I do not work for you sir. I do not work for this state. I work for the Nigerian Police Force. And I'll not obey your order. Especially the kind of order you just gave me"

The Governor explodes angrily,

"You'll do as I say. Or you can say goodbye to Lagos State!"

The Commissioner retorts with very suppressed anger,

"Good night your excellency".

He turns and walks towards the door as he mutters under his breath, '*shege danboroba*'.

The Governor, wide eyed, screams after him,

"Come back here Commissioner! I'm not finished with you!"

The Commissioner walks out of the room, and slams the door shut loudly.

The Governor slumps into his seat, exasperated, and in disbelief.

*

The Commissioner storms down the enormous hall way angrily as he calls out loudly,

"Captain Shehu!"

Captain Shehu, his aide-de-camp and driver, rushes out of the living room where he was waiting with Frank Audu and Chief

Badamasi. He answers sharply, alarmed by the Commissioner's tone,

"Yes sir?"

The Commissioner, without stopping, bellows angrily,

"Let's get out of here!"

Captain Shehu, jogging to catch up with the Commissioner, retorts, while glancing around furtively,

"Yes sir"

He walks side by side with the Commissioner as they leave the building, with several of the Governor's hangers-on watching them quietly with suspicion.

They step outside the building and hurry towards their nondescript vehicle parked in a corner. Captain Shehu opens the back door for the Commissioner, but he opens the front passenger door himself and plops into the seat. Captain Shehu closes the back door and hurries into the driver's seat. He guns the car and screeches off as the Commissioner dials numbers on the car phone. He puts the phone to his ear as it rings. And as someone answers, the Commissioner orders,

"Inspector Yakubu, I need you to move Hans Ludwig right away as discussed"

He listens briefly, and barks impatiently,

"No! Tonight. Get to it right away! Call me when it is done"

He hangs up the phone, glances at his wrist watch, and begins to dial another number, he stops dialing as Captain Shehu approaches the armed mopol officers on the tree lined road. Captain Shehu slows down the car, and flashes the lights briefly. The mopol officers on duty all jump up to attention, and salute briskly. He stops the car.

The Commissioner rolls down his window and speaks to the ranking officer,

"Sergeant Bello"

Sergeant Bello standing erect like a tree, salutes and answers very respectfully,

"Yes sir!"

The Commissioner smiles slightly and says,

"Keep your eyes open. I might call upon you soon. You and your men"

Sergeant Bello retorts with very strong conviction,

"We will bleed for you anytime sir. Day or night!"

The Commissioner nods and says,

"Carry on"

The Sergeant and all his men salute briskly. The Commissioner nods at Captain Shehu as he rolls up his window. Captain Shehu screeches off into the night.

Captain Shehu looks at the road impassively as he tears through the very light night traffic. The Commissioner glances at his wrist watch again and dials some numbers. He puts the phone to his ear and listens as it rings.

A voice answers gruffly,

"Hello?"

The Commissioner asks expectantly,

"Superintendent Mohamed?"

The voice replies,

"Yes. Who's this?"

"Superintendent, this's Commissioner Usman Danladi"

The voice, Superintendent Mohamed, another former mopol officer, relaxes and exclaims heartily,

"Commissioner sir! How's everything?"

The Commissioner smiles and retorts,

"Everything is everything"

Superintendent Mohamed chuckles and says,

"All correct sir"

"Superintendent I need your help", responds the Commissioner.

"Anything for you sir", says the Superintendent

"I want a meeting with the Inspector General as soon as possible", retorts the Commissioner

"Em… ok. Give me a few days and I'll make it happen sir", says the Superintendent.

The Commissioner smiles, and says,

"Do it quickly. It is very urgent"

The Superintendent retorts,

"Yes sir. Consider it done"

The Commissioner says,

"Over and out!" and hangs up.

*

The almost completely inebriated Governor of Lagos State, His Excellency Bode Adefarasi, is still seated behind the desk in his home office, his glass of whiskey in one hand; a telephone, glued to his ear, in the other hand. He is speaking very angrily with someone on the other end.

"You don't understand. The man is rude and very disrespectful. I want him gone immediately!"

The person on the other end is the Special Adviser to the President of the Federal Republic of Nigeria; a personal friend of the Governor of Lagos State, a former classmate, a fellow party stalwart. A very crafty fellow named Chief Tunji Durojaiye. He tries to reason with the Governor as he says tranquilly,

"Bode, the Police Commissioner is a good man. He's one of the very best police officers this country has ever known. His record is simply impeccable. We can't just fire a man like that?"

The Governor retorts angrily,

"Tunji are you kidding me? Are you for real?"

Chief Tunji Durojaiye replies,

"Bode I understand how you feel and…"

The Governor cuts him off,

"My friend I'm not sure about that"

Chief Durojaiye retorts,

"C'mon man. We've being friends for over fifty years. Since we were in diapers even. Give me the benefit of doubt at least"

The Governor grunts reluctantly,

"Yeah. Ok"

Chief Durojaiye continues reasonably,

"As I was saying, this's probably just a little misunderstanding. I'm sure we can reason with the man without having to fire him. Remember elections will be here soon. We don't need any scandal on our hands. Firing a very respected and highly decorated police commissioner won't do us any good"

The Governor shaking his head in disagreement, and fueled by all the whiskey flowing through his veins, retorts forcefully,

"You don't understand. The man told me to my face that he does not work for me. And that he will not take any order from me. I can't have that Tunji. That's blatant insubordination. We're the ruling party for God's sake!"

Chief Durojaiye says jokingly,

"But technically the man is a federal employee. Not Lagos state"

The Governor, who is not in the mood for jokes, retorts,

"Are you trying to be funny? I'm not joking Tunji"

Chief Durojaiye, unable to reason with the drunk and very upset Governor, asks quietly,

"So what do you want my friend?"

The Governor snaps angrily,

"I already told you! I want him gone! That's it! No negotiation"

Chief Durojaiye clears his throat uncomfortably and says,

"Ok then. I'll speak with the President about it in the morning. I'll advise him to inform the Inspector General of Police"

The Governor exclaims excitedly,

"Now that is my friend Tunji! Thank you"

Chief Durojaiye grins, and says jokingly,

"Piss off"

The Governor retorts,

"Whatever dude. Just get it done. Chikena!"

Chief Durojaiye says thoughtfully,

"I just hope this doesn't come back to bite us in the ass"

The Governor gulps some more whiskey and says arrogantly,

"We run this country man! Nothing is biting nowhere"

Chief Durojaiye replies,

"Go get some sleep my friend. I can tell you've been drinking"

The Governor grins and says playfully,

"Screw you!"

*

Within a matter of days, the Lagos State Police Commissioner, Usman Danladi, is summoned to a meeting with the Inspector General of Police, Audu Idris, at the Federal Police Headquarters.

The IGP is a man who has been around the corridor of power for many years. He is the type of man who always supports '*AGP – Any Government in Power*' shamelessly, regardless of how terrible the administration is. A complete original 'yes man'. He is not very intelligent and neither is he a very good police officer, but his blind loyalty to whoever is in power has kept him at the very top of the police force.

Many men and women within the Nigerian Police Force do not trust him at all. They whisper many disparaging things behind his back. And folks like Commissioner Usman Danladi only tolerate him because of his office, and reluctantly feign the perfunctory undeserving respect for him. A travesty, no doubt.

When the Commissioner receives the summons to appear before IGP Audu Idris he assumes his inside man, Superintendent Mohamed, has been able to arrange the meeting as he requested. And without wasting time he heads over to police headquarters to meet the IGP, accompanied by his very trusted driver and aide-de-camp, Captain Shehu. Both of them are formally dressed in their official, full, police uniform.

On their way to police headquarters, the Commissioner, deep in thought, with a frown etched on his face, reads a newspaper in the back seat. Captain Shehu glances at him intermittently through the rearview mirror even as he navigates the very harrowing and unpredictable Lagos traffic. Shortly after, they arrive at police headquarters.

*

They park the car and walk briskly towards the IGP's office on the fifteenth floor. They stop intermittently to exchange pleasantries with other police officers in the vicinity. They ride the elevator to the fifteenth floor, and arrive at the IGP's office. Captain Shehu is made to sit in the outer office while the Commissioner heads into the meeting with the IGP alone.

The very plump and out of shape IGP, who looks nothing like a police officer but akin to a rather stuffed and overfed politician, is plopped in a huge leather chair behind his massive desk. He looks up as the very dashing, trim, and athletic looking Police Commissioner.

The Police Commissioner, who looks like a prim and proper police officer, saunters in closing the door behind. Straight-faced, and at attention, he gives the obligatory crisp salute.

The IGP grunts impatiently,

"At ease commissioner. Have a seat"

The Commissioner relaxes and says,

"Thank you sir"

He sits on a chair across from the IGP, and looks at him quietly.

The IGP clears his throat uncomfortably and says,

"I won't keep you here longer than necessary"

The Commissioner looks on without a word.

The IGP continues quietly, almost whispering,

"It has been brought to my attention that your position as the Lagos State police commissioner is no longer tenable"

The Commissioner is impassive.

The IGP continues embarrassingly,

"You have two options. Either accept a new assignment. Or resign from the police force"

The Commissioner smiles sardonically without a word.

The IGP looks at him for a moment, then asks,

"What do you have to say?"

The Commissioner, trying to remain calm, quips sarcastically,

"You have made a decision without listening to my side of the matter. What else is there to say?"

The IGP retorts,

"You started an unnecessary battle with the governor of Lagos state. What did you expect?"

The Commissioner can not believe his ears. He asks quietly,

"Isn't investigating crime, no matter whose ox is gored, part of my job?"

The IGP clears his throat, and says shamelessly,

"Yes. Yes of course. But the people of Lagos state would rather you do that somewhere else"

The Commissioner retorts sarcastically,

"The people or the governor?"

The IGP quips impatiently,

"It makes no difference commissioner. Accept a new assignment, or resign from the police force. That's it"

The completely shocked Commissioner looks at him quietly, fighting hard not to explode. He knows the IGP is a 'yes man', but he did not realize what a complete bastard he is until now. How can this man sitting across from him and saying what he just heard be the inspector general of police, he wonders.

How can a man who condones this kind of shenanigan be the highest ranking police officer of this nation. This country is in serious trouble, he figures.

The IGP continues rudely,

"So what will it be commissioner?"

The Commissioner stands up,

"I don't know Mr. Audu Idris. Do whatever you want. After all, you're the inspector general"

He turns and starts to walk towards the door.

The IGP looks at him walk away wide eyed, both shocked and scared of the commissioner's reaction at the same time. He is mopol after all.

The Commissioner whispers under his breath, as he slams the door behind loudly,

"*Shege danboroba!*".

The IGP grunts to himself,

"Bloody mopol!".

The Commissioner, trailed by Captain Shehu, walks briskly towards the elevator. He turns to Captain Shehu and says matter of fact,

"This country is in serious trouble my friend. Serious trouble walahi!"

Captain Shehu looks at him, worried.

They ride the elevator without a word. They alight on the ground floor and walk to their car. They enter and drive off. Both men are lost in their own thoughts.

*

A few days later, Commissioner Usman Danladi receives his official reassignment order from the Inspector General of Police, Audu Idris. He is to become the new Commandant of the Police College; a demotion of sorts, an administrative position devoid of any particular influence in the scheme of things, except within the confines of the police academy.

He accepts the position without a fuss, realizing he has been outwitted by the corrupt politicians this time. He refuses to resign, he decides to stay on to fight another day. He knows he has lost this particular battle; but the war is just beginning, he reckons. He understands that there is a long war ahead.

He also understands that sometimes you need to take a step back in order to move forward. He reckons he would do his best as the Commandant of the Police College. And he vows to produce the very best officers possible as long as he is in charge of the college. His long time loyal friend, aide-de-camp, and driver, Captain Shehu follows him too.

Commissioner Usman Danladi knows when he is beaten. And he was beaten this time. He meets with Hans Ludwig to explain the development. He assures the man that this is not the end of his case, but that he should go home until there is an opportune moment to revisit the case. He explains to Mr. Ludwig that his life is in danger. That he should return to Germany where he would be safe until further notice. Hans Ludwig acquiesces and returns home, albeit reluctantly.

Days become weeks, and weeks become months. The erstwhile Police Commissioner Usman Danladi, assisted by his very able assistant, the indefatigable Captain Shehu, goes to work on revamping and reorganizing the Police College into a very efficient and effective organization.

The restructuring is easy because of the reputation of the no-nonsense new man in charge. Everyone knows what has to be done and it is done without prodding. His influence on the previously deteriorating police college is not unnoticed by all and sundry.

*

Meanwhile, Frank Audu and his cohorts continued to flourish unabated. Business is great, and could not be better. They are making more money than they can ever spend. There are too many greedy unsuspecting victims to scam around the world. They are making loads of money from all across the world, aided by very corrupt high powered government officials.

Frank Audu continues his philanthropic activities too. He is a 'Robin Hood' of sorts. Stealing with one hand and giving it away with the other hand. He is by now a household name across the country. He is helping the indigent, the needy, and the penurious. He never says no to anyone who needs his help.

Several songs are written about him. He is inundated with several respectable and honorary chieftaincy titles across the nation. He is the '*sun that shines on all*', as they say.

Frank Audu decides to actually do something more tangible for the downtrodden masses of the country. He starts sponsoring his friends and lackeys for political office. Some for the House of Representatives, and others for the Senate.

He reckons that when he has put enough minions in the

legislature then he would actually be able to influence the laws that are passed. And he is always in favor of laws for the people of Nigeria, favorable laws for the common man. Laws that will actually change their condition for the better. A noble ideal, no doubt.

With the help of Chief Badamasi, the fixer, the son of the soil, Frank Audu starts to make some long-lasting and far-reaching moves to take over the country completely. Chief Badamasi himself aspires to be president of the country as well, with Frank Audu's support.

As they plan and plot, other people have a different idea about the direction the country should be heading towards. And these other people are planning and plotting as well.

Within two years, Frank Audu has successfully put in several legislators and senators in the combined house. He is gaining very serious and palpable control of the legislative arm of government.

Even Frank Audu's former teacher and surrogate father, the evergreen Mr. Jonah, is now Senator Ovie Jonah; all thanks to Frank Audu. The once unknown, and unheard of, Mr. Jonah is now an elected Nigerian Senator.

And Chief Badamasi is closing in on a successful run for the office of President of the Federal Republic of Nigeria. The die is cast, and good to go.

It is the season of promises; it is election season when the corrupt politicians make every promise under the face of the sky. Promises they have absolutely no desire to keep. It is the season when the masses are lied to blatantly. It is the season when various alliances are formed, and several are dissolved.

It is the season when money is spent recklessly in the bid to win votes cum election. It is the season when people sell their conscience and their votes for peanuts, shamelessly.

The election is only a few weeks away, and the campaigning and politicking is at breakneck speed, and its acme. Aspersions are being cast up and down. People are getting death threats. Some are pulling out of the race, and others are taking their place. It is mayhem.

At this time Nigeria is in a very frightening precarious economic predicament, replete with immense uncertainty. The politicians in power, with their lackeys, have completely mismanaged the nation's affairs for the last four years. The masses are now hungry beggars in a country supposedly blessed with abundant natural resources.

Food is not readily available to the people. There is no tangible health care system in place. The educational system is spiraling down a very dark rabbit hole. The unemployment rate is at an all time high. Several states owe salary arrears for well over nine to twelve months. Whereas the so-called leaders continue to revel and squander money like there is no tomorrow. Government official residences have more parties and orgies than night clubs weekly. Streets are closed off by the politicians for wild parties regularly.

The political leaders reek of indiscipline and corruption. Wanton corruption. They spend money like it is going out of fashion. They throw endless parties for their lackeys, wasting away the nations resources on foolhardiness.

They spray money, hard to get currency, both foreign and domestic, with reckless abandon; for absolutely no good reason whatsoever. They treat the nation's coffer like their own personal money pot that they can just dip their accursed selfish thieving fingers into without regard for the suffering of the very poor disenfranchised masses.

The masses, scared out of their wits, just grumble under their breath; and remain unheard. They are too weak to protest, or act, or ask questions openly. To paraphrase Fela Anikulapo Kuti, Nigeria's afrobeat legend, 'my people fear too much. They don't want to die'.

They are too afraid to express themselves publicly because of fear, just like headless chickens. They hail the thieving politicians openly, but cry themselves to sleep every night. They are completely emasculated, and all they do is argue in bars drunkenly.

They go to bars, get drunk, argue endlessly, and go home to their beds with empty stomachs. The next day, they repeat the exact same scene from the day before. And so on and so forth. An endless vicious cycle, with no end or salvation in sight.

Nothing is working. The country is a broken machine. The economy is collapsing. The government of the day is completely inept and incompetent. The very fabric of the nation is being torn apart by a gang of buffoons and charlatans. And the crime rate is spiraling out of control.

'419' chieftains, con men, scam artists, and fraudsters, like Frank Audu, are all having a field day. They do as they please in the by now very lawless nation. They are brazenly conning and scamming millions of people out of their hard earned money all across the world. They drive around town in exotic cars bought with stolen loot.

They drive around town in convoys that cost more money than the budgets of several countries combined. They live in mansions that seem to have been ripped out of fantasy picture books. Structures that will make foreign kings and princes green with envy.

Meanwhile the very unscrupulous people tasked with the responsibility of upholding law and order in the country just collect bribes and look the other way.

They are all accomplices in the grand criminal enterprise. No one is ever prosecuted even when they are arrested with very conspicuous and glaring evidence. Criminals just spend their way out of every situation without fuss.

Most times the criminals just call their political accomplices, who are usually high ranking government officials or senior party stalwarts, and the case against them just mysteriously disappears.

The few honest police officers who refuse to cooperate with the criminals, in an attempt to uphold whatever is left of the law, are either reassigned, or let go completely.

At this time it is hard to tell who is worse between the politician and the criminal. Frankly, they are one and the same. No difference whatsoever.

It is total chaos!

14 THE GENERAL

"My people are useless. My people are senseless. My people are indiscipline"
– Major General Muhamadu Buhari

Then one early morning, shortly before the scheduled general election, Nigerians are rudely awakened by ominous martial music blaring from their radio and television sets at the break of dawn. Rumors started making rounds amongst neighbors. There has been a coup d'état overnight, they said.

The military has forcefully snatched power from the corrupt fingers of the dastardly politicians. Democracy is over just like that. The second republic has been cut short abruptly by a rather untimely death. It is over. C'est fini!

Telephone lines are all dead across the country. No phone calls can be completed to confirm or refute the frightening rumors. Families, huddle together inside their homes, whispering in hushed tones; too scared to step foot outdoor.

Then a frightfully terrifying military officer, Brigadier Sanu Aboki, wearing very dark goggles, comes on air in a live broadcast on every TV screen, and via every radio set, across the nation.

The fearsome looking man clears his throat somberly as he peers directly at every Nigerian, from behind his pitch-black sun shades, and bellows authoritatively,

"Fellow Nigerians, I, Brigadier Sanu Aboki, of the Nigerian Army hereby declare as follows:

There is a change of government effective immediately. The newly constituted Supreme Military Council is in charge of the affairs of this country.

The Federal Military Government, under the auspices of the Supreme Military Council, hereby decrees the immediate suspension of the hitherto Constitution of the Federal Republic of Nigeria.

The office of the President, State Governors, Federal and State Executive Councils, Special Assistants, the National Assembly, and the States Houses of Assembly are all hereby dissolved effective immediately.

All political parties, the formation of political parties, or political organizations, is hereby banned as of today.

Accordingly, the erstwhile President and Commander-in-Chief of the Armed Forces of Nigeria, Alhaji Shaka Umaru, therefore ceases to exist in that capacity, or in any capacity whatsoever.

All previous incumbents of all federal and state executive offices must vacate their official quarters, surrender all property belonging to the government in their possession, and must also report to the nearest police station within 7 days from today.

A dusk to dawn curfew from 7pm and 6am is hereby imposed, and in effect, as of this moment.

All airway flights across the country are hereby suspended immediately until further notice.

All airports, seaports, border posts – including land and water – are hereby closed effective immediately.

All external communication has been severed until further notice. All internal communication will be restored as at when it is deemed necessary.

Fellow Nigerians, this is a peaceful change in government. But everyone is hereby warned to remain law abiding in their own interest. The Federal Military Government expects your maximum cooperation. Any disturbance of public order will be met with full force summarily.

As customary, martial law will be declared immediately in any area where any disturbance occur. You have been warned.

You are to remain peaceful and very orderly as you await further instructions. Good morning to you my fellow country men and women".

Then on cue, all the TV screens across the nation return to a picture of a flying flag of Nigeria, and emblems cum logos of the armed forces with martial music blaring endlessly. All the radios start to blast martial music too.

*

It is a new day in Nigeria. The decadent politicians who once lived and carried on like demi-gods have been swept off their feet overnight. They have been relegated to the dustbin of history just like that.

Some try to escape the country through various means but they are all apprehended and thrown in prison pronto.

While a section of the population celebrate the sudden change of government, others, who are associates or beneficiaries of the debauchery, gnash their teeth and go into hiding immediately.

A very huge darkness has fallen and enveloped all the politicians of the second republic. It is a real tragicomedy.

Frank Audu and all his political coconspirators, completely unsure of what is to come, and fearing the worst, have all gone underground.

The governor's mansion that was once a very lively and booming entertainment center with endless obscenities, orgies, and parties, has suddenly become like a vampire's lair – frosty, quiet, and almost desolate, with no one in sight.

Most Nigerians across the nation remained indoors with eyes and ears glued to TV and radio sets with uncertain anticipation.

Several hours later, internal communication is restored and people are able to make phone calls again. And the frightful Brigadier Sanu Aboki announces the new people in power at every level across the nation.

With military precision, Major General Maman Baduru is appointed the new Head of State, Commander-in-Chief of the Armed Forces, and leader of the recently constituted Supreme Military Council.

Also, each state is to be governed by a military administrator who is either a brigadier, or colonel, or lieutenant colonel as the case may be.

But as soon as Frank Audu, who is sitting on a couch in his living room, with eyes glued to a television set, hears the announcement of the former Lagos State Police Commissioner, Usman Danladi, as the new Inspector General of Police, he knew right away his goose is cooked.

As he ponders what to do, his telephone rings loudly, cutting into his thoughts rudely.

He glances at the caller ID and answers weakly,

"Your excellency"

The former Governor of Lagos State, His Excellency Bode Adeferasi, who is on the phone, says tearfully,

"Did you hear about Usman Danladi?"

Frank closes his eyes as he answers painfully,

"Yes"

The former Governor says tearfully,

"Run Frank. Run away"

Frank retorts weakly,

"Run away to where?"

"Wherever my friend. Just get away. I'm leaving now. I should be at the Cotonou border within the hour"

Frank mutters,

"But I just can't run away"

The former Governor says with finality,

"Usman Danladi is a mopol. Mopol are very unforgiving. Lets not test his will. Get out before it's too late!"

Frank says quietly,

"Where will I go?"

The Governor retorts,

"Just get away from Lagos. Get away from Nigeria. That's it. I'm getting out now. Good bye my friend".

And with that he hangs up abruptly.

Frank looks at the dead phone in his hand, and blurts out angrily,

"This is nuts!"

He turns to John and Mr. Jonah who are both hovering around the living room thoughtfully, and asks rhetorically,

"What do we do now? We can't just run away. This is our country too"

Both John and Mr. Jonah look at him quietly with helpless resignation.

*

At the Governor's Mansion, the Governor and two of his long time aides are hurriedly loading luggage into a big SUV. They all enter the stuffed vehicle and head towards the tree lined road that leads out of the mansion. And as usual there are several armed mopol officers on duty. They flag down the SUV with guns pointing.

The ranking officer in charge, Sergeant Bello, the same officer that was in charge the night the former Lagos State Police Commissioner last visited, walks towards the rear door. The Governor rolls down his window, forcing a smile.

"Officer, let us through"

Sergeant Bello, without flinching, without saluting him either, blurts out coolly,

"Not today sir"

The Governor, wide eyed, retorts,

"Excuse me?"

Sergeant Bello quips,

"Nobody leaves or enters the premises"

The Governor attempting to bamboozle his way through, bellows,

"Do you know who you are speaking to?"

Sergeant Bello says impassively,

"I'm following orders sir"

The Governor, scared shitless, asks,

"Whose orders?"

Sergeant Bello grins,

"The Inspector General of Police, Usman Danladi"

The Governor blinks widely as he pleads,

"Officer listen to me. Have I not taken very good care of you and your men all the time you've been here?"

Sergeant Bello grins enthusiastically,

"Oh yes sir. You've been very kind and nice to us. You have always treated us very well sir"

The Governor relaxing slightly, smiles,

"Good"

Sergeant Bello retorts,

"Yes sir"

The Governor continues quietly,

"I need your help officer. I need to leave this place right away. Can I count on you?"

GENESIS OF THE NIGERIAN 419 SCAM

Sergeant Bello says quietly,

"I understand sir. But there is nothing I can do"

The Governor continues reasonably,

"All you have to do is let me through and I promise you will not regret it. I will make you the richest mopol officer in this country"

Sergeant Bello glances at his fellow mopol officers who are standing and looking on quietly. He looks back at the Governor and says coolly,

"That sounds really good sir. But how exactly are you going to do that?"

The Governor says hopefully,

"I'll take care of you and your men. If you let me through right now I'll wire money into your account right away"

Sergeant Bello asks wide eyed,

"Really?"

The Governor retorts,

"Yes. How much do you want? Five million? Ten million? Twenty million? Name your price officer"

Sergeant Bello is perplexed as he asks incredulously,

"Name my price?"

The Governor says,

"Yes. Name your price and I'll pay it immediately"

Sergeant Bello says quietly,

"I have just one question for you Mr. Governor"

The Governor blinks widely,

"What's that?"

Sergeant Bello asks, covering the name tag on his uniform with his hand,

"What's my name governor?"

The Governor blinks widely, totally floored, he stutters,

"Em... em..."

Sergeant Bello grins and says,

"Ding ding ding! Wrong answer"

The Governor blinks widely, totally floored.

Sergeant Bello says,

"You see Governor, you can't buy your way out of this. I'm a mopol officer. I have my order. Turn the car around and go back inside until further notice"

The Governor pleads,

"Please don't do this to me. I've been very good to you"
Sergeant Bello says forcefully,
"Turn around!"
The Governor says tearfully,
"Ok thirty million? Fifty million? Hundred million!"
Sergeant Bello looks at him and says with finality,
"Mr. Man, you don't understand. I don't care for your stolen money. And I won't say this again. Turn the car around now!"
He cocks his gun loudly and points it at the governor.
The Governor tells his driver fearfully, with tears streaming down from his eyes,
"Turn it around"
Sergeant Bello blurts out angrily,
"Shege danboroba!"
The SUV turns around and heads back inside.

*

Within hours, several politicians including executive and cabinet office holders have all been rounded up and arrested. The ones who turn themselves in to their local police stations, as ordered by Brigadier Sanu Aboki, are also detained. A few have successfully escaped the country through forests and rivers into neighboring Benin Republic, Niger, and the Cameroons.

Frank, John and Mr. Jonah are walking briskly towards an SUV in the middle of the massive compound. John goes behind the steering wheel, Frank opens the back passenger door for Mr. Jonah to enter. He shuts the door and moves to enter the front passenger seat beside John.

John starts the engine and maneuvers the car through the massive gate that opens electronically. He turns into the almost deserted Frank Audu Drive. As they drive down the road an unmarked car suddenly cuts them off.

John slams on the breaks to avoid hitting the car. He turns to Frank wide eyed. He tries to back up. Another unmarked car blocks them from behind. Frank smiles sardonically.

Frank turns to John and says quietly,
"Say nothing".
Three armed mopol officers, led by Sergeant Bello, alight from

both unmarked cars. They move to surround the SUV, pointing their guns precariously.

Frank rolls down his window and grins widely as he asks Sergeant Bello,

"Is there a problem officer?"

An impassive Sergeant Bello says matter of fact,

"Mr. Frank Audu get out of the car, you are under arrest!"

Frank, still smiling, says quietly,

"Barrister Frank Audu".

Sergeant Bello, unmoved, says dryly,

"Barrister Frank Audu you are under arrest sir"

Frank retorts,

"What is the charge?"

Sergeant Bello, irritated, says,

"My friend get out of the car now!"

Frank frowns slightly,

"Do you have an arrest warrant? Who ordered it?"

Sergeant Bello yanks Frank's door open and bellows angrily,

"Get out now or you'll have yourself to blame!"

Frank glances at John, then at Mr. Jonah. He turns to Sergeant Bello, smiles ruefully and says,

"Ok".

He steps out of the SUV.

One of the mopol officers steps forward to handcuff him,

"Hands behind your back!"

Frank turns to Sergeant Bello pleadingly,

"Is this necessary?"

Sergeant Bello looks at him angrily. Then stops the other mopol officer with a wave of his hand,

"No handcuffs. Take him to the car"

John alights from the car and asks loudly,

"Where're you taking him?"

Sergeant Bello retorts over his shoulder,

"None of your business!"

Frank calls out loudly,

"John, call my lawyer…"

John returns inside the SUV. He dials a number on the car phone. As it rings he maneuvers the car to follow Sergeant Bello and his men.

A voice answers the phone,

"Hello?"

"Nancy?"

"Yes?"

"This's John"

"Hey John, what's up?"

"Listen, they just arrested Frank?"

"What? Who? When?"

"Em… I'm not sure. Some mopol men just took him… and I'm following them right now"

"Where're they taking him?"

"They didn't say"

"What's the charge?"

"They didn't say either"

"Ok. Stay with them. Follow them wherever they go. And keep me posted"

"Ok"

Apparently Barrister Nancy Audu, Frank's lovely wife, is Frank's lawyer of record.

*

Frank is taken to the notorious federal prison in Lagos. A place known as Kirikiri prison. A nightmarish institution without doubt. Many people are thrown in there and completely forgotten. Nobody goes in there and comes back the same. Many lives are lost there too. It is a complete albatross.

Nancy, the dutiful wife and lawyer, goes to work on behalf of her husband and client. She leaves no stone unturned. But she is no match for the now very powerful and unbendable Police Inspector General Usman Danladi, who is hell bent on bringing the likes of Frank Audu to justice.

IGP Usman Danladi, with the utmost support of the Commander in Chief of the Nigerian Armed forces, makes it his personal mission to prosecute every criminal element in Nigeria. He invites Mr. Hans Ludwig back into the country and proceeds to build a water tight case against Frank Audu.

Although IGP Usman Danladi is a ruthless advocate for law and justice, he is also known and reputed for his fairness. He is a very fair man who would not be moved to action without palpable evidence. He recognizes that Hans Ludwig has been hoodwinked and duped, covertly or otherwise, but proving it is another matter.

There is really no evidence except for all the money that left Ludwig's account. Money which cannot be traced directly to Frank Audu in any way. A trace of the money is ice cold. The money has completely disappeared without trace. Some Nigerians can be exceptional money launderers.

Also the initial email, and then fax, Hans Ludwig received; which only serves to incriminate Ludwig in a grand scheme to defraud the government and people of the Federal Republic of Nigeria is another useless piece of evidence. It cannot be tracked to Frank Audu either. The email address and fax number are both bogus and a dead end.

Attempting to buy federal government property clandestinely is a crime. He should have reported the matter to the appropriate authority immediately, rather than agreeing to participate in the fraudulent business. Mr. Hans Ludwig is certainly not a saint, and not without blame in this matter, the IGP reckons.

Frank Audu claims his involvement is only as an attorney and adviser to Hans Ludwig. He received only a retainer from Ludwig, which is the only money traceable to him.

Frank Audu also claims that he advised Hans Ludwig not to go ahead with the so-called investment which seemed like a scam to him in the first place, but that Hans Ludwig was blinded by the perceived profit he thought he would gain despite all his warnings to him as his attorney. And he completely denies being the orchestrator of the supposed business transaction.

He also vehemently denies any knowledge of the other so-called participants. He only served as Hans Ludwig's attorney. He prepared letters and other documents as instructed by Mr. Hans Ludwig himself.

He also denies ever meeting with anyone else, or anywhere else, except with only Mr. Hans Ludwig within the confines of his law office in Surulere, Lagos. And that he never attended any meetings at the NNPC Headquarters or at any bank for that matter. He therefore challenges Mr. Hans Ludwig to show proof otherwise.

He accuses Mr. Hans Ludwig of only crying foul and looking for a scapegoat. He brands his claims a figment of his imagination. A total fabrication. He challenges Hans Ludwig to provide any evidence of his so-called involvement in the purported scam.

Hans Ludwig on the other hand is completely stunned by Frank Audu's defense. But the IGP asks Hans Ludwig to provide the names and identities of the so-called other participants. Something he cannot do.

There is no trace of them whatsoever. He doesn't even know them. The case against Frank Audu is therefore precarious at best. Almost improbable and unconvincing, the IGP reckons.

The IGP is a man of honor and is not in the habit of embarrassing himself by allowing anyone make a fool of him. Although he sympathizes with Hans Ludwig's loss, there isn't a way to actually prosecute Frank Audu successfully.

There is no proof. But he still keeps him detained at Kirikiri Prison hoping to find some evidence, or perhaps to eventually break Frank Audu into confessing his real involvement in the matter.

John, on a visit to see Frank in detention, is instructed to carry on with business as usual. Frank tells him to be careful and to keep things tight and organized. John acquiesces.

He becomes the interim boss. He keeps every one and every thing running like clockwork behind the scenes. So even while Frank Audu is locked up, his wealth and empire continues to grow, albeit mostly criminally.

Days become weeks, weeks turn into months, and Frank Audu continues to languish behind bars in Kirikiri Prison. Nancy continues to try everything within her power, and beyond, to get him out to no avail. She reaches out to all the traditional rulers and communities across the country that Frank has helped in the past.

She writes and petitions all the newspapers, television channels and radio stations across the nation. Strategic editorials and op-eds started asking questions about the detained Frank Audu.

All the people he helped across the country started to ask questions, and demand his release. They accuse the government of being in cohort with a foreign national in the abuse, disenfranchisement and denial of the rights of a Nigerian citizen.

People from all sections and sectors across the country, people that have been touched by Frank Audu's philanthropy and generosity, started to grumble. They started asking questions.

"Where is Frank Audu?"

"Try him or Release Him!"

"Justice for Frank Audu!"

IGP Usman Danladi being unable to build a watertight case against Frank Audu, once more, advises Hans Ludwig to return home to Germany until another opportune time. Hans Ludwig agrees because the IGP has proven himself to be a man of his word thus far. Hans returns home to Germany.

But the IGP still holds on to Frank Audu in Kirikiri prison, refusing to let him go, in spite of all the pleas and cries of all his supporters across the country.

*

Meanwhile, the new Nigerian military government has become a nightmare for the people of Nigeria. Having hijacked power from a democratically elected government, under the guise of delivering the people from the stranglehold of corruption; have themselves become cancerous, corrupt, and woeful just like their predecessors.

First of, all the previous political office holders have been in detention for many months without any trial. They are locked away behind bars in several prisons across the country, where they are subjected to inconceivable inhuman treatment.

The military administrators have become just as corrupt and wasteful as the politicians they kicked out of office. This is coupled with the fact that they have guns and absolute control of the people who are threatened with bodily harm and possible death if they fail to cooperate.

Several draconian decrees are enacted to stifle the people, especially the very despicable 'Decree 5' whose main purpose is to gag the press.

The press is no longer allowed to print or report any manner of story that is conceived to be critical of the military government in any shape or form, without dire consequences and retribution.

Therefore, the press, and the entire masses, become completely emasculated and stifled for fear of being victimized by the wayward soldiers that have been let loose on the people.

A particularly noteworthy victim of the military government's extreme highhandedness is a very popular musician and a rather strong critic of the government, both past and present – the one and only King of Afrobeat, the Abami Eda, Fela Anikulapo Kuti himself.

Fela is thrown into prison for supposedly laundering money.

He is arrested, charged, and imprisoned because they supposedly found a large sum of foreign currency on his person at the airport.

Mind you, he was traveling with his music band of well over thirty members. Frankly, as they say, he was muzzled for all his criticisms of the people in power through his music that is listened to all around the world, even to this day.

Fela Anikulapo Kuti goes on to say in one of his songs that the judge who tried and sentenced him to prison had in fact begged him for forgiveness afterwards. He claims the judge told him his hands were tied. That he was ordered to persecute him.

A story that only serves to further the veracity of the narrative that Fela was indeed muzzled, if only for a brief period of time. A very surreal tragicomedy, without doubt.

Ironically, and unfortunately too, many predictions Fela made about Nigeria; the corruption, wastefulness of resources, suffering and smiling of the people, authority stealing, etc. have all come to pass.

Fela is considered a prophet of sorts till this day because everything he said and made songs about have all come to pass. And are still happening today.

If you have not, you MUST make an effort to listen to Fela Anikulapo Kuti's songs. They are just as relevant today as they were yesterday. And even the day before. The man saw everything coming ever before the world noticed.

The military government also institutes several 'structural adjustment programs' that only make life worse for the common man, which is just like falling from the proverbial frying pan into the fire. They instruct the people to tighten their belts while they live large and grow fat on the nation's resources.

They tell the people to be prudent and extra cautious of their spending while they loot the treasury for their own gain. It is really just a change in attire, from civilian clothes to military uniform; the situation in the country is just as it was with the politicians, if not worse. Just really tragic!

The Head of State, and Commander in Chief of the Armed Forces of Nigeria, General Maman Baduru, tells the whole world at a United Nations conference that the problem with Nigeria is indiscipline. He claims Nigerians lack discipline and that is why the country is the way it is. And that he has the cure for that.

On his return to Nigeria, General Maman Baduru constitutes the infamous 'War Against Indiscipline' campaign. A real farcical fallacy. What a joke!

According to the Head of State, Nigerians must henceforth be extra orderly and cue at gas stations, bus stops, banks, etc. And they must also clean their homes, gutters, streets, etc. If found wanting, they are flogged mercilessly with the popular Nigerian horsewhip known as *koboko*.

They are beaten brutally and viciously by the mostly drunken soldiers and mopols who are usually high on *igbo*, weed, marijuana. The citizens are treated like animals and common criminals. This is General Maman Baduru's 'big plan', his 'grand plan', and supposed 'cure' to rid the country of indiscipline.

In his semi-illiterate mind, he figures cleaning gutters, streets, etc. and forming lines everywhere would somehow miraculously improve the life and the dire economic condition of the people. But it certainly doesn't do that. The people are still wallowing in poverty and squalor in a country that is one of the largest oil producers of the world.

The people are still starving. Many don't have the energy to clean gutters and streets because they are too hungry to do so. There are still no jobs. No food. No roads. No hospitals. Nothing. The economy is in the 'toilet', getting flushed down!

In contrast, military officers are living like kings and princes across the country. They are having parties and orgies everywhere, just like the charlatans before them.

The people start to grumble, albeit under their breath. The world notices the plight of the people. The draconian decrees et al. And the continued detention of the political class without any charges brought against them is too much for the civilized world to accept quietly.

People everywhere start to demand a change in tactics by the draconian dictator. It is too much for the citizens to bear.

*

At this time the global illegal drugs epidemic is sweeping across the world. And some brazen Nigerians refuse to be left out of the highly lucrative dastardly drug trade.

Many jobless young people are enlisted into the business as couriers and traffickers of the dangerous narcotics. The response of the Head of State, General Maman Baduru, is to promulgate another decree that stipulates death by hanging or firing squad for any person caught with narcotics. But that does not stop the menace.

The people are hungry and desperate. A hungry and desperate man is capable of anything. So the extremely dangerous but lucrative narcotics business thrives, regardless of the consequences.

Some people are caught and executed. But some still do it anyway, too hungry to be scared.

Then rumors about some supposedly top military officers' involvement in the narcotics business come to light. There are hushed whispers everywhere. It is reported that several top military officers are the brains behind the nefarious drug cartel in Nigeria.

It is rumored that military planes, trucks, and personnel, are used to facilitate the illegal business. Now this is a big blight on the image of the supposedly 'squeaky clean and very disciplined' Head of State, General Maman Baduru and his Supreme Military Council; the self appointed messiahs.

Disturbed by the unending rumors, and supposed campaign of calumny against his person and administration, General Maman Baduru addresses the nation. He promises to conduct a very thorough investigation of the rumors. And that if in fact military officers are involved in drug trafficking he would spare none of them. He would make sure they are dealt with like the criminals they are.

Days become more weeks. Weeks turn into many more months, and there is still no change in the status quo. The military brass continue to live large, while the people continue to wallow in poverty. Crime rate is at the highest level it has ever been. Millions of jobless folks turn to crime to make ends meet.

Many of the detained politicians are now very sick and almost dying. The Head of State and his cronies refuse to release them, claiming they are responsible for Nigeria's woes and economic predicament. They forget that they have been in charge for many months already and the economy has shown no improvement but only worsened under their watch. They have shown they lack any real solutions to the nation's myriad problems.

Frank Audu who shares a cell block with some of his former political juggernauts, including the erstwhile governor of Lagos State,

His Excellency Bode Adefarasi; has resorted to fate. He understands that the military is nothing but disaster for the country. They have taken the country back to the stone age with no constitution or rule of law.

The men in uniform have promulgated draconian decrees to serve their selfish interests. The judiciary and the press have been locked in a metal box. And the legislature has been discarded completely.

His wife, Nancy Audu, has tried every legal maneuver to spring him from prison but nothing has worked. No judge has the cojones, the balls, to act for fear of reprisal from the IGP and his military dictator. Although there is absolutely no legal reason why he should be held in prison, he understands that the IGP, Usman Danladi, is using extrajudicial power to continue to hold him, only to make a point. A needless point at that.

He continues to wallow in prison even though he never stole anything from the government. Heck, he has never even held a political office!

The IGP and his goons have tried every trick in the book to try to make him confess his involvement to no avail. They have threatened and tortured him ruthlessly, all illegally. Thank God he is not one to be frightened easily.

Matter of fact, everything they've tried reminds him of those days at the University of Ibadan when he was trying to get into the *Pyrates Confraternity*. After passing through the almost murderous drilling and torture from those faceless *Pyrates* in the middle of the night inside the very thick, dark, and dreadful forests; nothing else can ever possibly make him say or do what he chooses not to say or do.

As he reflects on that period of his life, a smile breaks across his face. He mutters to himself smugly,

"No fren, no foe. It could've been worse. I weep blood for you".

*

A few weeks later, the Head of State, General Maman Baduru addresses the nation again. This time very somberly. He says the rumors about the involvement of military officers in the extremely terrible and unconscionable narcotics trade in Nigeria is unfortunately true.

He goes further to say that his investigation has uncovered the involvement of very top high ranking officers in drug trafficking. And that he is a man of his word. He plans to bring them to book pronto, no matter whose ox is gored. He says several key changes are being made in the administration that will be announced shortly.

Many Nigerians are shocked to hear that. Others already knew of the involvement of top military officers in the narcotics trade. Yet still more are very surprised that the Head of State would publicly admit the rumors. They really thought he would sweep it under the carpet, as is typical in Nigeria.

The shocked masses look at General Maman Baduru differently. Perhaps this man is not as bad as we think? Maybe we should give him some more time to try to fix our country?

After all, if he can go against his own top military officers then surely he must mean well for the nation, they reckon. Let us support this General, he might just very well be the messiah we crave, they say.

But the military did not quite share that sentiment with the rest of the nation. Several secret meetings are held behind the Head of State. The military brass have been completely thrown off by the Head of State's address and acknowledgment of the military's complicity in drug trafficking. He apparently didn't run it by the Supreme Military Council, except with his very few trusted loyalists.

A few days later, Nigerians every where across the country wake up to another round of the diabolical staccato martial music blaring on their radios and television sets. There has been yet another coup, just like that.

What now? The people wonder.

15 THE OTHER GENERALS

"The man dies in him who keeps silent in the face of tyranny" — *Wole Soyinka*

Nigerians, both young and old, are rudely awaken once again to the uncertainty of yet another unsolicited change of government. This is a palace coup they say. A bloodless change of power.

A group of senior military officers who are unsatisfied by the actions, or inactions; as the case may be, of General Maman Baduru decide to send him off to an early retirement in a farm somewhere up North.

He is stripped of the office of Head of State unceremoniously, and immediately. Without fuss. Without any fighting. Not even a single bullet is fired.

It is like taking a piece of candy from a little baby in a crib. Just like they did to the last democratically elected government. Shameful. Embarrassing.

Nigeria is the laughing stock of the civilized world. It is becoming a place where folks with guns can just decide to take over power. Just like that. Tragic!

With lightning speed the new coup plotters make several changes. The new Head of State is going to be General Issa Babagarri.

General Issa Babagarri was General Maman Baduru's own Chief of Army Staff. He is a man who has always been somewhat involved in every coup plot that has ever taken place in Nigeria. Go figure!

The announcer of the previous coup, the fearful dark goggle wearing Brigadier Sanu Aboki, is also a key player of this new coup. He is immediately promoted to a General as well.

Several key changes are made throughout the country. But the immediate change that appeals to the citizenry the most is the release of all the previously detained politicians.

General Issa Babagarri turns out to be a genius of sorts. He knows how to work the people. He relaxes some of the overbearing decrees promulgated by the previous administration. An administration he was also a part of.

He appoints some civilians into very important positions. He assures the people that he is going to stay in power only briefly. That his goal is to conduct a free and fair election for a transitional process to return power to a democratically elected government.

Then the rumors started making the rounds that General Maman Baduru had been overthrown by his own inner caucus because of his attempt to prosecute some of them for drug trafficking.

It is widely reported that he had a list of top military officers to be axed and prosecuted on his desk before he was kicked out. The people say he dragged his feet. He took too long to act. That the criminals got together and planned the coup.

The rumor also indicts the likes of General Issa Babagarri, the current Head of State. It is rumored that General Babagarri is in fact the brain and mastermind behind the drug trafficking, and of course the coup to overthrow General Maman Baduru.

That General Issa Babagarri never had any interest in being Head of State. That he always liked to be in the shadows. In the background. But he had to step up this time when General Baduru came too close to kicking him off the army and perhaps also prosecuting him for drug trafficking.

The rumors are deafeningly loud. The press are writing all manner of innuendos. The question on everyone's lips is: can this really be true? Are we currently being ruled by a criminal minded dictator?

Then a big story breaks. Apparently, a domestic staff member of General Issa Babagarri's household is caught with narcotics at the airport. A rather large quantity they say. She is arrested and detained in prison, awaiting trial.

But somehow it is reported that she had mysteriously died in custody. Tragic, right? But a very respectable journalist runs into the supposedly dead woman in London, live and well. He interviews the woman, and is getting ready to publish the story. He tells the people of Nigeria that he has a mind blowing story coming up.

Alas, a few days later, the journalist is killed by a parcel bomb that is hand delivered to his office. For the very first time in the history of Nigeria, someone, a very popular and important journalist is murdered via a parcel bomb.

The country is completely aghast. And until this day, the question, who killed Dede Liwa, still remains unanswered.

All the same, life goes on under the new administration. Life seem a little easier without the constant fear of getting beaten mercilessly hanging over you every day. The new administration seem to have reined in the errant soldiers and mopols somewhat.

*

Nancy Audu learns that General Issa Babagarri's wife, Mariam Babagarri, is from the Niger-Delta Region; just like Frank. Matter of fact, they are from the same town. A little known fact until now.

Nancy finds a way to reach Mariam Babagarri through various contacts. She explains the situation to her. Mariam Babagarri is both shocked and angered to learn about how much time they have locked Frank up in prison without trial.

She immediately speaks to her husband, General Issa Babagarri, the Head of State of Nigeria, about the untoward maltreatment of her townsman – Frank Audu, by the unrelenting IGP, Usman Danladi.

The Head of State who does not joke with his very lovely and beautiful wife at all, invites the IGP to see him immediately. He orders the immediate release of Frank Audu, despite protests from the IGP. And shortly after that, the IGP is relieved of his office. He is sent abroad on a diplomatic mission, thereby ending his corruption fighting days.

Frank Audu is once again a free man, all thanks to his very tenacious and delectable wife Nancy; with help from the first lady of Nigeria – Mariam Babagarri, who is herself very well aware of all the good Frank Audu has done, and still does, for her people in the Niger-Delta Region.

Frank breaths a sigh of relief after a really horrendous sojourn in prison. Now spotting a beard, he looks much older and wiser than his age. He refuses to shave throughout his incarceration. But his mind is still as keen and sharp as ever.

He tries to resume living his life, as it were. He meets with John, and his other lieutenants to get a grip of the state of affairs of his business empire. Things are not great. And things are not bad either. The team has been threading very carefully and keeping things simple without raising eyebrows. They have maintained a low profile the last few months, just as Frank had instructed them to do. The machine is oiled and still profitable regardless.

Frank is invited to dinner with the first lady, Mariam Babagarri. He attends with Nancy. He expresses his immense gratitude for her help with springing him from prison. The Head of State is supposed to be attending some sort of economic conference in Geneva, Switzerland.

They sit down at the dining table, eating and making small talk when the Head of State, General Issa Babagarri, suddenly saunters in; unexpected. Frank and Nancy both jump up from their seats, very surprised to see him.

Mariam Babagarri grins cheerily to see her husband. She isn't expecting him really. He is supposed to be in Switzerland.

The General goes around the table to hug and kiss his wife lovingly.

She grins at him,

"What happened? I thought you were in Geneva"

He grins widely, and says,

"I was missing you and decided to come home early".

Frank and Nancy exchange uncomfortable glances.

The General turns to the couple who are still standing uncomfortably and bellows,

"Please sit down. Pardon my intrusion"

He moves around the desk to shake hands with the couple. First with Nancy, and then with Frank. All the time smiling very graciously.

He says to Frank, as he shakes his hand,

"I'm glad to see you're ok after the trauma of prison"

Frank manages to mutter,

"Thank you very much sir. I'm very grateful for your intervention"

The General waves it off. He holds his shoulder tenderly, and points to his chair,

"Please sit down".

He moves to the end of the table. He sits down and looks up at Mariam who is still smiling.

He asks playfully,

"Is there enough food for me darling? I'm famished"

Mariam chuckles as she stands up and moves to fix him a plate.

The General turns to Nancy and Frank, and says playfully,

"I hope you don't mind? I'm really hungry"

Frank and Nancy both chuckle, relaxing. They realize the General is really just a man after all, in spite of all the terrible stories they might have heard about him.

Mariam fixes her husband a plate.

He starts to gobble it up hungrily, while joking about his wife and how they met, etc.

He asks Frank how he met Nancy.

Frank says matter of fact,

"She is the first girl I met in Ibadan on my very first day in UI"

The General exclaims wide eyed,

"Really?"

Frank grins,

"Oh yes!"

The General grins,

"College sweethearts. That sounds interesting. Please tell me about it"

Mariam exclaims playfully,

"Issa!"

The General retorts playfully,

"What? Who doesn't like a good love story?"

They all laugh.

Frank tells the story. The General listens with very rapt interest, Mariam too; even as Nancy blushes shyly.

From this chance meeting with the Head of State of the Federal Republic of Nigeria, General Issa Babagarri, Frank Audu's life changes completely.

General Issa Babagarri takes immediate liking to Frank Audu. He invites him to come see him in his office. Frank does. And this goes on quite frequently.

Frank works his way into General Issa Babagarri's inner caucus very quickly. He becomes a very close associate, confidant, adviser, and also a business partner. Previously unthinkable and unimaginable doors are suddenly open to him. His power in Nigeria is quadrupled immediately. He is now known as General Issa Babagarri's boy. Frank calls him 'Uncle Issa', or General, or just 'Uncle'.

This power is transferred to Frank Audu's 419 empire, his kingdom of fraudsters. Anyone connected with Frank Audu becomes automatically untouchable, feared, and revered.

Frank is more powerful than state governors, even the new IGP, and many top military officers. Several top officers who want favors from the Head of State have to go through Frank Audu to be heard. You want something done? You have to see Frank Audu.

General Issa Babagarri, a very busy Head of State of a nation is readily accessible to Frank Audu any day of the week. Frank can call him any time of the day and he will answer immediately. Frank runs private and personal errands for the General. He's trusted completely and wholeheartedly.

Frank has dinners with the General anytime he wants. The General's wife, the First Lady of the country, is just like Frank Audu's big sister now. That is technically accurate. They both hail from the same town in the Niger-Delta Region.

The First Lady is now always seen in public with Nancy Audu, Frank's wife. Nancy works with her on several philanthropic and community development programs for the indigent. They're very close friends, and just like blood sisters. Go figure!

Finally bowing to pressure from his parents, Frank decides to start a family with his wife Nancy. She gets pregnant to everyone's pleasant relief.

They become parents when the time is right, without any complications. She gives birth to a very cute, bouncing, healthy, baby boy. They name the child Frank Audu, Jr.; which is very appropriate because he looks just like Frank.

Frank is over the moon with joy. He takes being a dad very seriously. And Nancy is just the kind of mom any child could ever wish to have. A very doting and dutiful mother.

*

With time, Frank Audu becomes the 'bag man', unofficial accountant and foreign investor, for General Issa Babagarri and several other top military officers.

He travels around the world at their behest to open several bank accounts for them. Millions of dollars are funneled into the accounts. All money stolen from the people of Nigeria. And Frank Audu helps them buy prime properties and real estate in the most exclusive communities around the globe with all the looted funds.

You can therefore see how important Frank Audu is to the General and his coconspirators. He is, matter of fact, indispensable and of utmost value; hence the power he wields. He knows their darkest secrets.

He has access to their wealth that is stowed away abroad. And he of course also profits immensely from this ignoble operation. He is making a killing doing this. Much more than he can ever make from scamming people. Thus, he sticks to it religiously.

Frank Audu is the conduit, the facilitator, fixer if you want. He makes it happen on their behalf with no questions asked. He does as he is told. He is past caring. After all, he was imprisoned for almost two years without course, he reckons. This is time to be paid back, he figures.

General Issa Babagarri and his gang of thieves all siphon the wealth of the country into their foreign private accounts while the people of Nigeria continue to wallow in squalor. It is the same vicious cycle, unending.

The global price of oil is good. Nigeria's oil – the Bonny light – is highly coveted and in great demand. Money is flowing in. Enough money to make Nigeria a real world power. A very developed country. But instead, the criminals in power – according to Fela Anikulapo Kuti, '*the Vagabonds in Power*' – steal everything from the common man.

General Issa Babagarri starts borrowing money from the international community. He signs Nigeria up for an IMF – International Monetary Fund – loan. Ironic isn't it? He sells the oil to the international community, they pay him, he shares the money with his gang. They put the money in their own private accounts abroad, and then ask for a loan from the same banks. Except that the loans are obtained in Nigeria's name.

So basically, the people of Nigeria; whose oil is sold in the first place, with no accountability, or benefit to them whatsoever, have to bear the brunt of eventually paying back a loan they never enjoy or gain from.

That is double jeopardy right there. And according to Fela Anikulapo Kuti, *'double wahala for dead body'*, which loosely translates as 'double trouble for a person who is already dead'. Really tragic!

Meanwhile, the international community, including the United Nations, et al; are all aware of this ongoing madness. This malady. But they all turn a blind eye. Switzerland especially, which is the haven, and hiding place, for all the money stolen by all the corrupt African leaders, both past and present.

The people of Nigeria grumble about the hardships, and question why things are not working. The press write all manner of stories, having been given more freedom of expression by General Issa Babagarri himself, ironically.

Students across the country and the Nigerian Labor Congress decide to demonstrate and protest the hardships in the country. Some are arrested and locked up. Some universities are shut down indefinitely. It is total chaos across the country once again.

General Issa Babagarri, President and Commander in Chief of the Nigerian Armed Forces, also appoints himself as the Minister of Defense. Yes, he does.

And his friend and loyalist, the former Brigadier Sanu Aboki, now Lt. General Sanu Aboki, is upgraded to Chief of Army Staff and Chairman, Joint Chiefs of Staff. He is basically the alpha dog of the combined armed forces of Nigeria. Not a small title by any measure.

One day, Nigerians hear that some senior military officers, including a very well liked and respected General, are under arrest for a coup attempt. In a matter of days, they are tried, sentenced to death, and summarily executed.

The world is in shock by this development. Several pleas for sparing the lives of the accused coup plotters is unheeded. And there are reports that the coup plotting charge is only a ruse to silence some officers who opposed General Issa Babagarri's dictatorship.

Now there is talk of General Issa Babagarri's desire, and attempt, to enroll Nigeria into OIC – the Organization for Islamic Countries.

A real travesty when you consider the fact that Nigeria has an almost equal population of Christians versus Muslims.

The southerners, who are predominantly Christians, are not enthused by this development whatsoever. They take to the streets to protest. And as always, they are subdued, arrested, and detained. Some die in the process.

Shortly afterwards, the rather cunning General Issa Babagarri, who understands how to manipulate the people of Nigeria, suddenly lifts the ban on politics. He literally throws the proverbial carrot to the people by allowing the formation of political parties. But the caveat was a ban of certain individuals who are prohibited from participating in the new political dispensation. Another travesty!

The General assures the people that his intentions are honorable. That he plans to follow through with the planned transition program to democratically elect a new government. That the people should consider him a coordinator and facilitator of sorts. That he has no reason to remain as Head of State beyond the set timetable.

To show his goodwill, the General, and the Armed Forces Ruling Council, go on to create a few new states. According to him, 'to better manage the country and its diverse communities'.

The easily cajoled political class go into a frenzy at full speed. They jump into the fray. They start to form alliances and parties with lightning speed. As always, they lie and attempt to undo each other.

The likes of Frank Audu; and the 'son of the soil', Chief Badamasi, who has been almost nonexistent up until now, suddenly reappears. They all jump right into the thick of things.

Chief Badamasi approaches Frank to feel his pulse about the new development, considering his relationship and status as 'General Issa Babagarri's Boy'. Frank assures the Chief that the General is going to go through with the plan to handover government to a democratically elected administration.

Frank Audu, as usual, refuses to run for office personally. This time he is going to install Mr. Jonah, his surrogate father, as the Governor of the newly created Delta State. A state that is very rich in oil and other natural resources. And he also plans to make his wife, Nancy, run for the Senate.

Very serious, respectable and astute aristocrats, businessmen, and career politicians all throw their hats into the political arena.

They all want to win the proposed forthcoming election. It is time to take back the country and set it on the right path, they reckon.

But a particular military officer who becomes privy to the General's real agenda discovers that he might not be sincere about relinquishing power at all.

The General had commissioned this particular army officer, a certain Lt. Colonel, to secretly work on a version of diarchy based on Egypt's Abdel Nasser's.

The Lt. Colonel discovers that the General is in fact goading and deceiving the populace with his promise of a transition program while he is secretly working on propagating himself on the Nigerian people forever. A real travesty, he reckons.

At this time, Frank and Nancy have their second child. A sweet beautiful daughter, named Amanda, who is a spitting image of Nancy. The couple couldn't be happier with their growing family.

Frank's parents, Philip and Stella, have both since moved into his mansion where they take extremely good care of their grandchildren with immense pride.

*

Then one early morning, the citizens of Nigeria wake up to that ever dastardly familiar staccato martial music. And the annoyingly idiotic 'fellow Nigerians' speech that follows.

There has been another coup overnight. A very feisty and fast talking army Major is on the airwaves talking very forcefully, almost pleading for the support of the citizens of Nigeria.

"I, Major Godwin Obar of the Nigerian army, hereby inform you of the change in government with immediate effect…"

This is a coup by mostly junior officers. The highest ranking participant is a Lt. Colonel. The others are Majors, Captains, Lieutenants, and below. This not a joke. Junior officers can be very bold, brave, dangerous, and blood thirsty.

Major Godwin Obar on the radio is already talking about excising and expelling five core northern states from the Federal Republic of Nigeria. He is blaming all the problems of the country on the predominantly senior military officers who are of northern descent.

As the people listen to all the orders, threats, and promises over the radio, they can still hear gun shots going off in the distance. Especially those who live near military installations. They realize that this is not a palace coup by any means. This is a very brutal and bloody coup happening.

Frank Audu can't believe what he is hearing over the radio in his living room. He starts dialing phone numbers frantically. He is surrounded by Nancy - his wife, his father - Philip, his mother - Stella, John, and Mr. Jonah. He starts pacing the floor with concern as the others look at him quietly.

Apparently the coup plotters attempted to overthrow the government by attacking the Head of State's official residence, the State House, inside Dodan Barracks in Obalende, Lagos. Their plan is to execute General Issa Babagarri and all the other senior military officers across the country. A very vicious and violent plan.

The coup plotters almost succeed. The Head of State narrowly escapes. His aide de camp is killed in a fierce gun battle. Several guards are killed. The Head of State is smuggled out to safety through a secret underground tunnel that leads to the National Arts Theater Complex several miles away in Iganmu, Lagos.

The fearsome Lt. General Sanu Aboki, the Chief of Army Staff and Chairman, Joint Chiefs of Staff; who is at the Flag Staff House in Ikoyi, makes concerted effort to ascertain the state of affairs in Dodan Barracks, and around all the key military installations in Lagos and across the country.

He is able to communicate with the Head of State directly to confirm he is alive and safe. He then mobilizes a counter attack with other units of the Nigerian army. Apparently the coup plotters failed, or perhaps forgot, to cut off communication.

The coup failed the very moment Lt. General Sanu Aboki is able to establish communication with the Head of State and other military commanders across the country.

Lt. General Sanu Aboki successfully crushes the coup attempt within hours. The seemingly very bloody coup attempt is over just like that. C'est fini!

Shortly afterwards, he addresses the nation about the day's events. He announces the end of hostilities and the capture of some of the coup plotters.

General Issa Babagarri also addresses the panicked citizens. He claims he is unharmed and well. He thanks all the loyal troops who fought off the insurrection. He assures the public of their safety, and asks them to carry on with their normal lives as usual.

Several military officers are subsequently arrested, court martialled and eventually executed. A few escape from the country successfully. Some others are also dishonorably discharged from the military.

It is reported that the most senior participant in the coup attempt is a certain Lt. Colonel; ironically, the same Lt. Colonel who worked on General Issa Babagarri's secret plan to install himself as lifetime president by using Egypt's Abdel Nasser's system.

The same theory Major Godwin Obar hammered on in his speech over the radio on the morning of the coup attempt. And this got the people thinking that the coup plotters may not have been crazy after all. That they probably knew what they were talking about.

Luckily for the Lt. Colonel, he is able to escape from the country unharmed. He is reported to be enjoying his freedom somewhere in Europe till this day.

Although General Issa Babagarri claims he is safe, sound, and completely unperturbed by the coup attempt; he makes certain there isn't going to be a repeat of the very close shave with death.

He knows very well that he came very close to death the last time. After all, his aide de camp and personal guard was killed in the imbroglio, and that's very close.

Several scholars also claim the Major Godwin Obar coup is the most brutal and violent so far in the history of Nigeria. And there have been quite a large number of coups, counter coups, and coup attempts in Nigeria over the years.

General Issa Babagarri subsequently moves the seat of government from Lagos to Abuja, a much more central location. An almost impenetrable fortress known as Aso Rock becomes the new Federal Capital Territory of Nigeria, the official headquarters of the Federal Government.

Frank Audu maintains his relationship with General Issa Babagarri. He immediately buys a nice house in Abuja, not too far from Aso Rock, on account of advice from General Issa Babagarri himself. He stays very close to the seat of power and the occupant of the seat as a matter of fact.

Although many questions about the sincerity of the General to hand over power to a civilian administration remain unanswered, the politicians and political aspirants continue to swarm like fleas and flies.

They pander on with their political genuflecting, having received assurances from the '*Maradonic*' General that the transition is still on, regardless of recent events.

So the politicians continue to hobnob and campaign fervently in preparation for the promised forthcoming election. A date is set for a national election. Several strong contenders extol their virtues. They toot their own horn as they make the most ridiculous promises to the people, as always.

But among the pack of wolves is a very well known philanthropist. A very educated man. A chartered accountant. A man who is known to care about the poor masses. A man who feeds the poor, who gives scholarships to indigent students, etc. A man known as Chief N. K. A. Abiodun. Chief Abiodun for short.

The people naturally stand behind this man wholeheartedly with the thinking that if he can do what he does for the people without any political office, then he can be trusted to actually deliver the people from economic quagmire when given the mantle of leadership.

From no where, Chief Abiodun's campaign explodes to life. He becomes the automatic frontrunner. He becomes the candidate to beat. Every man, woman, child, young, and old jumped behind him. Students, workers, et al. His victory in the forthcoming election is a foregone conclusion, they reckon. The signs are as clear as the sun on a bright, hot, summer day!

Even Frank Audu convinces his long time friend and collaborator, Chief Badamasi, to join forces with Chief Abiodun's campaign. Frank believes in Chief Abiodun like most of the country. Chief Badamasi reluctantly agrees.

Every where you turn, there is a poster of the ever smiling Chief Abiodun waving at you. Whether schools, offices, banks, hospitals, on buses, inside buses, on the side of the street, literally everywhere. The man is loved immensely, especially by all the poor downtrodden masses. He is their messiah, they reckon.

This a man who is a multimillionaire, a very successful businessman, who has never held any political office any day of his life. He is running for president so he can serve the people who have been repressed for so long, he claims. He wants to fix the problems of the people, he says.

He is completely believed and absolutely trusted by the masses. They flock and swarm around him like flies on honey. They sing his name everywhere. They make elaborate campaign materials, including clothing items, with his pictures. This is our time. The messiah is come, they say.

His message to the people is very simple,

"Hope. Farewell to poverty. How to make Nigeria a better place for all!"

General Issa Babagarri and his Armed Forces Ruling Council look on quietly. Not saying anything. Not disturbing the political process, as it were.

Over the last few months Frank Audu has deployed his personal resources to discretely campaign for, and support, Chief N. K. A. Abiodun's endeavor.

The day of reckoning finally comes. It is election day. Several foreign observers from far and near are present to observe the proceedings. The process has been so far civil and respectable up until this moment. And everyone is impressed by the civilized manner folks are going about electing a new government in Nigeria.

The citizens are up bright and early. They all troop out en masse to cast their vote for Chief Abiodun. There is no permutation anywhere on earth that does not predict a landslide victory for Chief Abiodun. All the polling experts around the world all agree that a victory for Chief Abiodun is a foregone conclusion. They all say it is not a question of whether he will win the election, but a matter of by what margin.

After all said and done. After all the votes are cast. The people return to wait in their homes with a very strong conviction that victory is most certainly assured for Chief N. K. A. Abiodun. The exit polls also point towards a very huge victory for the people's candidate.

Even the foreign observers who are present throughout the process are already reporting that this is one of the freest and fairest elections they have ever seen any where in the world. And that they are especially proud of Nigerians for being able to pull off such an open and credible election.

The masses, being unable to contain their excitement for being able to actually vote in a candidate of their choice, start the celebration early.

The people break out the bottles, all kinds of bottles, to celebrate. Local bars are packed full with very excited and exuberant patrons all waiting for the result of the elections.

There is singing and dancing on almost every street across the country by both young and old, in anticipation of the much anticipated victory of Chief Abiodun.

Minutes turn into hours, very many hours. Still no result. Some people are already slumped over bottles inside bars. The people wait. The singing and dancing starts to wind down. The people look at each other with uncertainty. The question on everyone's lips is: what's going on?

The following day, the people start to walk around like zombies lost in their own thoughts. A silent haze is over the entire nation. Nobody knows what to think. There's still no result. And no word from the electoral commission – FEDECO – the Federal Electoral Commission.

As the by now very weary citizens worry about what is happening, General Issa Babagarri comes on air to address the nation.

According to the General,

"The election is inclusive. And it's therefore annulled".

The people ask angrily,

"What?"

"Annulled?"

"Why?"

Unable to accept such travesty, they take to the streets to protest massively. Male, female, young, old, everybody took to the streets. The people have finally had enough, perhaps?

College students across the nation and the Labor Congress start another massive protest. It is wild. They start to burn anything in sight. Tires, cars, etc. There is massive rioting all across the country.

Lt.. General Sanu Aboki, the Chief of Army Staff and Chairman, Joint Chiefs of Staff, orders the military and police to quell the riots wherever they occur.

The soldiers and mopol who are mostly high on weed start to clash with the protesters everywhere. They lynched the people. The people fight back with bricks, stones, anything they can find. And Molotov cocktails are thrown at military vehicles to start fires.

As usual, several citizens are either killed, or maimed, or arrested, or all of the above. The people refuse to back down. Many are ready to lay down their life. They all demand that the election result be announced.

Frank Audu is devastated. He has been conned by a master conman, he reckons. Never in a million years would he think that General Issa Babagarri would lie to him without flinching. He asked him several times if this is for real. He said yes every time. How could he have been so stupid, he asks himself sadly.

The entire world reach out to change the General's decision. They try to prevail on him to conclude the election. General Issa Babagarri refuses to acquiesce. Instead, he unleashes the army and mopol on the citizens of Nigeria. He insists that the election has been annulled.

Chief Abiodun on the other hand refuses to accept the annulment. He tells General Babagarri that he must be declared the winner of the election or else he would do it himself and form his own government.

The people agree with Chief Abiodun, and they egg him on to do so.

They say to him,

"Declare yourself the winner"

"Form your government, we will follow you"

"You are our president"

"We want you to lead us"

"You're our only hope!"

Frank Audu tries to speak with the General. He calls him on his private direct line.

The General chides him gently, as a father would a son,

"Frank trust me, you don't want to get involved in politics. It's a dirty game"

Frank retorts,

"General you told me this is for real"

The General says,

"Yes Frank. I said so"

Baffled, Frank queries,

"So what happened? Why have you annulled the election?"

The General retorts,

"My boy, you won't understand"

Frank confused, says incredulously,

"General the people are very angry. I don't think you should've done that"

The General replies impatiently,

"Don't worry about the people Frank. They'll be fine"

Frank not believing his ears, asks,

"How?"

The General chuckles,

"Never mind that Frank. Come to the house. You and Nancy. Mariam misses you. I've to go now. Come to the house. Bring the kids too"

The General hangs up the phone abruptly. Frank is stunned out of his mind.

Chief Abiodun and the citizens of Nigeria refuse to back down. They will not accept the very criminal and unnecessary annulment of the freest and fairest election in the history of Nigeria whatsoever. The riots continue nationwide.

Chief Abiodun holds rallies across the nation with the support of the citizens. He has the full backing of the masses. They want him to be their president, either by crook or by hook.

The very eloquent Chief Abiodun makes several memorable speeches. Exciting and inspiring monologues that drive the people nuts.

Statements like,

"You can not shave my head in my absence"

"You can not throw away a child with the bath water"

"I must receive the mandate bestowed on me by the good people of Nigeria. All the suffering citizens!"

"The military must return to the barracks where they belong"

"Enough is enough!"

Seemingly very inciting statements that propel the masses into mass riots nationwide. The very enraged people take to the streets violently. Putting their lives in harm's way without any care.

He directly threatens General Issa Babagarri and his Armed Forces Ruling Council. He is charged with treason, and declared wanted by the General.

Chief Abiodun goes into hiding. He only suddenly pops up at very charged rallies unannounced. And as General Babagarri's security forces show up to arrest him, the very angered and militant masses prevent his arrest in very grave danger of their own lives.

Chief Abiodun, who is a man with very vast resources at his disposal, continues to threaten the General and his administration. He vows to fight the military government with his whole being to the end.

He threatens to bring in a private army to fight the General. He will not accept the ridiculous annulment for absolutely no reason. That is for cowards.

"I'm not a coward!", he says.

According to him,

"I will rather die before I accept the criminal annulment!"

"Over my dead body!"

"The military administration is a criminal enterprise. They can't get away with this terrible crime against the people of Nigeria", he declares.

"They must conclude the election immediately, or else I'll make this country completely ungovernable for them!", he threatens.

"These illiterate soldiers can't be allowed to continue to insult our intelligence. Enough is enough!", he says.

"Give us our mandate. No more, no less!", he bellows.

General Issa Babagarri and his Armed Forces Ruling Council quickly realize that the very vexed Chief N. K. A. Abiodun is not going anywhere anytime soon.

They have completely underestimated the very educated and highly intelligent man with almost limitless resources. A man who is backed by millions of angered Nigerians willing to lay down their lives for him.

The die is cast. The military government declares a state of emergency nationwide. They order everyone to stay away from the streets.

This is really just a ploy to make it easier to arrest the rather elusive Chief N. K. A. Abiodun. The people can see through their ruse. They refuse to obey.

They continue their relatively violent protests. Several lives are lost daily. Businesses are crippled and paralyzed. Several tertiary institutions are shut down for participating in the riots. The labor unions and their leaders are now pariahs. There is very palpable uncertainty in the air.

*

The Armed Forces Ruling Council are forced to convene an emergency meeting. Tempers are frayed. There is finger pointing. The senior officers must decide the way forward for the nation.

Afterwards, General Issa Babagarri addresses the country somberly.

"I've decided to step aside", he says.

"A new interim national council has been created", he continues.

"The interim government will be in charge until it's feasible to conduct another election", he adds.

"The interim administration is to be headed by Chief Edward Shonibare", he concludes.

Although Chief Edward Shonibare is a renowned lawyer, and a civilian, the people are still very furious about this development. This is yet another coup, albeit a palace coup it is still a coup, they reckon.

This is not what they want. They want a logical conclusion of the recently held election. They are not interested in a transitional administration. The country has been transitioning since independence. It has been an endless transition since 1960.

They protest loudly,

"No to the General"

"No to the military"

"The military belong in barracks!"

"No to any illegal interim administration"

"No to a civilian stooge of the military"

"No to endless transition!"

The citizens across all sections, across all sectors, both young and old, are done with the continued military incursion into politics in Nigeria.

Frank Audu, who is completely taken unawares by the sudden turn of events, drives straight to General Issa Babagarri's private residence.

Unable to contain himself, he starts to berate the General disrespectfully,

"Uncle Issa what have you done? How could you?"

The General checks him promptly,

"Watch yourself son. Remember whom you're speaking with"

Frank, suddenly realizing what a treacherous man he is dealing with, soft pedals.

He asks almost tearfully,

"What happens to Chief Abiodun now?"

The General grins cunningly, and mutters,

"I don't know Frank. I really don't"

Frank, bewildered, asks,

"What about his mandate?"

The General frowns and whispers through his gapped teeth,

"Fate"

Frank blurts out angrily,

"What the heck does that even mean?"

The General glares at him angrily.

Frank, cowed, slumps into a couch, deflated.

The General softens up,

"I understand how you feel"

Frank looks at him queerly and asks,

"You do?"

The General grins wickedly,

"Yes of course. You're upset. All the people are upset. And frankly, I'm upset too. But child, there're things that are larger than all of us. Things beyond our control"

He continues with his devilish 'maradonic' logic,

"What will be will be Frank. If it's Abiodun's fate to be president, he will be president some day. No one can prevent it"

As Frank listens to him he cannot be sure if he is listening to Lucifer himself. Or the renowned Niccolo Machiavelli, a man who the General adores greatly, and sometimes pretends to be.

The General continues to mete out his own brand of the 'Machiavellian maradonic' philosophy,

"Some times we must make very tough decisions for the greater good"

Frank finally finding his voice, says meekly,

"Whose good exactly?"

191

The General retorts,

"That remains to be seen my dear boy. Only time will tell"

Frank asks with concern,

"So the duty of the interim government is to carry out another election?"

The General grins effusively,

"Yes. That's correct"

Frank frowns,

"And you think Lt. General Sanu Aboki will let that happen?"

The General chuckles,

"Of course! That's the agreement"

Frank smiles sardonically, as he asks,

"The agreement. And you think it'll be honored?"

The General says matter of fact,

"I don't see why not Frank. We all agreed to it"

Frank grins,

"I see"

The General looks at him thoughtfully, and says,

"I trust Aboki with my life. He's a loyal friend"

Frank says seriously,

"Uncle, I've never heard of anyone who would give a ferocious lion a piece of meat for safe keeping. Sanu Aboki is a very ferocious lion"

The General frowns as he says thoughtfully,

"But he has shown he can be trusted in the past"

Frank retorts, enjoying himself,

"Trusted with protecting your life, yes. Absolutely! But with power? Really?"

The General is speechless.

To meet the terms of the supposed agreement, General Issa Babagarri summarily moves out of the official presidential residence, albeit reluctantly, to make way for the new occupant. He moves into his own palatial enclave. A place fit for only kings and queens.

Apparently, the General is forced to relinquish power by the Armed Forces Ruling Council. The soldiers, realizing that the people of Nigeria are not going to back down without an immediate solution to the very unexpected election annulment, under pressure, make General Issa Babagarri the scape goat.

But the supposed transitional Interim National Council which is created to replace the dastardly Armed Forces Ruling Council is DOA – Dead on Arrival. The people want nothing to do with it.

Chief N. K. A. Abiodun meets with the Interim President, Chief Edward Shonibare, to discuss a possibility of his revisiting the supposedly annulled election. An election that the entire world concludes is the freest and fairest election ever held in the history of Nigeria thus far.

But it turns out that Chief Shonibare, as suspected by the people of Nigeria, has no 'cojones' at all. He is nothing but a seat warmer with no authority whatsoever.

Making any meaningful decision isn't part of his job description in any way. Therefore, to expect him to be able to make a decision on the supposedly annulled election would be tantamount to wanting to squeeze water out of a piece of rock. Go figure!

Chief N. K. A. Abiodun go back and forth severally with Chief Edward Shonibare with no result whatsoever. It is a total waste of time, to say the least.

"My hands are tied", he says to Chief Abiodun.

"Untie your hands. Do the right thing", says Chief Abiodun.

"There's nothing I can do", says Chief Shonibare.

"So why're you here?", asks Chief Abiodun.

Chief Shonibare says unconvincingly,

"I'm here to serve the country"

Chief Abiodun asks rhetorically,

"To serve the country, or to serve the military?"

Chief Shonibare says sadly,

"I'm very sorry my brother. There's nothing I can do"

Chief Abiodun retorts angrily,

"I don't need your pity or sympathy. I just need you to do the right thing, brother"

Chief Shonibare shakes his head piteously as he whispers,

"I can't"

Chief Abiodun says condescendingly,

"What kind of man are you? I thought you were a lawyer? Does this seem fair to you? Where's the justice in this? Ehn brother?"

Chief Shonibare is silent.

Chief Abiodun glares at him angrily as he asks,

"How do you sleep at night my brother?"

Chief Shonibare is speechless as he looks at Chief Abiodun.

Ironically both Chief N. K. A. Abiodun and Chief Edward Shonibare hail from the same town. They are brothers of sorts.

O, the con of man!

*

Meanwhile the citizens of Nigeria continue to protest angrily. They are killed like animals on the streets. They are slaughtered by agents of the government led by the very inhuman and sadistic Chief of Army Staff, Lt. General Sanu Aboki.

But as soon as the interim regime takes office the people start to relax, believing that the interim President Shonibare might decide to do the 'needful' by concluding the botched election and declaring their candidate the winner.

After all, he is a learned man who should know to do the right thing for peace to reign in the country, they reckon. He is a lawyer by training, and most certainly understands fairness, equity, and justice, they figure.

The riots subside reasonably to give the interim government time. Time to get the justice they deserve. They stop all rioting in good faith, expecting a favorable resolution of the imbroglio.

Alas, that is not to be. Three months after General Issa Babagarri relinquishes power to the accursed transitional Interim National Council, which is led by the Interim President Chief Edward Shonibare, their goose is suddenly cooked.

The power hungry Lt. General Sanu Aboki only tolerates Chief Edward Shonibare and his Interim Administration for just ninety days before he gives them the boot.

Lt. General Sanu Aboki takes over power overnight with no fuss whatsoever in a classic case of the proverbial 'palace coup'. Not a single bullet is fired. No long thing. He constitutes the

Provisional Ruling Council that gives him complete and full dictatorial powers.

Chief Shonibare is suddenly relegated to the dustbin of history just like that, after only three months in office. Lt. General Sanu Aboki declares himself the Head of State and Commander in Chief of the Armed Forces of the Federal Republic of Nigeria.

Lt. General Sanu Aboki turns back the clock, literally. He reverts Nigeria to the stone age. There will be no transition. No election. No nothing. All politicians are once again banned. It is back to military rule in its purest form. To paraphrase the King of Afrobeat, Fela Anikulapo Kuti, "soldier go, soldier come".

The citizens of Nigeria once again take to the streets to protest violently. They are hounded like animals, arrested, detained, and killed like nothing.

The civilized world cry out loudly in disgust for the extreme barbarism and savagery. They are shocked by the barbarousness of the treatment of a people by their own rulers.

The ferociousness of the methods being employed by the accursed and repressive regime of the sadistic Lt. General Sanu Aboki, to annihilate his own people of Nigeria, is widely condemned worldwide.

Frank Audu calls General Issa Babagarri, who is now retired, on the telephone.

He asks tearfully,

"General, is this what you agreed on with your people? A total annihilation of our people?"

The retired General says very sadly,

"This is not the plan. I never agreed for this to happen"

Frank retorts angrily,

"It's happening General. People are dying like flies on the streets. Our own people sir! Are you going to just sit back with arms folded and do nothing?"

The General bites his lip and says painfully,

"What can I do Frank? I'm retired. They made me retire. I'm cut off completely. I've no say anymore"

Frank retorts,

"That's not good enough sir"

The General says sadly,

"What can I do with no power?"

Frank replies,

"Talk to your people. Talk to Aboki. He has lost his mind"

The General says somberly,

"You think I've not tried? He won't listen to me. He says this's his time. That my time is past. He has stopped taking my calls"

Frank pleads,

"Surely there must be something you can do. Don't you all say 'once a general, always a general'? Are you not a general? Don't you have your people in the army? Your loyalists?"

The General says with finality,

"You want me dead? Frank, I'm just a civilian now. Aboki made sure of that. He outsmarted me"

Frank says boldly,

"Sir, with all due respect, you're responsible for this madness. I love you like a father, but I must tell you the truth. You're responsible for this. And I hope you recognize that"

Frank hangs up angrily.

The retired General says weakly,

"Frank? Hello? Hello?"

The line is dead.

He mutters to himself,

"Da Allah. What have I done?"

He weeps quietly.

*

The very violent protests continue nationwide. The extra judicial killings by faceless agents of Lt. General Sanu Aboki, now full General Sanu Aboki, continues unabated, all in the name of quelling the supposed riots.

Nigeria becomes a full-fledged police state. It is under a total draconian dictatorship reminiscent of the diabolical stone age. Dusk to dawn curfew is imposed.

The people disregard it completely. They are past caring for their own lives and safety. They have had enough they say.

Finally recognizing that there was no way in the world the despotic dictator, General Sanu Aboki, would ever declare him the winner of the annulled election; Chief Abiodun, bowing to pressure both from within and beyond, decides to do it himself.

He declares himself the winner of the supposedly annulled election in a powerful speech he gives at a massive rally around the Epetedo area in Lagos.

He appoints himself the President and Commander in Chief of the Armed Forces of Nigeria in an administration he labels 'the Government of National Unity'.

He declares in his very fiery speech as follows,

"As of this moment, a new Government of National Unity is in power throughout every nook and cranny of this country. A new government led by me, Chief N. K. A. Abiodun as President and Commander in Chief"

The people in attendance explode with euphoria.

He continues strongly,

"The national assembly is reconvened immediately. all dismissed governors are hereby reinstated. All state assemblies and local government councils are hereby reconstituted"

The masses all jubilate wildly with excitement.

Frank Audu, his friend – John, and his surrogate father - Mr. Jonah are amongst the crowd; nodding their heads and clapping their hands in open energetic support of the declaration.

Chief Abiodun continues very forcefully,

"I hereby call on the usurping interloper, General Sanu Aboki, to tender his resignation effective immediately!"

The crowd cheer rapturously.

There is no stopping him now. The cat is out of the bag.

He bellows loudly,

"We will no longer have any devious soldiers masquerading as politicians in uniform. If they leave now and hand over quietly, they will be retired with all their entitlement intact"

The people applaud.

He continues boisterously,

"As of today, my Government of National Unity is the only legitimate, constituted authority in the Federal Republic of Nigeria"

The crowd is agog with joy.

He explodes with finality,

"Let us say goodbye to the 'minority rule' by the military forever. Enough is enough. Long live the Government of National Unity. Long live Nigeria!"

Frank Audu and his entourage are clapping effusively with teary eyes. There is very palpable excitement about the future of the country in the air.

Then about 200 police and military vehicles suddenly appear as if out of thin air, packed with countless officers who are armed to the teeth and ready to battle.

The crowd is livid with rage, but too powerless against such massive show of force. Hundreds scamper off in different directions. It is like a war zone.

Chief Abiodun is arrested and detained, by agents of General Sanu Aboki, for a charge of treason against the state.

Frank Audu who observes it all happen, immediately gets on the phone with retired General Issa Babagarri.

Frank, almost crying, mutters,

"They just took him, right in front of us"

The General retorts almost angrily,

"What did you expect? He has been making serious threats against the administration"

Frank says pleadingly,

"The man did nothing wrong. He has the people's mandate. You must help him General"

The General retorts,

"I already told you Frank. There's nothing I can do. I'm powerless"

Frank pursues the obviously fruitless cause,

"Speak to your friend. Your 'loyal friend'. Talk some sense into him. He must not harm Chief Abiodun"

The General says abruptly,

"Frank, do you know what you're dabbling in? Do you?"

Frank retorts,

"I'm asking you to right a wrong sir. Do the right thing General"

The General cuts him off,

"Stop it Frank. Stay away from Aboki and his administration. The man is very unpredictable. You don't want to be in his way, believe me"

Frank tries to speak,

"But he…"

The General cuts him off again,

"Forget it Frank. Come see me in Abuja. Bring the family with you. I want to see you. It's important"

He hangs up the phone.

Frank looks at the dead phone, and shakes his head sadly. He looks around at the almost deserted venue that held so much promise for the people of Nigeria only a few minutes ago.

He starts to walk towards John and Mr. Jonah who are standing in a corner together.

He takes faltering steps in their direction, dazedly, and browbeaten.

*

Chief N. K. A. Abiodun, the People's President, the hope for the masses, is taken to a federal prison in shackles and locked behind bars.

The masses of Nigeria, emboldened and fired up by anger, take to the streets yet again. They break out in violent riots across the country.

More universities are shut down. Labor unions who orchestrate the demonstrations are proscribed. The leaders are arrested and thrown in jail.

There is mayhem across the country. This goes on for weeks. The international community start to demand the release of the imprisoned Chief Abiodun. Citing human rights abuse, et al.

Religious leaders, traditional rulers, and elder statesmen across the nation all plead with General Sanu Aboki to no avail.

Frank Audu is livid with rage. He knows the state of affairs inside a Nigerian prison. He was a recent occupant of one. It is not a place for human beings, he reckons. He reaches out to General Issa Babagarri once again.

General Issa Babagarri makes it abundantly clear that he will not get involved in anything relating to General Sanu Aboki, or his administration.

Desperate, and in a bid to help the confined Chief Abiodun, Frank Audu reaches out to General Sanu Aboki himself. This is despite his immense dread for the man.

General Sanu Aboki agrees to meet with Frank.

Frank arrives at Aso Rock and proceeds to a meeting with General Sanu Aboki in his humongous office.

The General is sitting in a huge regal leather chair behind the equally gigantic mahogany desk majestically. His eyes, as always, are hidden behind a pair of very dark glasses.

Frank walks inside the office with trepidation, very unsure of himself. He clears his throat uncomfortably as he stops in front of the massive desk.

He mumbles,

"Good morning General"

General Aboki waves him to a chair without a word. His eyes staring at him through the very black glasses.

Frank feels him glaring at him through the spectacles that seem to never leave his face.

Frank wonders to himself,

"Does he sleep with this bloody thing on?"

He sits on the edge of a chair across from the General's desk in very palpable discomfort.

The General clasps his hands in front of his stomach impatiently. His bespectacled eyes not leaving Frank's face.

Frank breaks out in sweat.

The General glances at his wristwatch impatiently.

Frank clears his throat, finds his voice, and says,

"Em... General... I've come to plead with you"

The General is silent and very impassive.

Frank suddenly remembers a conversation he had with General Issa Babagarri some time ago.

General Issa Babagarri was saying,

"...people are afraid of Aboki for good reason. He doesn't speak. He acts. He listens. Then acts. He hates talking. He doesn't laugh either. I've known him for decades, and I've only seen him smile probably once or twice... twice I think. At his wedding. And when his first son was born"

Frank Audu shudders. Sweat breaks out across his forehead.

General Sanu Aboki glances at his watch again.

Frank wonders again, asking himself,

"Are you afraid of this man? He's only a man Frank! Get a grip"

He clears his throat again,

"Em... General sir. Please release Chief Abiodun from prison. I was in prison myself. It's a very horrible place to be in. Chief Abiodun can't survive in there. He doesn't have to die like that"

General Sanu Aboki just looks at him from behind his dark glasses. There is no change in his expression. Nothing. He just stares on.

Frank is tempted to ask,

"Did you hear what I just said?"

But instead he says,

"Sir, it won't look good on your person if something were to happen to him in prison. We all know you mean well for the country. You're a man of honor"

There is utter silence for a couple of minutes. A couple of minutes that seem like an eternity to Frank.

Frank is saying to himself,

"What the heck am I doing here? Why did I ever think I could reason with this man? This man is not human. He has no feeling. He doesn't feel anything whatsoever. I should've listened to Uncle Issa. What do I do now?"

Just then the General says quietly, in that somber, listless, and lifeless manner of his,

"Frank I agreed to see you because of our history. You and Issa Babagarri. You're Babagarri's boy. And he's like a brother to me. But I must tell you only this one time. Don't get involved in politics. Leave the politicking to the politicians"

Franks looks at him speechless momentarily.

Then he finds his voice,

"Your excellency, I'm not a politician. That's true. I've really never been interested in politics. But I just feel..."

The General cuts him off,

"So are you his lawyer then?"

Frank stutters slightly,

"No... I'm not his lawyer sir"

The General retorts matter of fact,

"The man committed a crime. He has been arrested. He will be tried like every other criminal who breaks the law. We must follow the law Frank. The police are currently investigating the matter. Like I said, don't concern yourself with this, unless you're his lawyer. Do you understand?"

Frank gets the hint,

"I understand sir"

The General spreads his hands,

"Is there anything else?"

Frank stands up, deflated,

"No sir. That'll be all"

The General grunts,

"Very well then. Thank you for coming"

Frank replies,

"Thank you for seeing me"

He turns and starts to walk towards the door.

General Sanu Aboki calls out,

"Frank"

Frank stops and turns to him.

The General says,

"I appreciate what you did for me. Running those errands for me and the others"

Frank nods and turns to leave.

And just then, Major Halim Maitama, General Sanu Aboki's aide-de-camp; walks through the door. He nods at Frank who is on his way out.

Major Maitama stops in front of the General's desk.

The General glances up at him.

Frank closes the door behind.

The General says quite frankly,

"Keep eyes on that boy, Frank. I don't trust him. I never liked him. I just tolerated him because of Babagarri"

Major Maitama says,

"Yes General"

Days turn into weeks. Weeks become several months.

Chief N. K. A. Abiodun is still in prison, deteriorating physically and mentally every passing day he is incarcerated.

The masses continue to protest across the country. The press demand his immediate release.

Several newspapers and magazines are shut down. Journalists and editors are thrown in prison. Anyone who complains, or criticize the government in any way, is summarily dealt with.

Several intellects are either killed brutally, or thrown into prison where they are left to rot behind bars. An example is the massacre of certain respected individuals in Ogoni, in the Niger-Delta region, for their protests over the maltreatment of their people. They are brutally executed for daring to ask for better conditions of living in their community.

Thousands of university undergraduates, and their unpaid lecturers, roam the streets with nothing else to do.

Businesses become caricatures. The economy is at a standstill. Nothing is working. The people feel the full weight of the accursed military government led by General Sanu Aboki.

Thousands of lecturers, unable to continue to wait for a reopening of their closed institutions of learning, while unpaid, start to leave the country in droves. Heralding the diabolic 'brain drain' era.

Thousands of Nigeria's most educated minds started migrating from the country in search of the proverbial golden fleece, taking their knowledge and expertise with them.

Doctors, lawyers, engineers, and professors of repute all start to leave the shores of Nigeria. Weakening the intellectual community in the process.

Thousands of undergraduates, the supposed future of the nation, all start to leave the country too. They spread across different nations of the world. Taking their keen minds with them.

The abandoned students who can not leave the country naturally turn to crime. All kinds of crime. Drug trafficking, robbery, stealing, fraud; anything to survive the very dire times.

Frank Audu's empire gladly welcomes these very angry and deprived group of people. The 419 conglomerate officially becomes the go to occupation for almost all the college drop outs, and unemployed graduates.

419 becomes a global entity with many of the emigrated Nigerians becoming facilitators of the very criminal operations.

Millions of people around the world are duped and tricked out of their hard earned money every day.

According to the fraudsters, *'mugu fall, guy man wack'*. Meaning if you take the bait it is your loss. Or, if you fall for the scam you will be fleeced.

The 419 scam, Nigeria's notorious export, soon becomes a very common practice around the world. People of all nationalities are indoctrinated into the global epidemic.

It is no longer a Nigerian thing. It is now a worldwide method of acquiring wealth, albeit fraudulently.

*

It is four years since Chief N. K. A. Abiodun was arrested. And he has been languishing in prison since that time. The very worst four years of his life without any doubt.

The masses of Nigeria have been browbeaten into submission by the very brutal regime of General Sanu Aboki. They now only whisper about the mandate and the people's president under their breath.

Even Chief Abiodun himself has been completely emasculated by the events of the last four years. Frankly, he is very fortunate to still be alive. Perhaps he has come to terms with his loss? And finally accepting of the sad reality that he would never be president? Only time can tell.

And surely, as time is the arbiter of all things here on earth; the time comes, not in the future, but around the fourth year of Chief Abiodun's incarceration when fortune seem to finally smile on him.

General Sanu Aboki suddenly dies, of a heart attack supposedly, while romping with two foreign and exotic prostitutes in the presidential chamber.

Oh yes, the feared General Aboki is a man deeply enamored by the pleasures of a *'ménage a trois'* – a threesome! He died while having a threesome with two imported 'ladies of the night'. Apparently that is something he is very famous for. Threesomes, sordid trysts, et al.

Believe it or not, the people of Nigeria, both young and old, upon hearing the news of the sudden death of General Sanu Aboki all break out on the streets in wild jubilation.

The people are ecstatic beyond reason as they jubilate wildly on the streets of Nigeria, while waving freshly cut palm fronds.

Never in the history of the country has there been anything like it. People breaking out in massive joy at the news of the death of a man. That indeed speaks volumes. Who celebrates the death of a man?

The Provincial Ruling Council meet promptly and immediately appoint General Abdel Abibi, the Defense Chief of Staff, as the new Head of State and Commander-in-Chief of the Armed Forces of Nigeria.

The people, buoyed by the sudden death of the tyrant, the dictator, the accursed General Sanu Aboki, start to make fresh demand for the conclusion of the last election. And the installation of the winner, the People's President, Chief N. K. A. Abiodun.

But the new Head of State, General Abdel Abibi, and the Provincial Ruling Council, refuse to acquiesce. Stating instead that there would be another election. The people don't buy that whatsoever. And the die is once again cast!

The international community try to convince the new man in charge to do the right thing. He will not bulge. But he agrees to allow some international groups meet him and also meet with Chief N. K. A. Abiodun as well.

Chief Abiodun is moved to a much better facility where he receives fairer treatment, et al.

Shortly afterwards, a couple of American Diplomats meet with General Abdel Abibi. They discuss some very important matters; including the release of Chief Abiodun from incarceration, and perhaps a revisiting of the botched election.

The American Diplomats also subsequently meet with Chief Abiodun inside the Presidential Villa in Aso Rock.

Chief Abiodun is cleaned up and brought to this meeting to specifically meet with the American Diplomats who seem to have a genuine interest in finally resolving the ongoing political imbroglio in the country.

At the meeting, which is facilitated by the Head of State, General Abdel Abibi, Chief Abiodun expresses his desire for the new man to do the right thing. That there is no need for another election when there is an inconclusive one hovering over their heads.

Tea is served at this meeting. Some of the participants, including Chief Abiodun and the American Diplomats, all drink this tea.

Chief Abiodun is reported to have suddenly collapsed midway into this meeting. He is rushed to the State Hospital inside Aso Rock.

Alas, he dies shortly afterwards.

Nigerians everywhere, as would be expected, believe he is poisoned. Some even accuse America of complicity in his death.

They say,

"They poisoned him with the tea!"

"They've killed our president!"

One asked angrily,

"Why did he even drink the tea?"

And someone else said,

"Chief N. K. A. Abiodun is the best president Nigeria never had!"

Nigerians across the country and beyond, still mourn his very untimely and extremely suspicious death until today.

Every year, they mourn the loss of the 'Hope of Nigeria', the best president that never was. They wonder about what could have been if he was allowed to rule the country.

16 HUMAN TRAFFICKING

"The best intentions are not always a guarantee of success" - Delia Salvi

The brain drain era is in full swing now. Nigerians, young and old, male and female, having completely lost faith in the entity called Nigeria; decide to flee the country in massive numbers.

All the foreign embassies across the nation are all packed full every day with folks looking to escape the country.

The Nigerian youth, the labor force, the supposed future of the country is ebbing away faster than any one could have imagined.

All the criminal acts of all the previous administrations have turned many youths into criminals; or into immigrants in different foreign lands across the globe.

While many countries educate and empower their youth, Nigeria destroys hers by all the atrocious and criminal acts of the rulers. The 'monkey see, monkey do' syndrome in all its glory.

The wealth of the nation is stowed away in a few personal, and private, bank accounts across the world, while the masses wallow in squalor.

The most educated Nigerians spread to every nook and cranny of the world. Wherever you go, wherever you see black people, there is a very high probability that one out of every four of them is a Nigerian.

Nigeria is, after al, the most populous black nation in the world; with a population of well over 150,000,000 (one hundred and fifty million) people. Some say it is closer to 200,000,000 (two hundred million). It is one of the fastest growing populations worldwide.

The self exiled Nigerians become anything to survive in these distant and at times strange lands. Many work their butts off doing honest menial labor in spite of all their education and smarts.

Others, who have become criminalized, attempt all manner of criminal activity including the accursed 419, and the blooming credit card, or identity theft fraud.

Many are caught and imprisoned. Literally going from the frying pan into a fire. Still others try their luck in the diabolic drug trade. Some are locked away, others are executed in countries where drug trafficking carries the death penalty.

Erstwhile lecturers and professors can be found working as cab drivers, security guards, or day laborers around the world. These are folks who should be imparting knowledge to, and developing, the future of Nigeria – the youths – but are instead forced to scrounge for a few dollars to survive.

Doctors, nurses, pharmacists, engineers, the very backbone of Nigeria are also all spread around the world like white on rice. Even lawyers, writers and artists too.

While local Nigerian hospitals lack the requisite professional manpower, Nigerian medical professionals can be found in an alarming number performing exploits in different medical facilities around the world.

The very best minds of Nigeria have abandoned the country. Not by choice, but as a means for survival.

The foregoing travesty, which should alarm the government and the people of Nigeria, and be a serious cause for concern, is instead encouraged and applauded.

Some families sell their homes to procure a means for their children to leave the shores of Nigeria. Some families even go as far as to give their young daughters away to the renowned 'madams' – the pimps who traffic young women around the world for prostitution.

These young women are bought and sold like meat despicably. They are forced into prostitution in Europe and other places, where they are turned into sex slaves who work for only the 'madams'.

The madams grow fat and live large on the blood and sweat of these trafficked young girls. They enrich themselves with all the proceeds from this accursed business while the poor girls suffer and die in silence.

Too scared to go to the authorities or to do anything about their situation they continue to suffer untold hardships. After al, some of their families are complicit in the dastardly arrangement. All for money!

Some work for years without ever been able to break free from the shackles of this modern day slavery. They are made to have sex with the very worst vermin of society.

Some are castrated and made to never be able to have children. Some are arrested and thrown in jail regularly. Some become drug addicts. A real vicious cycle, no doubt.

They can not run away either. The madams have their passports locked away in strong boxes. They must pay off the cost of bringing them to Europe with interest, says the madams. Something that they probably can't pay off even in 20 years!

Some are made to swear blood oaths in dingy shrines before they are trafficked. They must not break this oath of silence otherwise there would be dire consequences to them and to their family members left in Nigeria, says the madam.

A few stubborn ones break away from the so called madams and their fake oaths, and fake promises. And of course nothing happens to them.

Some report the abuse to the appropriate authority. And they get some form of help. Or they are deported back to Nigeria.

Some go on to live as normal as they can. Some find love, get married, and perhaps have children of their own. A few become advocates for trafficked women, in a bid to help others.

Yet others, completely cowed and scared shitless, do nothing at all. They live and die as prostitutes strung on all kinds of dangerous mind altering drugs.

They continue to pay these accursed madams until they die a horrible death from drug overdose, or by the hands of a 'john'. A 'lose lose' situation.

A very select few, against all odds, work very hard for a few years as prostitutes and some how miraculously pay off their madams and go off on their own. Some becoming madams themselves.

*

Osarentin Iyobosa was trafficked as a precocious 13 year old girl from the ancient city of Benin in the Niger-Delta region of Nigeria.

Osarentin, Osas for short, is an exceptionally beautiful and vivacious young girl who is way more intelligent than her peers, and overly mature for her age.

She is a young girl that could've gone on to be anything she wanted to be. Perhaps a scientist, or a doctor, or an engineer, or a lawyer, or an educator, or even a model; anything at all.

But alas, she is trafficked into the underbelly of the very repugnant international prostitution network. She becomes the property of Madam Eki Obasuyi, one of the pioneers of the illicit trade in Benin City.

She is amongst the very first batch of girls trafficked from Benin City in Edo State, Nigeria, to Italy. Done by a process they refer to as the 'Italo Connection' in the local Benin parlance.

Madam Eki Obasuyi on a visit to her hometown, is driving in the luxury of the back seat of her mint Mercedes Benz S-class, through the streets of Benin City, when she spots Osas walking on the side of the road carrying a bag of groceries.

The almost 6 feet tall young girl is nearly a head taller than everyone else in the vicinity. She walks very gracefully with her long elegant legs like a model on a runway.

She glides effortlessly like a gazelle. And her smooth cocoa butter skin is gleaming luxuriantly in the bright sunlight.

She can certainly pass for a high class model anywhere in the world. Whether in fashion, print or on a TV screen. She has all the attributes.

Madam Eki suddenly exclaims to her driver,

"Stop the car!"

The driver, Idemudia, stops the car abruptly.

He turns to her, confused.

He asks,

"Is everything alright madam?"

She turns in her seat to look at Osas who is walking away, oblivious of the attention.

She asks curiously,

"Who's that tall girl?"

Idemudia turns to look at Osas walking away.

She queries,

"Do you know her?"

He grins widely,

"Oh yes. That's Eghare's daughter, Osarentin. Everyone knows her. She runs very fast. She's a very good athlete. Nobody can defeat her"

Madam Eki turns to him,

"Go get her for me"

He frowns,

"Really?"

She retorts,

"Yes. Get her now!"

Confused, he asks,

"Now?"

She replies,

"Yes. Right now. I want to speak with her"

He parks the car, opens the door, and runs after Osas.

A moment later he returns with the young confused kid.

Madam Eki smiles at her very nicely.

Osas greets her respectfully,

"Good afternoon ma"

"Good afternoon my dear"

Osas glances at Idemudia who is standing beside her.

She looks at Madam Eki again, unsure of what is going on.

Madam Eki says patronizingly,

"You're Eghare's daughter Osarentin, right?"

Osas answers impassively,

"Yes ma"

Madam Eki smiles,

"I hear you're a very good athlete. Undefeated, right?"

Osas forces a smile,

"I like to run ma"

Idemudia laughs.

Madam Eki grins, and asks,

"How old are you now Osas?"

Osas answers matter of fact,

"13"

Madam Eki, not believing her ears, exclaims,

"Say what?"

Osas says shyly,

"I'm 13 years ma"
Idemudia shrugs nonchalantly.
Madam Eki continues incredulously,
"You can't be serious!"
Osas retorts,
"I turned 13 last month ma"
Madam Eki exclaims,
"Incredible!"
Idemudia says quietly,
"She's right. She's the same age as my nephew Osaze"
Madam Eki says, as she looks at Osas all over like a piece of
meat on display,
"You look very mature for your age. And you're so tall"
Osas smiles shyly.
Madam Eki asks,
"Where're you going?"
Osas says,
"I'm going home ma"
Madam Eki asks,
"Where're you coming from?"
Osas answers shyly,
"I went to get some food stuff from the market"
Madam Eki exclaims again,
"Wow! All by yourself?"
Osas retorts smiling,
"I do it all the time. My brothers don't like to go to the market.
They just like to eat the food"
Idemudia and Madam Eki both laugh out loud.
Madam Eki says nicely,
"Hop in. We'll give you a ride home"
Osas frowns slightly as she asks,
"Are you sure?"
Madam Eki laughs, and says,
"Yes I'm sure. C'mon in"
Osas glances at Idemudia furtively.
He nods at her, grinning.
Madam Eki says,
"Come seat with me here in the back. I want to speak with you"
Idemudia moves to open the back passenger door for her.

Osas, who has never ever dreamt of riding in a car this beautiful any day of her life, reluctantly enters the car. She puts her grocery bag on her thighs, uncomfortably.

Idemudia returns behind the wheel. He turns the car around and heads towards Uselu Quarters, Benin City, where Osas lives.

Madam Eki looks at Osas and says,

"Put the bag on the floor. Relax. I won't bite you. I just want to talk"

Osas smiles shyly and says,

"Ok"

She puts down the bag gingerly. She glances around the extremely beautiful interior of the very luxurious German engineered car which is nicknamed 'the beast' in Nigeria.

She wonders to herself,

"This's no beast. It's heaven on wheels. Who named it the beast is mad!"

Madam Eki asks,

"Is your father at home?"

Osas says matter of fact,

"He was home when I left. I don't know if he's still there"

Madam Eki smiles at her sweetly.

Osas reeks of both candor and innocence. After all, she is only just a child really. A 13 year old child. But this does not deter the cunning and devious Madam Eki.

She asks bluntly,

"Have you ever thought of going abroad?"

Osas turns to her and says with the naivety of a child her age,

"Yes. I'll like to go abroad when I'm older so I can help my family. Things are very hard for my family. My father has not worked for almost 2 years now. There's no work. He only farms on the small land he has"

Idemudia glances at her through the rearview mirror. He wipes a teardrop from the side of his eye.

Madam Eki continues,

"What about your mother?"

Osas says matter of fact,

"She sells some of the yams and cassava from my father's farm. And she plants some vegetables too"

Osas looks out throw the window of the moving vehicle, as she says tearfully,

"I really wish I was older so I can help my parents. I feel sorry for them"

Idemudia who is listening very intently, wipes away more tears from his eyes.

They drive in silence for a moment.

Then Madam Eki says quietly,

"Osas"

Osas turns to her,

"Ma?"

Madam Eki says matter of fact,

"What if I tell you that you don't have to be older before you can help your family?"

Osas frowns slightly, confused.

She says,

"I don't understand ma"

Madam Eki smiles ruefully,

"I can take you to Italy if you want"

"Italy?", asks Osas.

"Yes. You know where that is?", asks Madam Eki.

"It is in Europe. We studied it in geography", answers Osas.

Madam Eki smiles, impressed.

Osas glances at her. Then at Idemudia behind the wheel. Then at her again.

She asks innocently,

"When?"

Madam Eki says seriously,

"Within a month"

Osas retorts,

"But my parents don't have the money for that"

Madam Eki grins,

"Don't worry about that"

Osas frowns,

"No? Is it free?"

Madam Eki retorts,

"No it's not free. I'll pay for everything now. But you'll pay me back when you start working"

Osas thinks about it for a moment.

Then she asks,

"What kind of work will I be doing?"

Madam Eki says,

"There're different kinds of work in Italy. Babysitting, house help, etc. With your looks you can even be a model. You're very beautiful. You can be a model in Italy"

Osas says quietly,

"What if I can't pay you back? Won't it take long to pay you back? I'm sure it's very expensive to go abroad. I hear it costs a lot of money. Even more than the cost of a house"

Madam Eki says, placating,

"I can do it for you. So you can help your family. I'll take care of you Osas. Trust me"

Osas looks at Madam Eki with her big, beautiful, and bright innocent eyes without a word. Not sure what to say.

Madam Eki meets with Osas's father, Eghare Iyobosa. A man who has been through thick and thin. To hell and back too perhaps. A man pulverized by lack, penury and poverty just like his fellow country men and women.

Madam Eki dives straight to the point,

"Your daughter is an asset. She'll make you very rich!"

Eghare Iyobosa mulls the idea thoughtfully.

He turns to his wife Adesuwa, who is very quiet in a chair in a corner. As is customary in these parts when important decisions must be mad.

The man stands up and starts to pace around the floor of the very meager and dingy living room, deep in thought.

Adesuwa looks up at him impassively from the corner of her eyes. She cuts a very stoic image in her chair. She is a woman who has also been made to walk through fire and brimstone by life.

He stops and turns to Madam Eki who is looking at him quietly.

"What about school?"

Madam Eki grins and says,

"Of course she'll go to school"

Eghare moves to sit down near Madam Eki on the threadbare couch in the middle of the room.

He says pleadingly,

"Osas is only just a child. She needs to finish school at least"

Madam Eki retorts,

"Of course she'll go to school there. What do you take me for?"

He looks over at his wife Adesuwa.

She is silent and impassive as can be.

He says to himself,

"This's going to be my decision, sadly"

He stands up and paces around again briefly.

He turns to Madam Eki and says,

"Why don't you take Iyare instead?"

Madam Eki frowns,

"Who's that?"

Eghare mutters,

"My oldest daughter. She's ideal for something like this. And she's 21 already"

Madam Eki asks,

"Where's she?"

Eghare stutters,

"Em... em..."

He turns to his wife Adesuwa for help.

She looks away impassively.

He continues embarrassingly,

"Em... I'm not sure where she is right now. But I can find her. We can find her"

Madam Eki is surprised.

She mutters disapprovingly,

"You don't know where she is?"

He shakes his head sadly.

Madam Eki says matter of fact,

"Well, I don't know Iyare. You don't even know where she is. But I've spoken with Osas and she seems interested in doing it. So the decision is yours. After all, you're her father"

She stands up, and grabs her handbag from the couch, ready to leave.

He says,

"Give me some time to think things over. And perhaps find Iyare"

She grunts unsatisfied,

"Ok. But I'm in Benin for only a week. I leave for Lagos next week. From there I go back to Italy"

She points a finger at him,

"So the ball is in your court Mr. Eghare Iyobosa. This's a chance to change your family's situation for better. Think about that"

She looks at Adesuwa in the corner who remains unflinching.

She addresses her directly,

"You don't have anything to say about this?"

Adesuwa looks at her and shakes her head, unwavering.

Madam Eki grins,

"Wouldn't you like to change your life for the better?"

Adesuwa speaks for the first time,

"Who wouldn't want better?"

Madam Eki smiles. Then asks,

"So what do you think?"

Adesuwa glances over at her husband who is still standing beside Madam Eki. She looks back at Madam Eki.

She says resignedly,

"It's his decision"

Madam Eki frowns,

"Oh yes. I forgot. This's Edo Kingdom. This's Nigeria. The man rules the household, right?"

Adesuwa looks at her quietly with no response.

Madam Eki continues,

"But remember she's your daughter too. And it's your life also. Think about that"

Adesuwa bites her lip painfully.

Eghare grinds his teeth in annoyance.

Madam Eki calls out loudly,

"Where's the girl? Osas!"

Osas appears from behind a curtain. She was eavesdropping all this time. She heard every word spoken.

She whispers,

"Ma?"

Madam Eki smiles at her sweetly.

She rummages through her hand bag and pulls out a business card. She turns to Eghare and hands him the card.

"Here's my card. Call me when you've made a decision"

He takes it and says respectfully,

"Ok. Thank you ma"

She turns to Osas. She goes in her handbag again and pulls out a wad of naira bills. She hands the stack of money to Osas as she says,

"Here, take this. Buy yourself something nice"

Eghare and Adesuwa are both mouth agape as they stare at the wad of bills. They have not seen that much cash in a very long time.

Osas hesitates briefly, glancing at her father.

Madam Eki urges her, smiling,

"Don't be scared. Take it my dear!"

Osas glances at her father again.

He nods at her.

She looks up at Madam Eki.

Madam Eki smiles at her,

"Don't be shy"

Osas takes the money, kneeling down on the floor she says,

"Thank you very much ma"

Madam Eki pulls her up from the floor immediately,

"C'mon stand up. Don't do that. I'm not God. I'm just another human being like you"

She pulls Osas off the floor and hugs her.

Osas wipes away tears from her eyes. She has never seen that much money any day of her short life either.

She turns to her parents and says,

"Alright then. Let me know what you deicide"

She turns and starts to walk out of the living room.

Eghare escorts her outside to meet Idemudia who is waiting behind the wheel of her car.

Eghare exchanges pleasantries with Idemudia.

And inside the living room, Osas hands the stack of money to her mother Adesuwa.

They both plop on the couch.

Osas says wide eyed,

"Iye (mother), how much is that?"

Adesuwa, grinning, says with excitement,

"I'm not sure my child. But it looks like a lot!"

Osas grins,

"You want to count it?"

She frowns,

"No my child. Let us wait for your father"

Osas says under her breath, almost fearfully,

"Do we have to wait for him to know how much it is?"

Adesuwa looks at her big beautiful eyes.

She looks away and says sadly,

"It's tradition. He's the head of this house"

Osas bites her lips and asks again,

"Iye me (my mother), you think I should go to Italy?"

Adesuwa looks into her eyes again and whispers,

"Your father will decide my child"

Osas hugs her mother very close.

"But what do you think? I want to know what you think mother"

Adesuwa hugs her 13 year old daughter very tightly and says sadly, with closed teary eyes,

"What I think doesn't matter my child. It's your father's decision to make. That's our culture"

*

After all is said and done, Osas and eleven other young girls are then shipped off to Asti, Turin, in Italy, with Madam Eki Obasuyi. The ages of all the young girls range from Osas who is 13, the youngest, to the oldest who is 21.

The first course of action by Madam Eki Obasuyi is to forge a passport for Osas that claims she is 17 years old. An act that makes her a very prime victim of the illicit sex trade. A real travesty.

The 'dozen girls' are made to swear a blood oath in a 'juju shrine' before they embark on the journey. The oath specifies all the bad luck they will encounter in their lives if they reneged on their agreement to pay back Madam Eki every last penny.

The bad luck will also, supposedly, extend to every member of the girls family, according to the 'witch doctor' – the shrine owner. Hardships, massive suffering, horrible, and sudden, unexplainable, death will be invoked on any girl who runs away without fulfilling the said agreement.

Any girl who does anything as treacherous as to report their arrangement to the authorities will be barren for the rest of her life. She and her entire family will be miserable their entire life. She will never have any children, and she will die a very painful and horrible death, says the 'witch doctor'.

This is some very serious 'juju', the girls reckon. They must obey all the terms of the agreement, they figure. They are scared out of their wits!

The dozen girls arrive in Turin, Italy. They are taken to Madam Eki's house in Asti, where six other girls already reside. This first group of girls between the ages of 18 to 25 arrived only a few months before.

Ejiro, the oldest of the bunch, is a very feisty girl from Sapele, Delta State, Nigeria; although born and raised in Benin City. She is the unofficial leader of the 'army of girls'.

The fresh meat, the new girls, are introduced to the veterans. Their hopes of finding jobs and starting to change their lives is quickly dashed to shreds as Ejiro tells them point blank,

"This's Italy. We're prostitutes here. Forget everything you were told before you agreed to come. *We be ashewo for here*! (we're prostitutes here)"

The dozen new girls protest vehemently. We are not prostitutes they say. We can't be prostitutes. We are here to work as baby sitters or store clerks.

Ejiro laughs at them sarcastically as she says,

"*Who no go, no know*", meaning 'if you don't come here, you won't know. Basically, it is what it is.

Madam Eki is a completely different person from the very nice 'angel like woman' they met only a couple of weeks before. She is transformed into a real life jezebel, a very despicable and heartless monster.

She tells the girls there are many bills to pay. The rent, food, utilities, etc. Her investment must also be paid back too. And that the fastest way to accomplish all that is to stand in street corners and sell themselves. They are going to be prostitutes, full stop. No ifs, ands, or buts. There are no other jobs available for anyone.

They cry, they gnash their teeth, and they protest vehemently. All to no avail. What is done is done says Madam Eki. They must do it or face severe consequences. After all they agreed to do as she says. And she reminds them of their 'oath'.

Back home in Nigeria the families of these girls celebrate wildly, in anticipation of the largesse that will start rolling in soon. Some of them start to borrow money from neighbors and friends, promising to pay back with very generous interests.

Meanwhile, Iyare – Osas's elder sister, has been found. She had run away from home many months before because her father tried to force her into a marriage with a fat pot-bellied 60 year old local chief. A man whom her father owed money to. A man who is already married with two wives and thirteen children.

Iyare refused to be sold to the lecherous old man whom she finds very reprehensible for many reasons. Who can blame her? Except her parents of course. She left home and roamed from place to place for weeks.

The night she hears about her baby sister's voyage to Italy she immediately bursts into tears.

She wails loudly,

"Why? Why? Oh why?"

Her father Eghare screams at her angrily,

"Shut up you good for nothing child! What do you mean why?"

Her mother Adesuwa looks on confused.

Iyare throws her self on the ground and writhes about on the floor as she continues to wail in anguish,

"Why? Oh God why?"

Eghare snatches her off the floor angrily.

He shakes her violently and yells in her face,

"Be quiet! You'll wake up the neighbors. What's the matter with you? Haven't you embarrassed this family enough?"

Iyare looks at her father dead in the eye and asks with every pain she can muster from within her being,

"How could you do this Epa (father)?"

Eghare glances at Adesuwa, shocked.

He turns back to Iyare, wide eyed.

"You dare question me?"

He slaps her across the face.

"How dare you?", he says.

Iyare holds her assaulted cheek with both hands, sobbing.

Adesuwa stands up and moves in between father and daughter.

Iyare, whimpering and holding her face, whispers painfully,

"Do you know what they do there? Do you?"

Eghare, seething with anger, blinks wildly as he says,

"You say what now?"

He is ready to pounce on her again.

Adesuwa stops him.

She asks quietly,
"What do they do there my child?"
Iyare answers matter of fact,
"Ashewo. Prostitution"
Adesuwa grabs her and asks wide eyed,
"What did you say?"
Iyare sniffles and says,
"They force the girls to have sex with different men for money"
Eghare exclaims loudly,
"Liar! You're a liar. Shut up your mouth!"
Adesuwa turns to Iyare and asks painfully,
"Are you sure?"
Iyare nods.
Adesuwa asks again,
"How do you know this?"
Iyare answers,
"Somebody tried to take me too. But her brother told me not to go if I don't want to become a prostitute. He said all the girls they take to Italy become prostitutes. His sister is a madam. That's what she and all her friends do. They take girls from here to Italy for prostitution"
Adesuwa screams,
"Osanobua! (God!)"
She flings herself on the ground and rolls around on the floor, crying. Iyare goes over to her. She sits on the floor beside her.
Eghare paces the floor thoughtfully as he mutters loudly,
"This can't be true. You saw the woman. She's a very nice lady. She can't do something like that to my child. Can she?"
He stops pacing and looks at his wife and other daughter on the floor, pain is etched on his face.
He asks loudly,
"Can this really be true? My daughter an ashewo? A prostitute?"
Adesuwa cries out loud,
"She's only 13... only 13... she's only a child... only a child. Oh God why? Why me oh God?"
Iyare consoles her, crying herself.
Eghare plops himself on the threadbare couch and holds his head in his hands, tears start to stream down his face.
He mutters to himself bitterly,

"My young child is a prostitute?"

*

Months become years. Osas is about 18 going by her natural date of birth, but 22 according to her forged documents. She has lived in Italy for 5 years when she meets Nancy Audu – Frank Audu's delectable wife – at a symposium in Turin.

Nancy Audu is speaking at the symposium about the 'Human Trafficking Crisis in Nigeria', under the auspices of her Foundation for the Empowerment of Women – FEW. A project she started with the former First Lady of Nigeria, Mariam Babagarri.

Nancy gives her very moving speech about the ongoing annihilation and systematic destruction of the Nigerian girl child through sex trafficking. She implores everyone to join hands in the fight against the deplorable trafficking of Nigeria's vulnerable children.

Osas is sitting quietly in the conference hall amidst the crowd, inside the venue of the symposium. She is soaking up every word coming out of Nancy Audu's mouth with very rapt attention.

Nancy Audu ends her speech by saying,

"My team and I will be in Turin for at least another week. Our contact information is provided on the literature we handed out. If you're a victim, or you know any victim of human trafficking, please reach out to us. We'll protect your identity. Everything is very respectful and confidential. We'll do all we can to assist you. Or at the very least, direct you to where you can get some help. There's no judgment folks. We're here to help. Thank you"

The crowd rise up to their feet and applaud her rapturously.

Osas looks at the literature in her hand. Then she glances up at Nancy who is walking away from the podium. She is greeting and shaking hands with different people in her path.

Osas walks towards Nancy. She waits in line to greet her.

A moment later she reaches Osas.

Nancy smiles at her very warmly, stretching out her hand for a handshake, as she says,

"Hello dear. How're you doing today?"

Osas takes her hand in hers as she says tearfully,

"Can I speak with you privately ma'am?"

Nancy hugs her instinctively as she says dotingly,

"Of course my darling"

She takes her hand and leads her away from the crowd.

She says to the crowd nicely,

"Please pardon me"

Holding on to Osas's hand protectively she says,

"Come with me my dear"

Osas starts to sob inconsolably.

Nancy holds her tighter as they walk away together from the crowd. They are closely followed by two burly looking men. Nancy's bodyguard and driver respectively.

Nancy whispers to Osas lovingly,

"It's ok my darling. It's ok. Don't cry. Wipe your eyes. It's ok"

She stops briefly, holding Osas's shoulder tenderly as she says softly,

"Do you mind coming with me to my hotel where we can speak freely in private?"

Amidst sobs, Osas nods.

Nancy asks,

"Is that ok with you?"

Osas mutters,

"Yes ma'am"

Nancy smiles at her very warmly,

"Please call me Nancy, ok?"

Osas forces a smile,

"Ok"

Nancy says very sweetly,

"Don't worry. Whatever it is we can figure it out. Ok?"

Osas wipes her eyes and whispers,

"Ok aunty"

Nancy smiles and turns to her body guard who is hovering around. She says to him,

"Take us to the hotel"

He nods and starts to lead the way out of the conference hall.

*

Nancy and Osas are sitting alone inside the huge luxurious living room of her five star hotel suite somewhere on the outskirts of

Turin. She is listening to every word coming out of the young woman's mouth without interrupting her.

She is completely still like glass, not wanting to distract her in any way. Her face is impassive too. No expression whatsoever, only her complete attention.

Osas is saying softly,

"I was 13 at the time"

She glances at Nancy as she says,

"You must understand that I don't blame my parents for anything at all"

Nancy nods.

Osas continues as she looks away,

"It's not their fault. We were very poor. It was hard to eat. We needed help. And the woman lied to us. She deceived us. I believed her. My parents believed her too. She just took advantage of our situation"

She forces a smile as she continues quietly,

"She made many promises. She said I would go to school. That I would work as a babysitter. Or a store clerk. She lied about everything"

She glances at Nancy again, who is still unflinching.

"She never said I was going to be a prostitute. My parents would never have agreed if she told them that. You understand?"

Nancy nods again.

She continues sadly, wiping away tear drops.

"I was still a virgin when she brought me here. I was practically raped the first time...."

Her voice trails off as she sobs quietly.

Nancy, wiping her own teary eyes, moves over to hold her in a tender hug.

She whispers to her softly,

"It's ok my darling. It's ok"

"I was forced to have sex with all sorts of men. Young, old, dirty... you name it. They got me drunk first"

Nancy continues to hold her lovingly.

She continues softly,

"In the past 5 years I've seen all kinds of things here. Some girls have died from drug overdose, or slaughtered like animals. Some have committed suicide. And their families don't even know they're dead"

Nancy, completely moved, sobs quietly.

Osas continues sadly,

"Many girls are smuggled through Libya. They're kept in camps where they're raped and abused until they ship them here. Many die on the way. They just throw their bodies into the sea like dead animals"

Nancy mutters,

"My God"

Osas says softly,

"Aunty I wont lie, I've thought of killing myself too. When I couldn't take it anymore, I wanted to kill myself. I wanted to end it all. But when I think about my parents I change my mind"

They both sob quietly for a moment.

Osas whispers,

"My parents are the only reason I'm still alive today. I feel so sorry for them. Everything I've endured is because I want to help them. I just want to take care of them"

Nancy hugs her very tightly. They sob together quietly.

Several hours later, after listening to her dreadful story, Nancy would not let Osas out of her sight.

*

The following morning, very fired up, Nancy sends out a search party to go look for Madam Eki Obasuyi. They find her within the hour. And they bring her to Nancy.

Her driver and bodyguard, who are really very trained ex special forces personnel, both lead Madam Eki into the office where Nancy is sitting behind a massive desk, reminiscent of the 'Godfather' from Mario Puzo's 'The Godfather'.

She reeks of power as she sits quietly behind the elegant mahogany desk, dressed in a very sharp black suit, inside the very tastefully furnished and spacious office of the law firm she partners with in Turin.

Madam Eki who is flamboyantly dressed with excessive jewelry walks in tentatively, very unsure of her self.

The bodyguard closes the door shut.

Nancy points Madam Eki to the seat across from her desk without a word. Without any pleasantry. Godfather like.

Madam Eki sits down opposite Nancy.

She glances around furtively, visibly uncomfortable.

The bodyguard and the driver both walk over to sit on the couch beside the wall. Their eyes are trained on Madam Eki quietly, observing her every movement.

Nancy asks in a very straightforward manner,

"Do you know me?"

Madam Eki answers quietly,

"Yes I do ma"

Nancy frowns,

"How do you know me?"

Madam Eki clears her throat, forces a smile, and says respectfully,

"You're a household name ma'am. Everybody knows you"

Nancy retorts,

"That's not what I asked you. Eki Obasuyi, right?"

Madam Eki says quietly,

"Yes ma'am. Well, I do know you. I know you work with the former First Lady of Nigeria. And I also know your husband"

Nancy says impassively,

"Very well then. This'll be very short. I don't want you in my presence longer than necessary"

Madam Eki who was brought here under false pretense, and still completely unaware of the real reason for this meeting, forces a grin.

Agitated, she mutters softly,

"Oh oh. Is there a problem ma'am?"

Nancy blurts out,

"Yes I've a problem with you 'madam'. I've a problem with your type"

Madam Eki is wide eyed,

"I don't understand you ma'am"

Nancy quips,

"I'll go straight to the point. Today is the last day of your business. Do you understand me?"

Madam Eki glances around furtively, then says apprehensively,

"I really don't understand ma. I thought you brought me here to discuss one of your projects. Or something like that. I'm really surprised by your…"

Nancy cuts her off rudely,

"You traffic young girls from Nigeria to Italy for prostitution. Isn't it madam?"

Madam Eki blinks widely. Shocked.

Nancy continues aggressively,

"You deceive girls as young as 13 with all kinds of promises. You bring them here and sell them for sex, isn't it?"

Madam Eki finds her voice,

"You don't understand ma. I try to help…"

Nancy cuts her off again,

"Help who? You mean help yourself, isn't it? You turn poor innocent children into sex slaves while you enrich yourself. Is that how you help them?"

Madam Eki pleads,

"I help families. Some poor families back home can eat because of me"

Nancy retorts,

"Do you tell them you're bringing their young daughters here for prostitution? Do you?"

Madam Eki looks down at her feet, speechless.

Nancy continues,

"Who will give you their child for prostitution? Are you insane?"

Madam Eki whispers fearfully,

"I'm only trying to help…"

Nancy explodes angrily,

"Don't insult my intelligence woman!"

Madam Eki pleads,

"I'm sorry ma"

Nancy continues forcefully,

"Like I said. Your business ends today. You must release all the girls you control. I should pay you off. But I will not. I do not buy or sell people. I'm not a slave trader. But most importantly, you don't deserve a dime. Matter of fact, you should be locked away in prison. That's what you deserve!"

Madam Eki pleads tearfully,

"How am I supposed to do that? It cost money to bring them"

Nancy retorts,

"I don't give a crap about you woman. You're very evil and a total disgrace to women everywhere"

Madam Eki tries to speak,

"But..."

Nancy cuts her off,

"If you don't give up the girls. Or if you try to intimidate them, or their family, in any way, you'll have yourself to blame. I'll make sure you lose every penny you have. Everything you own, even the clothes on your back. Home and abroad. And I'll make sure you spend the remainder of your days behind bars. Do you understand me?"

Madam Eki looks up at her tearfully,

"Please understand..."

Nancy retorts,

"Do you know how much jail time you're looking at? At least 20 years per girl. And you have about 50 girls, right? Do the math woman!"

Madam Eki cries.

Nancy says without pity,

"If for whatever reason you fail to abide by my terms, or you try to be sleek, then you will really get to know me. Is that clear enough for you to understand?"

Madam Eki pleads,

"I beg you ma. Please don't do this to me"

Nancy explodes angrily,

"Get out of my sight. You disgust me!"

Her bodyguard jumps up promptly. He moves to escort Madam Eki out of the office.

Madam Eki tries to beg,

"Please ma..."

The bodyguard says forcefully,

"This way miss!"

He guides and leads her out of the office very quickly. He escorts her out of the building. She cries all the way out.

*

Osas becomes Nancy's surrogate daughter. Nancy takes her back home to Nigeria with her. She is welcomed into Nancy's home like any other family member.

Nancy enrolls her in school, and gets her several tutors. Osas wants to be a lawyer like her mentor Nancy. She wants to one day join Nancy's foundation, so she can help other trafficked women around the world.

Osas puts her insider knowledge of the sex trafficking ring at Nancy's disposal. Nancy sets up a fund to assist many of the trafficked girls. Some return to Nigeria and go back to school. Others learn various sponsored trades. Some remain in Europe to pursue other endeavors. Some find love and get married. They all try to find some semblance of a normal life.

Madam Eki, on the other hand, lets most of the girls go. But she hides a few of them in several brothels around Turin and Sicily. Nancy's investigators find out.

Nancy opens a case against her in Italy and Nigeria. She is found guilty of human sex trafficking. She is sentenced to 100 years in prison. All her property is confiscated and sold by the Nigerian government. The fund thereof is distributed to several NGOs – Non Governmental Organizations – that assist trafficked women.

As Frank often says,

"Nancy is the sweetest woman in the world; but she can also be the most vicious person if she chooses to be".

After all, his nickname for her is 'the wicked witch'.

Go figure!

17 GLOBAL EPIDEMIC

"Not doing what you feel like doing is freedom" - Swami Chinmayananda

The renowned 419 scam is certainly a product of Nigeria; but it has since traversed beyond the shores of the West African nation. Several practitioners of the dastardly act are spread all over the world today indiscriminately.

People as diverse as you can ever find are involved in the scheme. People of different nationalities, people of different heritages. People dispersed all across the face of the earth.

Some people who were scammed at some point have become scammers themselves. It is a very vicious cycle fueled by the innate greed of mankind. The inordinate desire of most people to want to reap where they have not sown is extremely powerful.

The diabolical plague is spread all over the world, even to places as farfetched as China, India and Malaysia. It is everywhere. It is in the north, south, east and west, all four corners of the world; constituting a very real global epidemic.

Michelle Delaney is a very bright, supposedly smart, 26 year old woman. She is a graduate student in the Master of Public Administration, Health Policy and Management program at New York University, in the 'Big Apple' – New York City.

She is in a class when her cell phone suddenly starts vibrating. She glances at the screen discretely, to see who is calling. It is an unknown number. She ignores it, letting the machine get a message if need be.

Later on, after the class, she gets a notification of a new voicemail. Her handbag is draped over her shoulder as she listens to the message on her way to grab some lunch.

The heavily accented voice on the machine says,

"This is Agent Dick Taylor of the IRS. This is to inform you of your past due debt to the IRS in the amount of six thousand dollars. You must pay the debt immediately or you will be arrested within 24 hours for failure to comply. To avoid getting arrested you must return this call to make a payment right away"

Michelle, confused and wide eyed, plays the message again. She listens hard, totally blown away. She glances around, frightened, with uncertainty plastered across her delectable face.

She has heard all kinds of frightening stories about the IRS – the Internal Revenue Service. She believes the IRS can be just as terrifying as the FBI – the Federal Bureau of Investigation.

But how in the world does she owe so much back taxes, she wonders. She has worked hard over the years, and she paid all her taxes, she reckons. Or did she? She asks herself, uncertain.

She moves to sit on a bench nearby. She pulls out a notepad and a pen from her hand bag. She plays the message again, and writes down the call back number.

She dials the number on her cellphone.

A thick accented voice answers gruffly,

"Hello?"

"Yes, hello. Is this the IRS?", she asks

"Yes yes yes", answers the voice.

"May I please speak with Agent Dick Taylor?", asks Michelle.

The voice retorts,

"This's Agent Taylor speaking. What can I do for you?"

"I received a message from you", says Michelle

"What does the message say?", asks Agent Taylor

"Well, it says that I owe the IRS"

"What's your name ma'am?"

"My name is Michelle Delaney"

"Give me a minute let me look that up"

"Ok"

Michelle is put on hold for a few seconds.

He comes back, and says,

"Yes Ms. Delaney. Our record show you owe six thousand dollars. Do you want to pay now?"

"But I don't have that kind of money sir. I'm a student", pleads Michelle.

"Well there is nothing I can do about that. If you don't pay, a warrant will be issued for your arrest within 24 hours. Do you understand?", says Agent Taylor.

"How am I supposed to pay six thousand dollars just like that?", she asks.

"How much can you pay right now?", he asks

"Em. Maybe three thousand?", she says

"Only three thousand?", he queries

"Yes. That's all I have in my account", she pleads.

"Ok. Because you called immediately I'll accept that payment today. And because you seem like a decent person I'll give you some time to pay the balance. You say you're a student, right?"

"Yes I'm a student sir"

"Ok. So how do you want to pay the $3,000 today?"

"How can I pay it?"

"Well, is there a shopping mall near you there? Like a Wal-Mart?"

Michelle frowns and queries,

"A Wal-Mart?"

He retorts,

"To expedite the process, and to prevent your immediate arrest I'll need you to send the payment via gift cards…"

She cuts in,

"Gift cards? Seriously?"

"Yes", he says.

She protests,

"That doesn't make sense. How…"

He cuts her off,

"Ma'am, do you want to be arrested?"

She answers meekly,

"No"

He says,

"Ok then. I'm only trying to prevent your arrest by helping you expedite the payment. There's a warrant already issued for your arrest. If you pay now, I'll call it off. Do you understand?"

She closes her eyes, inhales and exhales, then says,

"There's a Wal-Mart nearby. What do you want me to do?"

He says,

"Stay on the phone. Walk to the store. When you get there I'll tell you what to do?"

She asks,

"Now?"

He retorts,

"Yes, right now. Stay on the phone with me. Please do not hang up. I really want to help you today if you do exactly as I say, ok?"

She starts walking towards Wal-Mart as she says meekly,

"Ok"

He asks,

"Oh, you have your bank card with you, right?"

She answers,

"Yes"

He retorts,

"Very good"

Michelle is led to the Wal-Mart store like a sheep being led to the slaughter, by the faceless Agent Dick Taylor who is really a conman calling from India.

He instructs her to buy '*Apple iTunes Store*' gift cards with her bank card. $3,000.00 (three thousand dollars) worth of cards. She buys the cards reluctantly. She scratches the cards and gives him the numbers with the pin codes over the phone.

She becomes three thousand dollars poorer, and he becomes three thousand dollars richer, just like that; thousands of miles away. By the way, that is a lot of *rupees* if you ask me.

He takes her money and then asks when she can pay the balance of three thousand dollars, since the total amount is six thousand dollars. She says she will have to go borrow it from a friend or family member.

She asks for a week to pay the balance, he acquiesces because she is such a 'honest and reliable person'. Unbeknown to her, there is no 'Agent Dick Taylor of the IRS' anywhere in existence.

Matter of fact, the IRS has never, and will probably never ever ask for payment over the phone in the form of gift cards. That is ludicrous. And as bogus and farfetched as it sounds, many people have indeed fallen victim, and still fall victim to this total crap!

*

Elaine Molotov, a retired 75 year old lady, is sitting in her living room somewhere in rural Kentucky, knitting a sweater for her newest grandchild when her home phone suddenly rings shrilly.

She looks at the phone with annoyance, wondering who is disturbing her otherwise very quiet afternoon.

She picks up the phone and answers unenthused,

"Hello?"

A British sounding male voice on the other end says exuberantly,

"Hello and congratulations on winning the UK lottery drawing in the amount of two hundred and fifty thousand US dollars. That's American dollars!"

Elaine blinks, adjusts her glasses and asks,

"Say what now?"

The English voice says,

"Congratulations madam. You're a lottery winner!"

She queries suspiciously,

"What lottery? I didn't play any lottery? Are you sure you have the right person?"

The voice continues in the rich English brogue excitedly,

"Yes madam. Are you not Mrs. Elaine Molotov in Augusta, Kentucky?"

She replies,

"Well yes, that's me. But I…"

The voice cuts her off midsentence,

"Then congratulations are in order madam. You're a winner!"

She chuckles and asks with excitement,

"Really?"

"Oh yes madam! You're a winner of the two hundred and fifty thousand US dollars jackpot!"

"Oh wow! So what do I do now?", she asks incredulously

"Well, there's some processing fee involved before we can pay you your winnings. We'll also need some proof of identity. And you've to sign some documents as well", he says

"Alright then, lets get the horse on the road!", she says gleefully.

The voice chuckles and asks,

"How would you like to pay the processing fee today madam?"

She asks,

"How much is the processing fee?"

He says matter of fact,

"Considering your amount of winnings, the fee would be a ten percent surcharge of the entire winnings. Which will amount to twenty five thousand US dollars madam"

She whistles softly,

"Twenty five thousand dollars?"

"Yes madam"

"I don't have that kind of money anywhere"

"That will be pickle, I'm afraid", he says

"Can't you take it out of my winnings then?"

He retorts,

"The regulations prohibit that madam. Winners have to clear all fees before their prize can be released"

She mutters sadly,

"Well, I don't have twenty five thousand dollars. I'm retired"

He says charmingly,

"Very well then madam. We've to work something out with you, don't we?"

She whispers,

"Ok"

He says,

"For starters, how much can you put down today towards the twenty five thousand dollars surcharge?"

She says thoughtfully,

"I'm really not sure. I've to check my account balance"

He pursues,

"Very well then. Go ahead and check your account balance. And do you also carry any credit cards?"

She answers,

"Yes"

"You could put some of the cost on the cards. So once you get your winnings you can then go on to pay off the cards. You understand?"

She says weakly,

"I'm not sure about that"

He grins,

"I'm trying to work with you here madam. Let me help you. I want you to receive your money as quickly as possible"

"How long does the process take?", she asks

"Usually about 5 working days after we receive the processing fees", he answers.

They go back and forth until Elaine pays out $7,500.00 (seventy five hundred dollars), with a promise to raise another $10,000.00 within the next 7 days from her retirement account. That is a lot of money for a person with a fixed income to lose.

This very well spoken English voice on the phone is actually Trevor Wallace who lives in Kingston, Jamaica. He was recently deported from the United Kingdom for fraudulent activities. He is now preying on gullible old ladies across the United States with his suave English accent.

As you have already guessed by now, there is no lottery. She is not a winner of even a bad penny. She is the mark. She is fleeced out of her retirement income and savings.

Trevor Wallace, and many others like him, buy various mailing lists of potential victims from unscrupulous people online. The lists contain mailing addresses and telephone numbers of unsuspecting folks.

These telephone scam artistes call people from the list at random. Some people curse them out and hang up the phone immediately. The not so fortunate ones take the bait and get swindled out of their hard earned money.

*

Jacques Lemon is a small business owner in Las Vegas. He owns and operates a successful printing press. He prints a lot of the flyers and posters of events in the ever busy and electric city.

As is customary, most of Jacques work is done on a computer. His business is very dependent on modern, and up to date digital technology.

One morning he turns on his computer to begin another hectic work day, instead a banner with big red letters is splattered across his computer screen; with the following very cryptic message:

'You have been hacked. Call the number below to get your computer back'.

A phone number is provided with the message. He is completely bemused. He needs his computer system to do his work. And he is not in the mood for any ridiculous games, he reckons.

He calls the phone number provided and finds out he must pay $50,000.00 to regain control of his computer.

They tell him going to the authorities will not help him since they were operating from some remote location in a faraway corner of the earth.

The hackers had apparently gained control of his system after he downloaded a media file from a fraudulent website.

*

Several organizations have also been victims of this computer hacking for ransom. Hackers attack their network and take control of their system. They must pay a huge fee or they will lose all their data forever.

The hackers usually demand payment in 'bitcoin cryptocurrency', which is some kind of digital razzmatazz; basically an underground means of extorting money from innocent victims worldwide.

Some people have also had the misfortune of being targeted after they visit lewd and inappropriate websites. A certain computer virus or software is remotely installed on the user's computer. They send him an email with his private information and threaten to reveal all the details of his indiscretion to his family and friends, unless he pays them with bitcoin.

Some times the hacker just threatens that he has compromising information on the target. That he has been secretly collecting information and dirt on him via his webcam.

That he has videos of him pleasuring himself, and a list of all the porn sites he has visited in the last few months. That he has videos of him indulging in activities the victim would rather keep private. That he would reveal all that to his associates if he doesn't pay up. Scared and afraid of embarrassment, he pays up. Sometimes endless payments are demanded.

But, of course, if you have nothing to hide, or nothing to be embarrassed about then you can just call their bluff and tell them to take a hike; or you go to the authorities to report the matter, otherwise it could cost you dearly.

To be safe, practice appropriate behavior on and off line. Safeguard your computer and digital devices with all the appropriate measures provided by the manufacturer. Don't download anything from any questionable websites. And also avoid questionable behavior yourself.

Do not try to reap where you've not sown. There's no where on earth you can win a lottery without ever playing, or participating in, the lottery. You can't eat a boiled egg if it's not cooked.

Remember every time you receive an email or phone call promising to give you anything for free, it has a 99.99% chance of being a total falsehood. A classic scam.

18 THE THIRD REPUBLIC

"Don't ask someone else to do what you can do yourself" - Mike Carroll

After the sudden but widely celebrated death of General Sanu Aboki, the rather unfortunate and untimely death of Chief N. K. A. Abiodun, the new Head of State and Commander in Chief of Nigeria's Armed Forces, General Abdel Abibi, announces on national television that there would be a transition to a civilian and democratic rule.

He says to the people, who listen to him with a pinch of salt,

"Nigerians want nothing less than a true democracy in a peaceful and united nation. There will be no interim transition period. This administration has no plan to succeed itself. We're committed to handing over to a democratically elected government"

To show good will, he releases many activists, including some of the folks from Ogoni, who were previously detained, to the pleasant surprise of the people.

But the masses remain very skeptical, unable to trust the military who have proven themselves to be very untrustworthy in the past.

General Abdel Abibi surprises the masses still with his announcement that an independent autopsy would be carried out on the late Chief N. K. A. Abiodun.

And true to his words, an autopsy is carried out. The team of international investigators find no foul play. They conclude that Chief N. K. A. Abiodun died of a heart attack.

The people are still not satisfied. They argue that had he not been imprisoned in the first place he would not have died of a heart attack or anything else.

They say his confinement prevented him from getting access to his personal doctors who could have seen any signs of a failing heart, if there was any.

Meanwhile General Abdel Abibi is a very close friend of the former Head of State and Commander in Chief of the Armed Forces of Nigeria, General Issa Babagarri, retired. The evil genius 'Maradona' himself, Frank Audu's mentor.

So once again, General Issa Babagarri, although retired, becomes relevant and powerful yet again. General Abdel Abibi meets and consults with him regularly. General Abibi makes no move without running it by General Babagarri first.

General Abdel Abibi goes on to constitute a legal process against the estate of the late General Sanu Aboki, perhaps on the advice of General Issa Babagarri, perhaps not. He sues the family of the deceased in a bid to recover Nigeria's stolen funds in their possession.

He successfully reclaims $750 million that had been stolen from the national treasury. A very tiny portion of the total amount stolen, no doubt.

General Abibi proceeds with the promised political transition process. Several newcomers toss their hats in the political arena since the serious folks refuse to be bothered with yet another political process.

Still seething with anger about the last botched election, the intellects and folks with real political and economic prowess refuse to participate in this new political dispensation.

The refusal of competent people to participate creates a vacuum that is filled by hooligans and hoodlums. Former motor park touts, meat butchers, drunks, people with very little or no education at all become politicians overnight.

Some of the very worst vermin of the society take advantage of the absence of the real educated and competent political class. Elections are held within months, and these charlatans gain power.

Local government council chairmen and councilors, are either, until recently, former meat butchers or motor park touts and thugs. These are criminals popularly known as 'agberos', total vermin with no political or administrative knowledge whatsoever. These folks with no worthy experience become the new political leaders.

At the federal level, General Abdel Abibi hand picks a former Head of State, the retired General Oluseye Obatan, as the new President of Nigeria. On the advice of retired General Issa Babagarri of course.

This completes the vicious cycle described by the late Afrobeat King, Fela Anikulapo Kuti, as 'soldier go, soldier come'.

General Abdel Abibi who could not wait to run away from 'Aso Rock', in a hurry to relinquish the leadership of Nigeria, carries out a very flawed election. He hands over the reins of the country to yet another General who now wears civilian clothes within a year. Retired or not, they say 'once a general, always a general'.

So by all intents and purposes Nigeria is still under military rule, albeit in civilian garb. And this is all orchestrated by the master mind, the evil genius, retired General Issa Babagarri.

The supposed winner of the presidential election, retired General Oluseye Obatan forms the new so-called democratic government. The third republic is, therefore, up and running. A total farce without doubt.

Frankly, it is business as usual in a nutshell. Corruption and 'authority stealing', as Fela Kuti would say, is at an all time high yet again. The criminal minded 'agberos' at the local level do nothing but divide all the local government funds amongst themselves.

No community development. No roads are built or repaired, no schools are maintained or cared for, no healthcare systems developed, no power supply; no development whatsoever. They just receive money from the state and share it amongst themselves blatantly.

The state government is exactly the same. They receive huge funds from the federal account and share it amongst themselves with no regard for the plight of the common man whatsoever. Government workers don't even get paid their salaries on time.

At the federal level the story is not different. The powers that be, sell Nigeria's oil and pocket the proceeds. No infrastructural development. The President and his cohorts divvy up the resources of the nation amongst themselves.

Federal entities are getting sold to private individuals. Oil blocks are assigned to friends and cronies. The masses continue to groan in poverty and penury while the so called leaders enrich themselves without any care in the world.

Frank Audu's empire continues to grow unchallenged. After all, his mentor and benefactor, General Issa Babagarri, still pulls the strings in the general scheme of things, albeit retired. He controls several oil blocks himself. And he can make anything happen.

*

In Delta State, in the Niger-Delta Region, one of the supposed richest states of the nation, that receives a huge federal allocation every year, the story is simply asinine.

The State Governor turns the State House into his own personal family compound. He appoints several of his cousins, nephews, and other relatives as 'Special Assistants'. Special Assistants whose preoccupation is to organize wild parties and orgies around the state.

These Special Assistants contribute absolutely nothing to the State. Their office and position is totally redundant; completely superfluous and unnecessary. All they do is to drive around town in official government vehicles with sirens blaring and trunks full of cash.

Yes, they drive around town with huge stacks of money stowed away in the trunks of their vehicles. They hop from bars to clubs every night splashing and squandering away money they have not earned. Money stolen from the people of Delta State.

They live extremely extravagant lives while the masses suffer in silence. These are evil seeds spurn by the devil himself. Heartless criminals, all of them!

With all the money Delta State receives every year, from Federal allocation, and from taxes paid by all the huge multinational oil companies operating within the area, the state should be a paradise; no kidding.

But Delta State, just like everywhere else in the country, is still terribly underdeveloped to this day because of the greed and selfishness of the wantonly corrupt leaders from top to bottom. The people are cursed with criminals for leaders.

From north, to south, to east, to west the story is the same. The people are inundated with criminals all across. The phrase 'civil service' is completely lost on the people of Nigeria. Selfless service is completely non-existent in Nigeria.

Ninety-nine percent of the people who aspire to power or leadership position in Nigeria do so for solely one reason, to enrich themselves.

Everyone who runs for office is just looking for a way to go steal and enrich himself, period. They don't care about nobody else but themselves. This is the very acme of selfishness and utter greed.

The 'chop chop', 'chop and quench', 'owambe' culture; which all mean the wasteful culture, continues across the country unabated. The politicians steal so much that the economy tanks again, worse than before.

Hungry and angry, the youth continue in their quest for survival by any means necessary. The crime rate spikes up even more. Many more flee the country, others stay reluctantly. They continue to commit all manner of crimes around the world flagrantly.

And as is customary with the 'Nigerian soldier' who gets power and refuses to relinquish it, the former Head of State, the retired General, and current President of the country, Mr. Oluseye Obatan; having completed two terms as president, as allowed by the constitution, decides he wants to do a third term. Imagine the travesty!

This is a man who failed woefully as a military Head of State, and is also sadly failing yet again as a civilian president, and he has the effrontery to demand a third term. This man must really think very highly of himself. But luckily the average Nigerian does not share that thought.

The legislators and senators put their corrupt feet down for once and overruled the very selfish and greedy Oluseye Obatan. They refuse to acquiesce to his third term bid. He is voted out of office.

He hands over to another civilian administration. An historic feat really. It is the first time in the history of Nigeria where an elected civilian administration hands over to another elected civilian administration without fuss. Go figure!

But alas, this new administration is just as bad as the previous one. If not worse that is.

The new President Mumuni Yayade turns out to be a rather sickly man. He is travelling all over Europe for treatment, an indictment of all the past governments for their failure to establish a proper health care system in the country.

It is a monumental disgrace and complete embarrassment that Nigeria, one of the richest oil producing nations of the world, the most populous black nation in the globe, need to send their president abroad for treatment. Is it a lack of the proper infrastructure? Or a lack of the manpower? Or perhaps it is both. Whichever way, it is a very big disgrace. Shameful and very embarrassing!

Mr. Mumuni Yayade eventually dies after a brief and turbulent time as President. His Vice President, Badluck Josiah, is sworn in as President.

The crap totally hits the fan under this man that many describe as 'clueless', 'drunk', 'incompetent', 'foolish', 'nonsensical', and a 'purveyor of corruption'.

Under Badluck Josiah's watch things just explode out of control. The wanton corruption of the political class is serious cause for concern for all and sundry. Authority stealing by top office holders is at epic proportions. Massive embezzlement is the order of the day.

There is a very palpable fear hanging over the people. A fear of a return of the military. The current state of the country is reminiscent of the infamous 'fellow Nigerians' speech days. And absolutely nobody wants that.

But they realize that the current state of affairs could warrant, or perhaps lead to, something like that. A forceful military takeover of the government yet again. So what must be done to prevent that? That is the question on everyone's lips.

Absolutely no one is interested in having soldiers back in charge of the country. That is tantamount to falling from the proverbial 'pan into the fire' as they say.

Nigeria since gaining her independence in 1960 has been ruled by various draconian military juntas over the years. The progress of the nation has been severely stunted by that unfortunate ill luck.

Half educated and extremely corrupt folks have dragged the once prosperous country through the mud of history. The once great 'giant of Africa' has since metamorphosed into the beleaguered 'ant of Africa' today.

The people, in consideration of the foregoing, decide to vote out the widely despised and derided Badluck Josiah at the national polls.

The people choose a former military dictator who runs as a politician in a democratic process.

The choice of the ex military dictator over the incumbent Badluck Josiah is not because of love, or for an overwhelming conviction that the ex soldier has the solutions to the problems of the nation either, not at all. That is very far from the truth.

It is just for the simple fact that the people were fed up with Badluck Josiah and his wantonly corrupt administration. The people will, at this point, vote for anyone, or anything else, but Badluck Josiah, they say.

19 SOCIAL MEDIA

"The only place success comes before work is in the dictionary"
— Vince Lombardi

To paraphrase Vince Lombardi, 'success only comes before work in the dictionary'; but apparently, many young people these days don't seem to realize that. They all want instant success without putting in any kind of work. Alas, that is the sign of the times we live in today.

Social media is both the golden gift and virulent curse of the twenty-first century. The possibilities social media has made available is completely mind boggling. Both positive and negative attributes no less, I might add.

Social media, like Facebook for instance, has opened doors that would otherwise be closed. People around the world are connecting effortlessly with only a few clicks on their computers or mobile devices.

The virtues of social media cannot be overemphasized. But then, the ills and dangers thereof cannot be understated either. A real albatross I must say. It is a very real conundrum.

People who are very far from home are able to communicate and stay in touch with family and friends anywhere in the world. The real time capability of the social media platform has made staying in touch 'easy like Sunday morning', as they say.

People are now able to support, and participate in causes dear to them more easily than ever. Transmission of information globally is as easy as a few clicks on a smartphone for example.

Folks can see things happening in any part of the world as it is happening in real time. People can make comments on all kinds of posts. Digital media is also easily shared more than ever before.

And with all the aforementioned benefits comes the dangers and risks associated with this so called social media platform. It can make or break you very easily.

Many very positive relationships are established on social media every day. And as it is human nature, very many dastardly ones too.

Many have found long lasting friendship, love, relationship, and even marriage. Many also have started all manner of businesses with help and ideas they find on social media.

The criminally minded have also found a niche on social media. They're crawling all over the various platforms in search of unsuspecting victims.

If you act gullible for a second you will be feasted on by these virulent charlatans. You cannot 'blink your eyes' on social media. You must be alert, cautious, and extra careful or else you'll become another statistic.

*

Many people promise all kinds of things on social media. Every time you turn around there is some promise here and there. Examples include things like,

'Earn $150,000 in 30 days'

'Earn six figures with only a $100 investment'

'Be a deal closer and make millions every year'

'Become a successful self published author in 30 days'

'Sell $25,000 worth of books with $100 investment'

The promises are endless. Nobody knows if anyone has really achieved any success from these self acclaimed gurus on social media.

Many go so far as to offer supposedly free webinars. And at the end of the webinar they try to sell you a product for hundreds of dollars. Total bullocks. Something that won't help you in anyway.

That right there is another scam if you ask me. The last time I checked, hard work is still the only foolproof method of making money; real money.

Be very scared when you hear the words 'free' and 'help you' on social media. That is how they suck you in.

'Come get free this, or free that'

'I want to help you do such and such'

How are you helping me if I have to pay you for something? That is not helping me in any way. That is selling me stuff. It is usually crap that I don't need, and that can't help me in any way whatsoever.

Folks be very careful on social media. Don't splurge your hard earned money on ridiculousness. Remember if it is too good to be true, then it is. Run away with your money in your pocket.

*

The most hilarious aspect of the 'social media scam' is the automatic assumption that every man on there is looking for some type of sexual or romantic alliance.

But the truth is that many people are really just there to network, and perhaps do some business too. And there is absolutely nothing wrong with that.

It is very common place to see pictures of scantily dressed voluptuous females exposing their 'front' and 'back' sides. These very erotic pictures are splashed all over the place.

You cannot be on Facebook or Instagram for a minute without getting visually assaulted by these very suggestive images. Some of the images are so over the top you wonder if you are on a porn site.

Thousands of Facebook accounts have nothing but pictures of large bosoms and extra big butts. Every picture on those pages is a close up, or extreme close up shot of humongous boobs or enormous ass; and nothing else.

Many of these supposedly 'gifted' females can not even construct a proper sentence. Many claim to be undergraduates yet you can not find one single picture of them in class or with a book. All their pictures are showing their indecently covered 'assets'.

Other pictures show them holding very expensive designer handbags and shoes. Yet others show them posing in front of exotic cars owned by only God knows who.

You only see pictures of their insanely disproportional 'front' and 'back' sides, or of them striking a very seductive pose with someone's car, or of them getting drunk and wasted. Is this the next generation? What future does the world have with people like this?

Some have several videos of partying, or drinking, and dancing but never a picture or video of them in class, or even on the campus of the school they claim they attend.

Two things come to mind here. Either they don't attend the school they claim they attend, or they are embarrassed by the school. My guess is they have never stepped foot on the soil of the school they claim they attend.

Another very puzzling phenomenon is that all these girls with 'big boobs' and 'gigantic behinds' are all born between 1990 and 1994, according to their profiles.

Another weird social media culture is having to pay for saying hi, or hello, to a female. These supposedly beautiful girls, or women, send you a friend request. You accept the request perhaps because they are already friends with one or two of your friends.

Shortly afterwards they hit you with,

"Hi"

You respond,

"Hi"

They go,

"Hello"

You chuckle, and maybe respond with a hello as well. Or perhaps you just ignore the redundancy.

But they persist with all manner of interrogation. They proceed to cross-examine you with all manner of ridiculous questions. You try to be nice, perhaps at that moment you have some free time and you just go along with the mindless chit-chat.

You finally get a chance to say,

"How're you doing?"

They reply,

"Not good"

You ask,

"Why? What's wrong?"

Then they say,

"I'm broke. I've not eaten since morning. I've not paid my rent. I've not paid my school fees. Things are very bad"

You sigh and try to empathize,

"Wow. I'm sorry to hear that"

And they say,

"Please give me money. I really need money"

They blurt that out just like that within five or ten minutes of chatting with them. This is someone you have never even met before.

Don't get me wrong. I don't have a problem with helping someone, even if I have never ever met them. But asking someone for money after only five minutes of conversing with them is just very low.

Agreed, they probably have a legitimate need. But who is to tell this isn't another 'cat fishing' expedition. No? How can you tell?

*

Edward Badmus is a dashing young man with a very active social media presence. He lives in New York City with his family. All his social media accounts very clearly show his relationship status as married.

Edward is bombarded every day with friend requests from various people, but mostly from women. Most of the requests are usually from the scantily dressed variety. The young women with the very 'sinful curves'. The ones who like to flaunt their gigantic front and back sides, real or not.

He mostly ignores the requests, especially if it is from someone he has no friends in common with. The total strangers.

When he gets a request and he has some time, he clicks on the requester's profile to see if there is any connection, or any need for him to accept the request. And usually he doesn't accept, but sometimes does if there're similar interests with the person.

He also gets 'poked' by some half naked women who are apparently 'sex workers' advertising their goods and services. He blocks those right away without any contemplation.

Then he gets a request from a very pretty young woman who seems very decent in appearance. She is clothed respectably. No half naked pictures on her page. No pictures of partying or alcoholic binges. No phony pictures of designer handbags and shoes either.

The first thought that crosses Edward's mind is,

"Wow. She looks really good. I can work with her. Lemme see what she does".

Edward Badmus is a filmmaker. He writes, produces, and directs motion pictures. So he is thinking of this very pretty young woman as a potential cast for a film. Yes, she looks that good in all her pictures.

So Edward accepts her request.

Her name is Benny. Short for Benedicta, she says.

They chat briefly on Facebook messenger, then Benny asks,

"Are you on Whatsapp?"

Edward replies,

"Yes"

"Can I have your number?", she responds.

"Ok. What's yours?", he says.

They exchange phone numbers and move on to Whatsapp.

Benny says she is a second year Theatre Arts student at the University of Benin, Benin City. Edward finds that interesting since his intention is to explore the possibility of working with Benny on a film.

He talks to her about his film project, and asks if it was possible to meet in person when he visits Nigeria shortly for a location recce for the proposed film project. She acquiesces.

Edward notices that in spite of all the beautiful photos Benny has on Facebook she does not even have a profile picture on Whatsapp. She has an image of a pair of caricature hands as her display picture.

He asks,

"How come you ain't got a picture of you here?"

She says,

"I'm not really a picture freak. Plus I don't really see the need of being an unnecessary cliché with regards to putting up pictures on Facebook and doing the same thing on Whatsapp. It's needless redundancy"

Edward, surprised by the seemingly ironic spiel, says,

"Not pictures. Just a profile picture"

She says,

"I know. It's the same thing"

He says,

"I'm not sure how a pair of hands represents anyone"

She says, or rather types,

"Lol (Laugh out loud)"

He says,

"True talk"

She says,

"That's my hands begging the father in heaven"

He says,

"I see. But they're not even your hands"

She laughs and says,

"Yeah, that's why it's figurative"

He says thoughtfully,

"Interesting"

He wonders why this person is being dodgy over a simple thing as a profile picture. He asks himself,

"Why does she have so many beautiful pictures on Facebook but is reluctant to even have a single profile picture on Whatsapp?"

Apparently this doesn't add up for Edward who is naturally very inquisitive and overtly wary of people and their intentions generally. And his bullshit detecting antennas go up defensively.

Cautious now, he says,

"I'm curious. Why did you add me as a friend on Facebook?"

She laughs, and says,

"I honestly don't know. I just felt a pull"

He responds,

"Mmm... a pull? What kinda pull?"

She 'laughs out loud' and says,

"It's personal?"

He presses her,

"C'mon, you can tell me. I promise I won't tell anyone"

She says,

"No"

He says,

"Don't be like that"

And she says,

"I don't really know. I just liked you as I saw you on my suggested list"

He responds,

"Ok. Fair enough. Don't worry, your secret is safe with me"

They both 'laugh out loud'.

They chitchat some more about their interests, including movies, books, places, etc. for a little bit and then bid each other farewell.

He signs off by saying,

"It's been a pleasure chatting with you. Except for having to stare at a pair of caricature hands"

They 'laugh out loud' again.

She says,

"I'll send you some pictures"

He says,

"Oh. Ok. But you really don't have to do that"

She laughs and says,

"I want to"

He responds,

"Oh. Ok then"

They sign off.

A couple of days later she hits him up on Whatsapp again. She sends him a ton of pictures. Many of the pictures are the same ones she has on her Facebook page.

He says cheerily,

"Oh wow! Tons of pictures to feast my eyes on"

She 'laughs out loud', and says,

"Yes. That's all I have on my memory card. I have a bad phone. Barely managing it right now"

He asks,

"How're you doing?"

She says,

"I'm sponsoring myself in school. It's really hard right now"

He asks,

"Where're your folks?"

She replies,

"Mom and my younger brother are in Warri"

"And your dad?"

"In Port Harcourt. They're not together"

"I see", he mutters.

"Yeah", she responds.

"Do you see them often?", he asks

"A bit", she answers.

"Ok", he says.

Then she says sadly,

"I've been sick lately. I think it's malnutrition"

He replies,

"Oops. What're you sick of?"

She says,

"Typhoid fever. The usual. My immune system is very weak now"

He says,

"Oh oh. How come? Typhoid fever is still a thing?"

She says,

"Yeah it is. No idea how it came around"

He says,

"Sorry to hear that. You should get some rest"

They chat for a couple more minutes. He encourages her to get some rest. She acquiesces.

The following day, Edward, still with a nagging feeling in his gut, places a video call to Benny from out of the blue. She hangs up immediately.

He sends her a message that says,

"What's up with you? I just tried to video call you. You hung up. What's up with that?"

She replies,

"I think I answered though. I told you my phone isn't in top condition"

He says, his 'spidery sense' tingling,

"I see"

He does a voice call to her. She answers.

She doesn't sound quite right to him at all. He cocks his ear, listening intently. They speak for a couple of minutes, then he hangs up. He mutters to himself,

"Drats!"

Later that evening, Benny sends him a message that says,

"I wanted to tell you something on the phone but there was no time. And I was too embarrassed to say it. Can't hide it anymore"

He reads the message a few times then replies,

"Yeah? What's it?"

She writes,

"I can't even sleep. I got a letter from my landlord yesterday and it's really bad. I've been keeping it to myself thinking I could handle it all on my own. But my hands are tied now. And my back is against the wall. I'm utterly confused because I've run out of time"

She sends a picture of a document with the message.

He reads the message, looks at the attached document carefully, then replies,

"Mmmm…"

She sends a couple of emojis with pleading hands and tears.

He ponders this briefly then writes,

"I'll be in Lagos next week. Can you meet me there?"

And just as he suspected she would do, she replies with,

"I'm supposed to be at my pastor's daughter's wedding working then. It's a bit tight from there on out because it's close to the festive period. I congested my timetable to try to see if I can make a little cash because of pending issues on ground"

Total garbage, reckons Edward. He concludes, as he has suspected all along, that this was a scam. This is 'cat fishing' he concludes, chuckling to himself.

He replies,

"I see"

She sends another couple of emojis.

He ignores them.

The following day she hits him up with,

"Good morning sir. Happy weekend!"

He reluctantly replies,

"Right back at ya!"

She says,

"How're you doing today?"

He says,

"I'm well. You?"

She replies,

"I'm alright"

He doesn't say anything else.

A few minutes later she writes,

"You've been off"

He retorts,

"Off how?"

She says,

"Offline"

He ignores her again.

She sends a sad face emoji. He doesn't respond.

The following day she writes,

"Good morning dear. How was your night?"

He ignores her.

The next morning she writes again,

"Good morning sir"

He still doesn't respond.

Then two days later she writes,

"Good afternoon sir"

He writes back,

"Hello"

She says,

"Seems you've been busy"

He retorts,

"Yep!"

She writes,

"Please what about what I told you?"

He doesn't respond.

She sends a couple of emojis, then writes,

"I'm running out of time"

He responds very curtly,

"Dude, I ain't got time for your lil' con game. Good luck to you. And goodbye!"

She writes back,

"Mmmm"

He says nothing.

She writes again,

"Okay sir. Please I admit that I'm wrong. But don't assume I'm as evil as you think please"

She continues,

"Hear me out. Please. I wanna be open with you. I wanna tell you the truth"

He says nothing.

She continues embarrassingly,

"I wanna be honest from this moment. Give me a second chance please. Even if I'm not what you thought I was"

He still doesn't say anything.

She continues shamelessly,

"Me being a male doesn't make me useless to you please"

She sends two emojis.

He is silent.

She says,

"I didn't just wake up randomly to do this. Give me a chance please. I want to make amends"

She sends another emoji, and writes,

"As a father or an uncle, give me a chance"

Curious, he asks,

"Make amends how?"

She sends a clasped pair of hands emoji and says,

"I want to be honest with you from today. No lies. No pretense. Only the truth please"

He says,

"I just have a question for you. Who is that person in all the pictures you post and send as your own?"

She says,

"Just some random girl sir"

He asks,

"Random girl from where?"

She replies,

"I don't really know her personally. I just saw her pictures on Facebook"

He mutters,

"I see"

She says,

"That's the truth sir"

He retorts,

"And you think it's ok to use her pictures for something like this?"

She answers,

"No sir. It's wrong and I'm really sorry about that sir. I never wanted to do it sir. Circumstances forced my hand. I'm running out of time as we speak"

He says thoughtfully,

"So tell me about your real self. Who are you? Where're you? Where're you from?"

She replies,

"I'm scared sir. I'm scared you're still mad at me"
He retorts,
"Scared of what?"
She says,
"Please understand that I'm really sorry sir"
He says coolly,
"If you're really sorry then you should answer my questions"
She replies,
"I'm scared of you arresting me being the rich man you are. I'm just a poor fellow. I'd just die if you arrest me"
He says nothing to that.
She continues,
"I'll tell you everything. My name is Vincent sir. I'm in Edo State. I'm from Rivers State sir. Ask me anything sir"
He asks, she answers.
"How old are you?"
"I'm 22 sir"
He says,
"Send me a picture of you"
She replies,
"I'm very scared sir. I'm choosing to tell you the truth because I'm feeling guilty. Not because I got caught. But because I know what I was doing is wrong"
He says matter of fact,
"Believe me, I realized you were a dude when I spoke to you on the phone. No woman sounds like you did on the phone"
She sends some emojis, then says,
"Mmmmmm"
He retorts,
"I'm really not sure why you're scared"
She says,
"You're a rich man. I'm scared of you arresting me. If you were in my shoes sir wouldn't you be scared too? Please be honest sir"
He says,
"Nobody is arresting anybody"
She says,
"I wanna take you for your word sir. Just like I want you to take me for mine. I've got nothing to give except my word to you sir. Even if I was very wrong earlier sir"

He says,

"I see"

She continues,

"I'm still capable of being truthful and keeping to my word sir"

He says,

"I see"

She says,

"Okay sir. Lemme do that now"

She sends him a picture.

He looks at it for a moment and asks,

"Is this really you, or someone else?"

She says,

"This is me sir. For real"

He says,

"Ok then"

She says,

"I already promised not to lie to you again sir"

He replies,

"So how many other people have you done this to? Posing as a beautiful girl?"

She replies,

"I just newly started sir because of my current situation"

He says,

"I see"

She says,

"Yes sir"

He asks,

"So why do you do this?"

She responds,

"Sir if I tell you my current situation you'd still think I'm lying"

He retorts,

"So I'm your first victim?"

She replies,

"Please sir, you're not my victim"

He asks rhetorically,

"So what am I then?"

She says,

"Mmmm please sir"

He replies,

"Please what?"

She says meekly,

"I said you're not a victim sir"

He says angrily,

"It's not what you say, but what the fact is"

She answers,

"Mmmmm fine. You're not my first victim sir but my fourth"

He replies,

"I see. So how much did you make from those victims?"

She says shamelessly,

"I'm aspiring to go to college that's why I did this in the first place. That's how I paid for all the exams. Now I'm trying to raise money for college. I just recently gained admission for a degree program. I've gained admission but because I'm penniless it's gonna go to waste. I just want to go to school to see if I can make it in life by God's grace. That's just the way it is sir"

Edward explodes angrily,

"By God's grace? Seriously? How do you pretend to be a girl to con folks out of their money and you still have the nerve to use God's name? Are you serious?"

She says,

"I'm sorry about that sir. But even when I did that I still prayed to God to forgive me. If there was another way I would've taken it. But there is other way"

Edward, seething with anger, asks,

"I've got another question for you. The poor girl whose pictures you use so despicably, do you realize what danger you're putting her in by pretending to be her?"

She answers,

"I do sir. I can't stress how sorry I am even if you don't believe me sir. But that's the truth"

He replies,

"Do you even care about what can happen to her?"

She says,

"I'm truly sorry even if my apologies can't get to her"

He asks,

"Do these other folks you've taken money from know this? Have you confessed to them as well? Or do they still think you're that girl?"

She replies,

"They don't talk to me anymore sir because they said they don't really have much this period. I told them I understand. And I didn't ask for anymore"

He asks,

"But they're still under the impression that you're that girl?"

She responds,

"I tried confessing to a certain man but he refused to give me a listening ear. He simply refused to believe the truth. Then he stopped talking to me"

He queries,

"Do you've sisters? Or female cousins?"

She says,

"Yes sir, I do. I have two younger sisters, and an older one too"

Edward asks incredulously,

"You have three sisters?"

She answers,

"Yes sir"

He pursues,

"What if someone does what you you've done with any of your sister's pictures? How would you feel about that?"

She says,

"I'd feel bad naturally sir. But another thing is that my siblings are not as beautiful. That's why no one would really bother to use them or their pictures for any thing sir. I don't mean to be cocky, smug, or irritating sir. But that's the truth"

Filled with very palpable disgust, he says,

"I see"

He wonders about the situation for a moment and says,

"Just so you know, the real victim in this whole thing is that young woman in the pictures. She's walking around without realizing that someone is using her pictures for a scam. She's in real danger"

She says,

"Believe me sir I know. And I wish I could express my apologies to her. That's why I'm apologizing to you"

He recoils and says,

"Apologizing to me? She's the one in a life threatening danger because someone wants to make some money"

She says,

"I don't think she'd ever forgive me. I was desperate sir"

He asks,

"Do you have a girlfriend?"

He responds,

"I used to sir. But she left me because I didn't have any money. We broke up January 2nd this year"

He asks,

"Why didn't you use your girlfriend's pictures? She's not pretty enough?

She says,

"She's not pretty enough sir. Plus she's too desperate for money"

He says,

"I see"

He ponders everything for a moment then asks,

"I ask you again, I want the truth this time. Why did you pick me for this?"

She answers truthfully,

"I didn't wake up to pick you sir. It was just a random friend request on Facebook with the hope that you will be a victim sir. There's no specific blueprint for you sir. It's all random and left to chance"

He mutters,

"I see. But what criteria do you use to pick people?"

She answers,

"Well, mature people who look well to do. People who will not pay attention to details, or care if the girl is real or not. Greedy or lustful men once the conversation picks up"

He says coolly,

"I see. And you believe I meet all that?"

She replies,

"Just the first part sir"

He asks,

"Only that?"

She responds,

"You're neither greedy nor lustful. Plus you're very brilliant too"

He says,

"I see"

He thinks momentarily and says,

"You seem like a really smart kid. Why haven't you thought of another way of making a living? Why not a legitimate way? Why this?"

She responds,

"I have tried to do so. It's not been working out for me. I have done many different odd jobs over the years. But the peanuts are not enough to take care of my expenses. I even dropped out of high school. I wrote WAEC with junior secondary school knowledge. But by God's grace I've passed all the required exams so far. In spite of all my sins, I know it's all by His grace"

He says matter of fact,

"Like I said, you seem like a really smart guy. You should be doing something else. Certainly not this"

She says,

"I'm doing this because men won't help fellow men or boys. They only help girls, and only beautiful girls at that. My back is against the wall"

He retorts,

"That's not true. There're many men who will help out another man if he comes correct with no lies!"

She pleads,

"I've not even eaten for several days now. My landlord has given me an eviction notice. I'm not lying sir"

He retorts,

"So you say"

She responds with,

"What reason would I have to lie now?"

He says coolly,

"You must admit that it's very hard to believe anything you say now. It's human nature. And I'm human after all"

For the next couple of days she, or perhaps 'he' which is the appropriate pronoun for Vincent the 'cat-fisher' at this point, sends several messages to Edward. He ignores all of them.

Edward wonders about how he could reach out to the young woman whose pictures and identity have been so blatantly violated. He realizes the young woman is in serious danger.

A crazed person who is cat-fished with her pictures might run into her somewhere and only God knows what can result from that, he reckons.

Then Vincent, aka Benny the 'cat-fisher', sends the following very cryptic message to Edward one early morning,

"Good morning sir. Please help me. I'm dying. I'm broke. I don't even have money to eat. I haven't eaten since yesterday and you didn't even bother to ask. Please help me. I don't wanna make the wrong decision tonight please. I'm tired of life"

Edward responds very angrily,

"Are you out of your freaking mind? I didn't bother to ask? Are you freaking kidding me?

Vincent replies,

"I'm sorry about that sir. I was just confused"

20 IT IS WHAT IT IS

"It does not matter how long you live, but how well you do it"
– Martin Luther King, Jr.

The socio-economic situation around the world is worsening daily, especially for the disadvantaged, and this creates a very fertile ground for all kinds of fraudulent activities. As the divide between the haves and the have-nots widens, so will criminal activities continue to grow exponentially.

This is especially so for the African continent because the supposed leaders continue to rob the people blind, and leave the populace to devise their own means of sustenance.

Scam or fraud, or whatever you choose to call it, is here to stay with us. Politicians scam the electorate all the time. Leaders defraud the led all day, every day. People take advantage of their kith and kin with reckless abandon all the time. Even parents scam their own children too. The list goes on and on. It is what it is.

The worst aspect of the global epidemic is the legal and acceptable aspect of the 'scam'. There are countless supposedly legitimate scams going on all around the world today.

What do you call the greedy wall street executives who fleece the common man of their hard earned money through 'legal' and 'legitimate' means? What about the huge pharmaceutical companies who prey on sick people for profit? How about the telephone and cable TV companies who reap off their customers? Go figure!

Have you met anyone who is completely satisfied with their cable TV or telephone provider? I haven't. Or are you familiar with anyone who is very pleased with their health or car insurance carrier?

The list of legal and legitimate scams is endless. Some overt, and others covert. But it is really the same. People just need to protect themselves by making the right decisions. Like it or not, you will be scammed one way or the other. It is what it is!

Every day law makers around the world make laws and legislation that is not very helpful to the majority of the populace. And this is especially true in the supposedly third world nations of the world.

In Nigeria for example, the law makers pass bills and laws that guarantees them huge salaries even when they retire; whereas the common man has no constant electricity, no good roads, no health care, and the education system is collapsing alarmingly.

It is a real tragicomedy to watch as Nigerian law makers fight amongst themselves about how much they should be paid, and their benefits; while the average Nigerian stews in poverty and penury. A real travesty no doubt.

It is a very known fact that Nigerian legislators and senators earn more income than any other law maker anywhere else in the world. They have even managed to write laws protecting their greed and thievery in a nation where more than 90% of the population live in squalor.

They live very opulent lives while their constituents wallow in abject lack and decadence. The robbed, deprived, and discarded constituents have no other choice but to resort to criminal activities.

The foreign banks around the world continue to aide and abet this grand fraud and scam being perpetrated on the abused people of the so-called third world countries.

The question is: why do these big banks continue to accept stolen money from these very corrupt and thieving African political leaders? Why do they continue to help the criminals hide their loot? And when will it end?

The simple truth is that as long as the third world political criminals continue to rob their people blind, the people will continue to find ways to steal from the developed nations. Sadly, the innocent citizens of the supposedly developed nations would be the scapegoats.

The average citizens of the developed nations who know nothing about the criminal third world politicians, who are in collusion with their 'big foreign banks' cohorts; are usually the ones targeted by all the fraudulent schemes engineered by the third world citizens. That is the fact. It is what it is!

The fraudsters don't write or call folks in other third world countries, they write and call citizens of developed countries like the United States of America, the United Kingdom, Germany, France, etc. They target innocent citizens of the supposedly developed countries.

These supposedly third world citizens who perpetrate the scams presume that the citizens of the developed countries have money spilling out of their ears, a complete nonsensical belief by the way; and they attempt to get some of that free money. But the truth is that the average citizens of these developed nations have their own hardships and issues to contend with.

Nobody plucks money from trees, or pick up money from the streets. People work very hard for their money. But the fraudsters think otherwise. And rather than demanding equity and fairness from their thieving leaders, they become criminals themselves.

They target the citizens of the developed countries who they perceive to be rich, and supposedly living in cities flowing in milk mixed with honey. Oh, how far that is from the truth is another subject entirely.

Thousands of innocent citizens dwelling in these developed nations are victimized every year. Many lose their life savings and go on to commit suicide. Some suffer severe depression and become vegetables.

Some people have lost millions to these scam artistes. Many are currently indebted to banks and other financial institutions. Many businesses have become bankrupt because the owners became victims of various scams.

The governments of the civilized and developed countries really need to do something about the continued victimization of their innocent citizens. They can start by prohibiting any financial business with the thieving third world political office holders.

They must stop their banks from accepting money stolen from the indigent people of the third world countries. And perhaps when the criminals in power see they can't hide any stolen money abroad they will get some sense and start to do the right thing.

Also, they should seize all property bought with stolen wealth within their countries. The property should be sold and the proceeds returned to the deprived people of the third world nations.

The developed countries should also stop being a safe haven for any criminal political leader of any third world country. The buck has to stop somewhere.

If the developed nations do not adopt these prescribed measures, then their citizens will continue to be targeted by criminal elements created by the dire conditions in the third world countries.

Curtailing the excesses of all the criminal elements holding political office in the third world nations is a good method of reducing the flagrant criminal enterprise.

If the leaders of these deprived nations are held accountable, they will be forced to provide for their people and the crime rate will therefore drop palpably. And that is how the developed countries can help their own citizens.

Frankly, it is everyone's responsibility to find a lasting solution to the ongoing infamous criminal enterprise.

The people of the third world countries must stop being docile and take decisive actions against their corrupt leaders. Enough is enough already! They must start to hold their leaders accountable. They must say no to all the corruption and looting of their national treasuries.

The citizens of the developed countries, who are the unfortunate victims of all the criminal activities, must also demand that their governments do something about the situation. They must lobby their law makers to pass laws that will disable 'authority stealing' in the third world nations.

They will be protecting their hard earned money by demanding that their governments protect them from the 'third word' criminals. This can be achieved by enacting laws that makes stealing from the third world countries, and hiding the money in their financial institutions, almost impossible.

If the 'third world' citizens are not robbed anymore perhaps they won't have to rob citizens of the developed world anymore. Therefore, it will become a win-win scenario.

*

Frank Audu has since transformed into a man reminiscent of Don Corleone in Mario Puzo's *The Godfather*; powerful, famous, and extremely wealthy.

He has successfully built an incredibly immense business empire. A multinational business empire to be exact. He has a hand in every profitable economic venture imaginable, covertly or overtly.

He owns a commercial airline company amongst others. He is the chairman of the board of a very profitable oil and gas conglomerate, all thanks to his benefactor General Issa Babagarri, retired. To paraphrase his mentor, Mr. Jonah, 'he has really made good'.

After his very painful 2 year stint in prison, he has since branched off into many various 'legitimate' businesses. He is a trained and certified lawyer after all.

He has prospered and profited immensely from his association with the indefatigable General Issa Babagarri, his own godfather. And he is now a godfather and benefactor to very many people across the world.

He has never forgotten his past. He remembers every detail of his journey to where he is today.

He has always stayed very close to, and kept in touch with, his very humble beginning. And he is helping everyone who needs help in his path, without discriminating against anyone.

Frank Audu has done a lot more for several thousands of people, and hundreds of communities around the country than the government has ever done for them since Nigeria gained independence from the British in 1960.

He has built schools, libraries, hospitals, roads, water projects, housing projects, you name it. He has also given away millions of dollars to people for everything they have asked for.

He creates factories and job training programs for people who want that. He has done it all for the masses of the country.

He continues to provide scholarships to thousands of indigent students across the country, to any level of education they crave. He remains an unwavering 'Robin Hood' of sorts.

His life long friend John, is now happily married to a lovely wife; and they have four healthy and beautiful children.

John who would go to the end of the world, and beyond, with Frank is still in the mix of everything. He remains very loyal and does as he is asked to do; with unalloyed love and unbridled steadfastness to Frank. He recently bagged his MBA with honors, all by himself. And he is considering getting a PhD too. He says he likes the sound of 'Dr. John Okhide'.

The days of scam letter writing and fraudulent activities are way past them. They are now very serious and 'legitimate' business men. They are very respectable entrepreneurs who provide a means of livelihood for thousands of families nationwide.

Mr. Jonah, Frank's former teacher and mentor; a one time Nigerian senator too, remains as an adviser to his mentee. His role as surrogate father is impeccable. Always has, always will be.

Frank Audu's parents, Philip and Stella, have always known what manner of son they have even from when he was just an infant. To say they are happy and pleased with him is a very mild interpretation of how they actually feel about him.

*

Nancy Audu, Frank Audu's wife, has since metamorphosed into a very steadfast rock. She has become the doyen of philanthropy in Nigeria. She works with all the disenfranchised people, especially women.

She is the face of the movement for a better life for the masses of Nigeria. No small feat without a doubt.

EPILOGUE

"You must be the change you want to see in the world" – *Mahatma Gandhi*

The realities of our time makes it almost impossible to completely stamp out the scourge of fraud, or fraudulent activities. The fraudsters around the world are motivated by the innate human greed and desire to want to reap where they have not sown.

The continued repression of a large proportion of the world's population by a few selfish brigands continues to facilitate the criminal climate. Deprived people will always try to find a way to even the scores or eke out a means of survival, just like water that will always find its level no matter what.

The way forward is for everyone to join hands together. Governments and citizens everywhere must pull their weight. The citizens of the third world countries must start to demand accountability from their rulers.

The citizens of the developed countries must demand that their governments protect them by taking action against the corrupt regimes of the third world countries.

The world powers, the developed nations, must help everybody by taking decisive action against the very corrupt rulers of the third world countries. They can not continue to fold their arms while the thieves in power run wild, unabated.

They must stop aiding and abetting the political thieves. All their foreign accounts must be frozen, and the money should be repatriated to the real owners, the masses of the third world countries.

To paraphrase Mahatma Gandhi, 'we must be the change we want to see in the world'.

LEGACY

ABOUT THE AUTHOR

Ernest Bhabor is a filmmaker who lives in New York City with his wife and two sons.

He was born, raised, and educated in Nigeria. He is one of the pioneers of the fledgling Nigerian film industry, which is popularly known as *'Nollywood'* - the 3rd largest entertainment industry in the world.

He is a founding member of both the Directors Guild of Nigeria (DGN) and the Writers Guild of Nigeria (WGN).

He is an avid reader, writer, and a connoisseur of sorts. He is a huge soccer enthusiast and sports pundit.

Made in the USA
Middletown, DE
07 December 2018